# Smartphone, Dumb User

# Smartphone, Dumb User

Lisa R. Schoolcraft

Printed in the United States of America

First Printing, 2019

ISBN: 978-1-7339709-0-7

Publisher: Schoolcraft Ink LLC

Visit the author's website at www.schoolcraftink.com

# Dedication

*To my family and friends, for always believing in me.*

# Table of Contents

# Chapter 1

Ravyn Shaw was angry with herself for not starting the profile story on Marc Linder sooner.

The story was due to Atlanta Trend magazine in two weeks – plenty of time if she had already started the interviews, which she hadn't.

That seemed to be the way with freelance work. It was either feast or famine.

Four weeks ago, she had no assignments and two bills overdue. Then five assignments came in, all of which had to be turned in on short deadlines. She'd gotten the assignment for the profile piece on the CEO of LindMark four weeks ago, but those other four freelance jobs were due ahead of it.

Ravyn was starting this assignment feeling deadline pressure already.

If only she could reach Marc Linder to set up his interview.

But the man was proving to be elusive. And his public relations consultant Laura Lucas was being less than helpful.

Ravyn, propped up in her queen-sized bed with her laptop computer, had done some background work already for the story as her cup of Earl Grey tea had gone cold beside her.

"How had anyone done in-depth writing before the internet?" she wondered to herself.

Marc Linder was 39, handsome, divorced, and driven. He'd founded LindMark, a startup technology company in Atlanta, five years ago in 2008, just before the economy had started to crater.

He'd managed to keep his company afloat when many others like his filed for bankruptcy, or simply unplugged their phones and closed their doors.

Linder was one of the rising stars of the city's entrepreneurs, which is exactly why Atlanta Trend wanted the 2,000-word profile on him for its "Rising Stars" issue.

Now if she could just reach him to schedule the interview.

Ravyn had never missed a deadline. She prided herself on that – not in the six years she had worked for the Atlanta Daily Tribune, the city's daily newspaper.

And she had not missed a deadline since she was laid off in 2010 from that job and had been forced into freelance work.

Although the transition had been painful, truthfully, Ravyn found she was quite happy to be her own boss.

Well, happy to be her own boss when the freelance work was steady and the clients paid on time. Atlanta Trend paid on time.

"This profile story will be turned in on time," she muttered to herself.

Her bedside clock read 12:43 a.m.

Ravyn stretched and rubbed the back of her stiff neck. She had been up late gathering as much background on Marc Linder as she could through the internet, piecing together scraps of information about a man who didn't have a lot written about him. Her other checks had been through some public documents, which is how she knew his age and marital status, and when he had started his company.

But his own company's website had just scant information about him.

"You'd think a CEO would at least have a bio on his own company's website!" she thought, flustered.

Ravyn was about to shut down her laptop and call it a night when she did one final Google search, but this time searching for Mark Linder, spelled with a "K" rather than the correct letter "C."

She found a couple of blogs that mentioned Mark Linder, one of which listed a phone number for the LindMark CEO.

On a whim, Ravyn picked up her smartphone and dialed it.

Ravyn was startled by the deep voice answering, "Hello."

"Hello. Is this Marc Linder?" she asked.

"Speaking."

"Mr. Linder, this is Ravyn Shaw. I've been trying to reach you to set up our interview for the upcoming 'Rising Stars' profile for Atlanta Trend. You are being featured in the upcoming issue with some other CEOs."

"Please call my PR consultant Laura Lucas to set that up, Miss... Shaw, did you say?"

"Yes, Mr. Linder," Ravyn rushed on. "I've left several messages with Ms. Lucas, but I haven't gotten any response and I need to get started."

"You realize, Miss Shaw, it is 1 a.m.?" Marc said, not hiding his irritation. "I am not prepared to get started now."

"Oh!" Ravyn said, looking again at her bedside clock and realizing the time. "I'm so sorry. Is there a number where I can reach you in the morning? I really must get started. The deadline is in two weeks."

"This is my private cell number," he said flatly. "How did you get it?"

"I found it on a blog site."

"Right," Marc said, angrily. "Call me later." And he hung up.

"Crap," thought Ravyn. "That was not a good way to start an interview."

Ravyn's cell phone was ringing at 8 a.m. the next day.

"Hello?" she answered sleepily.

"How *dare* you call Marc Linder directly!" hissed Laura Lucas. "You need to set up your interview through me."

Ravyn could feel herself getting angry at Laura Lucas's attitude, but Ravyn had dealt with her before, and knew this was just Laura's style.

Laura Lucas was a public relations consultant who believed it was her job not only to be a consultant, but also a gatekeeper. And Laura kept the gates closed, most of the time.

"Laura, I would not have had to call Mr. Linder directly if you had simply returned any of the five phone calls I've made to you and five voicemails I've left," Ravyn answered icily. "If you want your client to get a nice profile story in Atlanta Trend, then you had better help me get in front of him soon for the interview."

"Mr. Linder can see you next week," Laura said.

"No, Laura. I need to see him this week. I need to interview other people about him, too, but I'd like to talk to him first to get this started."

"I'll see what I can do," Laura said. "How much time will you need? Thirty minutes?"

"Laura, you know for an in-depth profile piece I'm going to need at least an hour. And that's just for the initial interview. I must have access to him for follow-up questions. Ideally, I'd like to shadow him at his office for a couple of hours to see how he works, too."

"He can't allow that," Laura sniffed.

"How do you know that?" Ravyn asked, very angry. "You haven't even asked him!"

"Mr. Linder is a very busy man and he doesn't have that kind of time for you."

"Ask him," Ravyn said, more forcefully. "I need to hear back from you today."

The call ended, but Ravyn felt that she already knew the answer she was going to get from Laura Lucas.

Ravyn immediately redialed the private cell number to Marc Linder she had run across last night on the internet.

"Hello," said the deep voice, this time a bit less sleepy.

"Mr. Linder, good morning. This is Ravyn Shaw again, calling at a better time for you, I hope."

Ravyn tried to sound as if last night's call was some hilarious mistaken drunk dial between friends.

"Miss Shaw, this is neither a good time, nor a bad time."

Inwardly, Ravyn groaned. This profile piece was really not starting out well.

"Mr. Linder, I would just like to set up an appointment for our interview. You did tell me to call you this morning."

"I believe my PR consultant will be calling you," Linder said, coolly.

"Mr. Linder, I have always found it best to go straight to the source, and that source is you. Are you free at all today or tomorrow? I would just need an hour for the initial interview, and I'd like you to provide some contacts, both professional and personal, that I may contact to interview about you."

"This sounds like a very elaborate piece," he said.

"Sir, I'd like it to be as well-rounded and complete as possible."

"Miss Shaw, my first-grade teacher is not available, but my second-grade teacher probably still is."

Ravyn could not help letting a small giggle escape.

"Be at my office at 2:30 p.m. tomorrow," Linder said and hung up.

Ravyn met her friend Julie Montgomery for lunch that afternoon at Carolyn's Café in Midtown Atlanta.

"You are not going to believe my day today!" Ravyn said, flopping down across from Julie in the booth.

Julie brushed back her long, blond hair and put on her best sympathetic smile. "Hello to you, too."

"Sorry, Jules. Hello. I'm glad we could meet for lunch today, but I have to keep it short," Ravyn said. "I've been summoned to the office of Marc Linder tomorrow for that profile story and I've still got some preparation and research to do."

Ravyn sighed. "But, a girl's gotta eat, right?"

The friends smiled and laughed. Ravyn ordered the turkey and brie sandwich with a side salad. Julie ordered a Cuban sandwich with a side of plantains.

Carolyn's Café was one of their favorite Midtown Atlanta lunch spots that catered mostly to locals. Off a busy street with a tucked away parking lot behind the restaurant, few tourists knew how to find it.

Between bites, Ravyn explained the last 24 hours and the faux pas phone call to Marc Linder early that morning.

"You did not call that man at one o'clock in the morning!" Julie blurted.

"I did," Ravyn said, pulling out her iPhone and waving it at Julie. "Smartphone, dumb user," tapping the phone to her own head.

"What's worse is I got a call seven hours later from Laura Lucas, bitching me out about calling Mr. Linder," Ravyn said. "That man must not sleep. Maybe that's the theme of this profile. I write that he's a vampire or something."

"Why would Laura Lucas call you?" Julie asked.

Julie, a recovering journalist herself, knew Laura Lucas and her reputation of being tough as nails and more than a bit acerbic.

"Linder is using Laura as his PR consultant," Ravyn said, rolling her blue eyes. "Just my luck. She tried to chew me a new one this morning. And I hadn't even had my first cup of coffee."

"Oh, that's grounds for a fist fight, or at least a couple of pins in a voodoo doll," Julie said, and both women laughed.

But dealing with Laura Lucas was no laughing matter. She was a consummate control freak.

Laura had a number of high-profile clients in Atlanta. At one time she catered mostly to real estate developers, but when the real estate market collapsed around the country, and rather spectacularly in Atlanta, she reinvented herself.

Now she had clients in the technology field, the hospitality industry, and even one major hospital in town.

Clients seemed to appreciate what she could do for them, but the working media didn't always appreciate *her*.

Rather than provide reporters or writers with information, Laura seemed to make it her mission to control that information, which meant she sometimes just flat out denied access to her clients. Ravyn knew that, and it made her worry about getting the Linder profile story done on time.

"So, what are you going to do about Laura?" Julie asked.

"Well, right after I hung up with Laura, I called Mr. Linder back on that cell number I found online last night," Ravyn said.

"And?"

"And I have a meeting with him tomorrow," Ravyn said, taking another bite of her sandwich.

"Does Laura know?" Julie asked, almost worried.

"I have no idea, but I'd bet money she does," Ravyn said, irritated. "She doesn't miss much."

The next morning, Ravyn was up early, finding herself nervous about the upcoming interview with Marc Linder. The whole thing had gotten off to such a bad start. It left her unsettled.

She arrived at LindMark's Midtown Atlanta office 30 minutes ahead of time, her questions arranged on note cards, her laptop fully charged.

The elevator opened on the sixth floor and Ravyn turned right toward LindMark's office. The startup company's office was down a hallway punctuated by nondescript office doors. A nameplate on a beige wall to the right side of the door let her know she was at the right one.

She sat in the reception area of LindMark's small office and looked around. The reception area was sparse. A few pieces of bland art hung on the wall, all nature scenes. They looked like they could have come from a motel's surplus sale. A couple of plants, neither of which looked too neglected, sat in one corner on a brown side table. Ravyn smiled and thought the table had come from the same motel's surplus sale.

A young receptionist had offered Ravyn either coffee or water, but Ravyn was too nervous to drink. She had been too nervous to eat lunch, too.

That could prove embarrassing if her stomach suddenly decided it wanted food and started to growl half way through the interview.

"Calm down!" Ravyn thought to herself.

Ravyn was smartly dressed for the interview. She wore her black pinstripe skirt suit and a dusky blue blouse that brought out the blue in her blue gray eyes. For once her mousy brown hair seemed to be behaving. Stick straight and baby fine, Ravyn's hair never seemed to want to hold any type of style. She usually just pulled it back into a ponytail, or wore it shoulder length and tucked behind her ears. A low-heeled black sandal finished out the wardrobe.

Rather absent-mindedly, Ravyn touched the jeweled flower brooch on her suit jacket's lapel. The brooch had belonged to her late grandmother Margaret, to whom she had been very close. Ravyn took a deep breath and felt calmer.

Ravyn heard Laura Lucas's voice and looked up, trying not to show her displeasure.

"Damn," Ravyn thought. "I do not want her manipulating this interview."

Ravyn stood up, put on her best fake smile and shook Laura's hand.

"Good to see you, Laura," Ravyn lied.

"We're ready for the interview," Laura replied, as they walked down a short office corridor. "Mr. Linder is on a very tight schedule and you won't get more than 30 minutes."

"Laura, this is an important profile story, I might need more than 30 minutes," Ravyn said, a little too sharply.

"You have 30 minutes," Laura snapped, and opened the door to Marc Linder's office.

Linder stood up from behind his dark wood desk, which held only a few items and some papers tucked neatly inside plain manila file folders. It was all very neat, very arranged.

Ravyn was not entirely prepared for how handsome LindMark's CEO was.

Tall and broad shouldered, Marc Linder had what could only be described as classic Roman features, with a full head of dark wavy brown hair and hazel eyes that had a hint of green in them.

He moved around the desk to shake her hand.

"Hello, Miss Shaw," he said. "Good to see you keep daylight hours."

Ravyn smiled. "Sorry about that. Thank you for seeing me today."

Linder gestured for Ravyn to sit down, and she moved to sit down in the chair that would be closest to him, but Laura swiftly sat down in that chair. Ravyn fumed inwardly.

Laura reached into her bag and handed Ravyn what looked to be Marc Linder's biography. "Here," Laura said. "This is some of what you said you needed for the profile."

Ravyn glanced over it quickly and saw it was hardly any more information than she'd already gleaned from the internet. She took out her notebook and began, checking the questions on the note cards balanced in her lap.

"First, Mr. Linder, tell me a little about your company, and why you founded it," Ravyn began.

Linder smiled. "Please, call me Marc."

Ravyn nodded and smiled.

"I studied to become a lawyer, and at first I found it very rewarding, working mostly at small firms," he started. "I eventually took a job at Kramer & Spelling, but I quickly realized real estate law, or any kind of law, wasn't holding my attention. Ten years after being a practicing lawyer, I realized I didn't want to be a practicing lawyer."

Instead, Marc went on, he was fascinated by the burgeoning technology industry. Atlanta, following the 1996 Summer Olympic Games, saw a huge number of startup tech companies form in the city and its northern suburbs.

Then in 2000, the technology bubble burst and many dot com companies became known as dot bomb companies, closing their doors.

Atlanta's technology industry struggled in the years that followed, but it was not dead, and as technology became more and more entwined in everyone's lives, entrepreneurs like Marc Linder wanted more and more to be a part of that world.

Marc explained that he quit Kramer & Spelling, one of Atlanta's oldest and most respected law firms, to start LindMark, which started out developing software to help retail businesses better track inventory.

Marc's eyes practically twinkled as he recounted the early years of the business, blowing through all of his savings to keep his fledgling company afloat.

LindMark got a few, small clients, and Marc kept putting the company's profit, meager as it was, back into LindMark, for better software development, better ideas, better employees.

He was really only a little over a year into his business in 2009, and just starting to see more profits and clients, when the economy truly tanked, Atlanta's housing market collapsed and companies large and small laid off thousands.

Ravyn nearly winced as he talked about the thousands laid off in the city. She had been one of them.

With people out of work, retailers saw sales slump, and LindMark saw its clients fall away.

"I was lucky. I had been smart and had run a lean and tight company, even when we were starting to make a profit," Marc said. "We took a blow, but we did not close. And we didn't lay anyone off."

Nearly four years later, LindMark was still a lean and tight company, but the struggles of the young company continued.

LindMark was still developing software for the retail industry, but now it was also working on applications for those retailers who wanted to tap into the new generation of shoppers who went to their smartphones for information, discounts and products.

"Is there anything new LindMark is working on that you can share with Atlanta Trend readers?" Ravyn asked.

Marc's hazel eyes darkened for just a moment, she noticed.

"LindMark is currently working on a new software product, but we will need some venture capital to see it through," Marc said. "I'm sorry. I can't tell you more than that."

"Is the new product still in the retail field?" Ravyn asked.

"Ravyn!" Laura shot. "Marc said he couldn't tell you more about it."

Marc and Ravyn both looked at Laura.

"Sorry, Mr. Linder," Laura said, catching herself.

"Has the company turned a profit in the past year?" Ravyn asked.

"Mr. Linder isn't going to answer that!" Laura snapped.

"Well, my editor will want to know that I asked it," Ravyn said firmly. "This is a business publication, read by business leaders in this city. They want to know about a company's revenue and profit, as well as its leader."

Laura glared at Ravyn and Marc looked a little puzzled.

"Should I answer that?" Marc asked Laura.

"I don't think you should," Laura answered. "You don't want your competitors to know too much about your revenue at this stage of the game."

"Sorry," Marc turned to Ravyn. "No comment."

Ravyn caught Laura's small smile and fumed, but she continued with the interview.

"What do you do outside of work, Mr. Lin..., Marc?"

"Is there an outside of work?" Marc asked, bemused. "Well, before LindMark started working on the new software, I was running and biking a lot more. I was hoping to train for my next triathlon, but I just don't have time right now. If I can, I get in a quick run, or bike ride."

"What book are you reading right now?" Ravyn asked, hoping some answers could be used to pepper more personal things about Marc Linder for the profile. She expected Marc to answer that he was reading some dry business book.

"I'm rereading 'Fellowship of the Ring,'" he answered, referring to the first book of The Lord of the Rings trilogy by J.R.R Tolkien. "But it is slow going. I don't have much time for reading, either."

"Oh! Fellowship!" Ravyn said and laughed.

"What's so funny?"

"Oh, nothing at all," Ravyn said, shaking her head. "I happened to be named by my parents because of those Tolkien books."

"Ah," Marc said. "I wondered about your name. Raven, like the bird?"

"R-A-V-Y-N, with a Y, because, well, because they could. I think they realized their folly later," Ravyn said. "My younger sister is named Jane. We suspect after Jane Austen, but my parents have never said so. Do you have family, Marc?"

"My parents are nearing retirement. I have a younger sister, too."

"Are you married? Do you have children?" Ravyn asked.

"Divorced, no children," he said, flatly.

"Would you like to name your parents and sister in the profile story?" Ravyn asked.

She knew some profile subjects, particularly successful business men and women, were a little touchy about naming family, for fear they would get unsolicited calls from readers who hoped the family member could help get them a job or give them money, or be a long-lost cousin looking for a free ride.

"I'd rather not," Marc said, and again his hazel eyes briefly darkened.

"I think I have some of the other background information to use for the biographical box that goes with the profile," Ravyn said, moving on. "But what about your competition? Who do you consider your competition and how does LindMark stay ahead?"

"I like to think LindMark has no competition," Marc said. "But certainly, there are companies that like to think they compete with *us*. We stay ahead because we have innovative products for our customers, we are responsive to our customers, and we treat our customers fairly."

"So, you don't consider Bradford Cunningham's company a rival?" Ravyn asked, knowing that it was.

Marc looked surprised at the question.

"I'm sure Mr. Cunningham believes he competes with us, but …" Marc began to say.

"Time's up!" Laura announced sharply.

Ravyn looked up, clearly displeased. "But I'm not finished with the interview."

"Yes, you are," Laura said. "I told you. You only had 30 minutes. Time's up."

Marc looked as if he was going to say something, but Laura cut him off. "Mr. Linder has a tight schedule today."

"Mr. Linder, may I call for some follow-up questions?" Ravyn asked, standing up, trying to keep the piece of paper with Marc's bio Laura had given her from falling to the floor. "This has only just gotten me started on my information gathering. I know I will have some follow-up questions."

Marc Linder, somewhat puzzled, looked at Laura Lucas, who mouthed the words "to me."

"You can run those by Ms. Lucas," Marc said.

Ravyn glared at Laura and then turned back to Marc.

"I'd rather run them by you," she said, rather adamantly.

"You run them by me," Laura said, as she ushered Ravyn out of Marc's office.

"Laura, I was nowhere near finished and you know it," Ravyn said when they reached the front door and were out of Marc's earshot. "This biography you handed me is meager, at best," she said, waving the half-page sheet at Laura. "And I need those contact names and numbers to call about Mr. Linder. I didn't get those. Don't sabotage this profile story."

"Not my fault if you can't write a decent profile article, Ravyn," Laura shot back.

"What do you mean by that?!" Ravyn nearly shouted.

"I mean exactly what I say," Laura snipped, shutting the office door in Ravyn's stunned face.

# Chapter 2

Ravyn was full on fuming when she left LindMark's office. She was almost shaking she was so angry.

"God! I'd like to wring her scrawny little neck!" Ravyn thought as she stomped to her car.

Getting in, she took some deep breaths, trying to calm down. She looked at her phone to check the time, realizing Julie's children would be getting home soon.

As a stay-at-home mother, Julie usually was always available to Ravyn for lunch or commiseration, but only while her two daughters were in school. Once they were home, Julie was busy getting them to soccer, swimming, gymnastics or any number of other events.

Julie liked to joke that her daughters had a fuller social life than she did, but that wasn't true. Hers was just on a different time schedule than her working friends.

Ravyn sat in her car in the office building's parking deck and dialed Julie's number anyway and heard her stomach growl. Now she realized how hungry she was.

"Ravyn! How did the interview go?" Julie asked.

"Well, I was really just getting into some of the meat of the interview and Laura Lucas shut me down," Ravyn said. "She only set up 30 minutes for the interview. Thirty minutes! That's barely enough time to get some of the pleasantries out of the way. And she was her usual bitchy self. Told me it wouldn't be her fault if the profile piece was bad. Bad! What the hell? He's her client! You'd think she'd do everything she could to help me write a great article. I'm so pissed."

"Wow! Sorry to hear that," Julie said. "Will you be able to do the profile piece?"

"I'll get the piece done, but I wish it had all gone smoother," she answered. "Sorry to blow off steam at you. Laura Lucas just pushed my buttons."

"Oh, I know how she is. But tell me, how was Marc Linder?" Julie asked. "I've seen some photos of him in some of the Atlanta magazines. He looks like a real dreamy CEO. And I hear he's single."

Julie practically sang the word *single*.

"Julie, just because you are happily married to a man you met while doing a story, doesn't mean I'm going to find a mate that way!" Ravyn laughed. "But yes, he is really good looking. If I'd had more time during the interview I might have been able to flirt with him," she added, only half joking.

"Well, you'll have some follow-up questions, I'm sure," Julie said. "If you don't, I'll make some up for you, and then you can flirt away."

Just then, Ravyn could hear young girlish voices calling "Mommy!" in the background.

"Sorry, Ravyn, the girls need to get to Girl Scouts," Julie said. "I'll have to get back to you. Chin up, girlfriend."

"Bye, Jules. Give the girls a hug from me."

Ravyn decided on a late lunch/early dinner at a restaurant not far from LindMark's offices.

The place was fuller than she expected for almost 4 p.m.

Ravyn was seated toward the front of the restaurant and glanced around. Shocked, she spied Laura Lucas and Marc Linder deep in conversation at a table toward the back.

"Probably debriefing him," Ravyn thought. Except it looked like a more intense discussion.

Marc's back was to Ravyn, but she could see Laura's face and Laura's face did not look happy at all.

"Hmm. I wonder what that is all about," Ravyn thought. "Wish I was a fly on that wall."

Ravyn ordered and tried not to keep staring back toward Marc and Laura's table, but she just couldn't help herself.

"No, Laura," Ravyn heard Marc say rather forcefully. Laura looked crushed.

Was he firing her? Ravyn wondered. Then she saw Marc put his hand on Laura's, a rather intimate gesture, Ravyn thought.

Suddenly, it occurred to Ravyn. They looked like a couple that was breaking up.

"Well, well, Laura Lucas, you sly she-devil, you," Ravyn thought. "Playing with fire again, I see."

Ravyn had heard the rumors about Laura, of course.

A party girl from Miami, Laura had many clients, but most of them were men. The whispers around Atlanta were that she got a little too close to some of her clients, including the married ones.

Although she did not personally like Laura, Ravyn could see how men would.

Laura was petite with a trim, beautiful figure. Dark hair and eyes and a toothy smile, Laura could be quite charming, but not to women. Almost always toward men, though.

Ravyn's food arrived just as Marc and Laura stood up to leave.

Laura wound through the tables toward the front door with Marc right behind her.

Marc spotted Ravyn and stopped, dropping his hand from Laura's elbow.

"Hello, Miss Shaw, what brings you here?" he asked. Laura turned to see who Marc was talking to, saw it was Ravyn and narrowed her eyes.

"Late lunch, early dinner," Ravyn said. "Then it will be a long night of work on your profile piece."

"Well, call me if you have any more questions," he said.

"I sure will. Thanks, Mr. Linder. Oh, I mean, Marc," she replied, smiling. Marc smiled back.

Laura shot Ravyn a look that was deadly.

Ravyn got back to her one-bedroom condominium, dropped her purse and mail, which she noticed was mostly bills, on the kitchen counter and placed her laptop on the kitchen table.

Ravyn's tomcat Felix came around the corner, giving a little chirp hello. She reached down to scratch his head.

"Hi, Felix," she said. "Are you hungry?"

Ravyn poured some cat food for Felix, who began to eat greedily.

She then poured a diet cola for herself and plugged in the laptop. She always knew it was best to type up her notes while they were fresh in her mind. Although she always brought her laptop to interviews, she rarely took notes on it while conducting interviews.

So, she scribbled furiously in a note pad, trying to keep up during the interviews. She knew it was ridiculous. She could type faster than she could write. But Ravyn felt the laptop created a barrier between her and her subject that the small note pad did not. And she didn't like to rely solely on a recording device for interviews either. She'd once conducted a long interview, only to get back to her newspaper desk and find she'd pressed the wrong button and nothing had recorded.

Ravyn opened her notes and began to type, trying to recall Marc Linder's office, his manners, and writing those impressions down, too.

She began to think about him, his hazel eyes, those broad shoulders, those hands. What it might feel like if he touched her with those hands.

Ravyn shook her head to clear away those thoughts.

"I've got to get a hold of myself," she thought. "Keep things professional, Ravyn. You are not Laura Lucas."

Less than an hour later she stopped and stretched. The interview notes looked thin. But she also had her research notes and would pull information into the story from those.

Since Laura Lucas hadn't provided any other professional or personal contacts for Ravyn to call, she was going to have to dig up a few on her own.

One contact who might have a very different perspective on Marc Linder was Bradford Cunningham. Ravyn quickly looked up Cunningham's contact information on his company's website and made a note to call him tomorrow.

Ravyn decided to call it quits for the night and closed the files on the profile piece before she poured herself a glass of red wine.

She logged onto the internet to check on her friends on Facebook when her cell phone rang. Ravyn didn't recognize the number.

"Hello?" she said.

"Miss Shaw, Marc Linder," said the deep voice on the other end. "Is this a bad time?"

"No! Not at all," Ravyn said.

"I wanted to apologize for the shortened time for the interview today," Marc said. "It won't happen again. Do you have time to meet tomorrow? I can give you all the time you need."

"Yes, that would be perfect," Ravyn said, sighing with relief.

There was a pause in the conversation, with Ravyn waiting for Marc to tell her what time to meet at his office.

"Have you had dinner tonight?" he asked.

The question caught Ravyn off guard, but she quickly recovered.

"No," she answered, looking at the time on a digital wall clock in her kitchen. It read 7:30 p.m. "I thought that late lunch would hold me, but I'm a little hungry again."

"How about dinner?" Marc asked. "My way of apologizing. There's no conflict in my taking you to dinner, is there?"

"Mr. Linder," Ravyn said for effect, "If you think you will get a better profile piece because you treat me to dinner, you are sadly mistaken. But just the same, I'd prefer to meet somewhere where I can pay my share."

"How about Tin Lizzy's?" Marc suggested. "The one on Crescent Avenue in Midtown."

Tin Lizzy's Cantina was a funky little Tex-Mex place not too far from Ravyn's condo.

"Sounds great," she said. "In an hour?"

"See you there," Marc said.

The second she hung up with Marc, Ravyn felt panicked. Could she be ready in an hour?

She looked down at her clothes. She was still in her business suit – minus the strappy black sandals.

Ravyn got up and hustled into her bedroom.

"What to wear? What to wear?" Ravyn thought, as she opened the closet.

This wasn't exactly a date, she knew, but it suddenly felt like a date. She needed something between business attire and date attire.

Ravyn took a couple of outfits out of her closet and held them up to her body as she looked in the full-length mirror before she decided on black pants and a turquoise blouse that she knew flattered her. She donned a funky necklace, brushed back her hair, freshened her makeup and she was ready.

Ravyn got to the restaurant first and got a table on the outside patio.

Despite the onset of fall, the night was warm in Atlanta. The outside patio, lit with white fairy lights, was full and Ravyn was glad to have snagged a table. Ravyn sent a quick text message to Marc to let him know she was outside on the patio.

Marc arrived about ten minutes later, wearing beige khaki pants, a dark green polo shirt and loafers. Ravyn stood up to shake his hand and could smell his spicy cologne. He smelled great and looked even better, she thought.

"How was the rest of your day?" Ravyn asked.

"Are we on or off the record?" Marc asked.

"We're off the record," Ravyn said, truthfully, holding up her hands. "See, no note pad. If you say anything tonight I want to use, I'll run it by you tomorrow."

"Fair enough," he said. "Have you always been a freelance writer?"

"No," Ravyn answered, noticing he had deflected her question. "I started out as a working journalist, first at a small newspaper in Southeast Georgia, then at a larger paper in Jacksonville, Florida. Finally, I landed here in Atlanta."

Ravyn looked down and shifted in her chair before continuing.

"I got laid off by the daily paper a little over three years ago," she answered, rather quietly. "I kind of became a freelance writer by default."

"Did you go to UGA?" Marc asked, referring to the state's major university.

"No again," Ravyn said. Everyone assumed she had gone to the University of Georgia's Grady School of Journalism, since she lived in Atlanta.

"I went to the University of Missouri," Ravyn continued. "It's the number one journalism school in the nation. Go Tigers."

"All the way out to the Midwest?" Marc asked, intrigued.

"Well, a lot of my family is from the Midwest, so it wasn't a stretch," she said. "And I loved it there. I had a wonderful college experience."

"If you loved it so much, what brought you back to Atlanta?" Marc asked.

"Hey, who is the interviewer here?" Ravyn asked, laughing. She smiled. "Family. Family brought me back. My father had a health scare while I was in college and I wanted to live closer to my parents."

"They live in Atlanta?" Marc asked.

"No. They live in South Carolina, so close enough that I can get there quickly if I need to."

The waiter arrived and Marc and Ravyn agreed to split a pitcher of margaritas. Ravyn ordered the fish tacos and Marc ordered the beef burrito.

"What about you, Marc? What brought you to Atlanta?"

"I grew up here."

"Really? You don't find too many native Atlantans in Atlanta anymore," she said.

"I know. But I was raised in Dunwoody," he said. "I went to The University of Georgia for undergrad and law school. I got my first job back here."

The pitcher of drinks arrived and Marc poured for both of them. Once again, Ravyn looked at his hands and felt her heart skip.

Marc then took a long drink from his margarita.

"I envy those who have seen a little more of the world than I have," he said. "The only real distance I've traveled was on my honeymoon to Mexico."

"No traveling the world?" Ravyn asked, as she sipped her drink. "I think that's what the working class expects of CEOs."

"I'm about to head to California to try to get some venture capital for the company," he said, taking another long drink, then refilling his glass and topping off Ravyn's glass from the pitcher. "It's imperative for my company to get some capital for this new project."

Maybe it was the balmy night, or the salty margaritas, but Ravyn felt herself beginning to relax next to Marc. It almost started to feel like a date. But Ravyn reminded herself it wasn't. Not really.

Yet Marc was the first man she'd been out to dinner with in months. Her last boyfriend had lasted just a short three months and when it was over, she wasn't all that upset about it.

And quite frankly, she felt like she was working so hard to keep her bills paid that she really didn't have enough time for a serious boyfriend. She'd had a series of casual dating with guys here and there. Someone she'd met at the gym, or in a club, not that she went to the clubs that much anymore. She couldn't really justify the cover charges. Not when the power bill was overdue.

Tonight feels nice, Ravyn thought as she smiled.

"What's that smile for" Marc asked.

"I was just thinking it is not often that I have a nice dinner interview with an Atlanta CEO," she said. "It's really quite nice. I must request this for all my future interviews."

Marc laughed and the food arrived.

Their conversation shifted to small talk during the meal.

Ravyn chatted about her parents, two professors at Clemson University, and Marc chatted about his triathlon last year, in which he placed ninth in his age group.

As they finished their meals, Marc signaled for another pitcher of margaritas. When it arrived and their glasses were refilled, Ravyn asked, "What keeps you up at night?"

"Other than phone calls from pretty reporters at 1 a.m.?" Marc asked, smiling.

Ravyn felt her heart skip another beat, and blushed. "Other than that."

"I guess it's keeping my company going," Marc said, suddenly serious. "It's been a hard five years. The economy has been tough and getting every client has been tough. To take LindMark to the next level, it's going to take capital – venture capital. I realize I need a partner to take the company to that next level. I think the company could be a second-tier player, maybe even a first-tier player, in the tech industry, but I can't do it alone."

He paused and took another long drink. "That's what keeps me up at night, Ravyn. Do you mind if I call you Ravyn?"

"Not at all," she said.

"What happens if you don't get the venture capital?" Ravyn asked.

Marc's voice lowered as he asked again, "Are we off the record?"

Ravyn nodded.

"My company may not continue without the capital," he said, looking sad. Then he seemed to pull himself together. "But I'm really hopeful about my chances. It's not a sure thing, and certainly there are other companies that want and need the money. But our new product is pretty far along in development, which makes me more confident we'll get some capital. Venture capital investors want something a little more than promising, something that is proving itself, and something they think they can make a profit on. That's what we have."

This was exactly the kind of information Ravyn knew she would need in the profile story.

"I'd like to talk to you about all of this – on the record – tomorrow," she said.

"I'm not sure I'm comfortable with that," Marc answered. "It could scare off some of the potential investors."

"Let's not discuss it now," Ravyn said. "Sleep on it and let's talk about it tomorrow. What time should I be at your office?"

Marc reached for is cell phone, checking its calendar. "Let's make it 11 a.m."

"Great," Ravyn said, pulling out her phone and inputting the appointment. "I'll be there."

The conversation had reached the point where Ravyn knew the evening was over. Their plates had been cleared a while ago, and although there was still half a pitcher of margaritas left, neither of them had refilled their glasses.

Ravyn wondered where the check was and commented on the waiter being slow with the bill.

"Oh, I took care of it," Marc said.

Ravyn started to protest, but he stopped her.

"I know what you said, but this was just my way of making up for today," Marc said.

"Well, you must let me make it up to you," Ravyn said as she got up from the table. "Let me get dinner next time."

"I'd love that," he said, walking with her toward the patio exit. "Bacchanalia next time?"

Bacchanalia was one of Atlanta's finest, and most expensive, restaurants. Marc then started to laugh.

Ravyn laughed, too, and started to have the odd feeling of just having been on a date with Marc, with plans having been made for a second one.

Ravyn was up early the next day, going over her research notes, her interview notes with Marc and her prepared questions for that morning's interview before she hopped in the shower.

She was nearly finished drying her hair when she noticed the missed call and voicemail on her phone.

"Miss Shaw," the professional female voice said. "Mr. Linder has been called out of the office today. He said he is very sorry, but he will have to reschedule today's appointment."

The professional voice went on to leave LindMark's office number and instructions to call back to reset the meeting.

Ravyn sighed. "Well, onward and upward."

She pulled out her notes and found the number she had for Bradford Cunningham. She dialed and was surprised when he answered.

"Mr. Cunningham, this is Ravyn Shaw," she began. "I'm a freelance writer for Atlanta Trend magazine, doing a profile piece on Marc Linder and I'd like to talk to you about him and his company for the story."

"Why aren't you doing a profile piece on me?" Bradford asked brusquely. "Why not my company?"

"Well, Mr. Cunningham, I don't make the assignments. But you and your company will certainly be mentioned in the story if you discuss Marc Linder and LindMark with me."

"I can't do this now," he said.

"I could meet you at your office any time today."

"How about in two hours," he replied.

"See you then and thank you."

Ravyn sat in the reception area of BC Enterprises Inc. noticing right away the differences between this one and the one at LindMark.

Where LindMark's office had been sparse, BC Enterprises looked like it had been done by a top designer. The furniture was plush, fresh cut flowers sat atop a glass coffee table, and the wall colors and lighting fixtures were trendy.

Several business newspapers and magazines, including Atlanta Trend, sat on the coffee table.

The receptionist walked Ravyn back to Bradford Cunningham's corner office, which was just as put together as his office's reception area.

Bradford, who looked to be in his late 30s or early 40s, was tall and blond, with a bit of a preppy, frat boy look to him. His golden tan showed off his very white teeth and deep blue eyes.

"Why are we talking about LindMark and Marc Linder?" Bradford asked by way of introduction. "In another year, his company won't be around. My company will still be here and I'll have increased profits by 15 percent. Nobody's getting double digit profits these days, and I am. You should be writing about me."

Ravyn immediately felt put off by Bradford, but his brusque, to-the-point style might be the very reason his company was doing so well – if he wasn't just blowing smoke to impress her.

"Mr. Cunningham," she started.

"Call me Bradford, Ravyn," he interrupted. "You don't mind if I call you Ravyn do you?"

In truth, Ravyn didn't mind if anyone was informal and called her by her first name, but the way Bradford asked, she rather *did* mind.

"That's fine," she heard herself saying, and taking a seat, quickly taking out her small notebook. "Why do you say LindMark will be gone in a year?"

"Linder needs money, and he's not going to get it. His company is younger than mine. I'm more established and investors want a sure bet, not a young company with no track record to speak of."

"Do you know Marc Linder personally? What can you tell me about him?"

"We're not pals or anything, but we travel in the same circles," Bradford said. "I know he was a good lawyer who got bored with it and decided to try to be a tech entrepreneur. You know, he's gotten himself on the right boards on the right charitable organizations, but they're not helping him. There are lots of local businessmen on those boards who are potential investors and they won't invest in him or his company. He's got to go to California to try to get funding. What does that tell you?"

"I thought venture capital in Atlanta was fairly limited," Ravyn said, thinking of the research she had done about VC and angel funding. "Isn't most of the venture capital still on the West Coast?"

"Yes, venture capital in Atlanta is limited, but investors are everywhere, New York, Chicago, even Davenport, Iowa, if you have the right product in the right company. Marc Linder is not drawing the interest of local investors."

"Why is it hard to get venture capital right now?" Ravyn asked.

"It's not hard, if you have the right product. Investors want to invest. How else do they make money? But where are they going to put their money right now? Real estate? That's bust in Atlanta for the next few years. The stock market? Be prepared to accept losses. No, investors want to put their money in proven companies like mine. We've rolled out two new technologies this year alone, and adapted one technology to make it better, more user friendly, that will increase revenues for the third straight year. Ask Marc Linder if his company had growing revenue over the last three years, or if he's turned a profit. I don't think he has. In fact, I know he hasn't. He had some success early on, but his company is stagnant right now. He's not worth your ink."

"I get the sense you don't like Marc Linder or LindMark much," Ravyn said.

"I don't dislike him," Bradford said. "I just don't think he should be made out as this wildly successful business man and some sort of tech wunderkind. He's not."

Bradford Cunningham spent the next 10 minutes talking about his company, BC Enterprises, and its history and successes. Ravyn tried to steer Bradford back to talking about LindMark, but it was no use. He was not interested in talking about his rival, unless it was to downplay the company and its founder.

Ravyn wrapped up the interview, giving Bradford Cunningham her number and asking him to call her if he thought of anything more to say about Marc Linder or his company, but she doubted he'd call. Still, she left feeling slightly uneasy.

Marc's flight landed in LAX around 4 p.m. and he quickly moved to pick up his rental car.

He hadn't expected to be in California so soon, but a voicemail from the head of the venture capital firm the night before meant hopping a flight from Atlanta first thing that morning.

He felt bad he would miss seeing Ravyn, but he knew he'd be back by the end of the week.

At least he hoped so, and with something to celebrate.

Ravyn was sure she would hear from Marc to reschedule the second interview, but a few days passed, then a week, and still she'd heard nothing, despite calling his office every day and leaving voicemail messages on his private cell phone.

Ravyn was surprised at herself for feeling disappointed that Marc hadn't called, that she wouldn't get to see him again in person.

She called a few other technology business leaders in town she knew would know Marc. They were much kinder in their assessment of Marc and his company than Bradford Cunningham had been.

As the deadline for the piece neared, Ravyn realized she was going to have to write the story with very limited access to the profile subject.

She spent two days writing and rewriting the piece before turning it in to Atlanta Trend – on time, of course.

The day after she turned in the story, Marc called.

"I'm sorry I've been so hard to get hold of," he said. "I've been out in California meeting all week with potential investors. I can meet with you this week to finish the interview."

"Marc, the story was due yesterday. I turned it in already. I used what information I had from our interview and talked to others in the community who know you to finish it."

"I see."

"The article should come out in six weeks, but I may get some questions from the editor during the edit process, so I'm glad you are in town in case I need to reach you."

"Well then, call me if you need me."

Ravyn found herself hoping she would.

As if on cue, two days later the editor sent an email with some minor questions and Ravyn immediately called Marc.

"I've got some follow-up questions," she said. "Do you have a few minutes?"

"I'm just headed out to grab a quick lunch. Why don't you meet me? How about Murphy's?"

Ravyn loved Murphy's and she had recently done a profile for Foodie Finds e-zine on the new chef there and got to sample some of the new menu items, so she agreed readily.

This time Marc had arrived first and got a table in the corner, which was good because the place was packed. "Not bad for a Tuesday afternoon," Ravyn thought.

Marc was in beige khakis and a deep green shirt. "Green really is his color," she said to herself, and blushed a little.

"How did the story turn out?" Marc asked as Ravyn sat down.

"I think it turned out well," she said. "But I'm sure you will be the judge of that."

Ravyn meant for that to be a bit of a joke, but Marc looked at her without cracking a smile.

"How come I didn't get to see it before it went to print?" Marc asked.

"Very few publications allow pre-publication review," Ravyn said matter-of-factly. She'd been asked that question so many times as a journalist for the daily paper. "You have to trust I know how to do my job, just as I trust you know how to do yours."

Marc seemed a little put off. "It's just you never know how a reporter is going to spin a story."

"I admit, there are publications that have certain slants, or political viewpoints, and the writers there present an article a certain way, but Atlanta Trend is a business publication. The story is a profile story on you and your business, not how you voted in the last Presidential election or how you feel about gun rights."

Ravyn knew she was sounding defensive, and quickly changed the subject.

"How was the trip to California? Did you get the capital you needed?"

"I had a lot of good meetings while I was there," Marc said. "But I didn't come home with a check, if that's what you are asking."

"Were you out there for the whole week in meetings? I tried calling you nearly every day to see if we could talk again for the story."

"I am sorry I didn't get back to you," Marc said. "I had to take care of some personal business while I was out there that I didn't expect."

Ravyn was curious as to what that personal business might have been, but she didn't feel she could ask.

The waiter arrived and they ordered. Ravyn got the mango chicken salad, while Marc ordered a burger.

Ravyn pulled out a small note pad and began to ask a few questions the editor had sent over. They were mostly questions about the company, again about the company's revenue and profit, and a question about the last triathlon Marc had entered.

Marc's answers weren't more elaborate than when Ravyn had interviewed him nearly two weeks ago. And again he would not answer any questions about his company's financial health. He didn't even seem to want to talk about the triathlon.

Ravyn wondered if Marc was hiding something. Maybe Bradford Cunningham was right about Marc and LindMark. Maybe the company would not be around in a year and the profile would make her and Atlanta Trend look bad in the business community.

Marc must have seen the concerned look on Ravyn's face.

"I'm not trying to be evasive," he said. "I'm just hesitant to disclose too much, since I have potential investors I'm dealing with. I don't want them to read something about the company's financials in Atlanta Trend that they think I haven't told them."

"Where did you stay in California?"

"Los Angeles, mostly, but I did spend a few days down in Laguna Beach."

"Was that for pleasure?"

"I wish," Marc said, his face growing dark. "Just some… personal business I had to clear up."

The food arrived and they both shifted into small talk between bites.

Ravyn told Marc about the very unglamorous life of a freelance writer, always having to hunt for more assignments to keep the bills paid.

Marc told her about running a business with a staff of just five, which meant he had to do a lot of extra duties, including making his own copies on a 10-year-old copy machine that was held together with baling wire and chewing gum.

Ravyn laughed at that, picturing Marc fighting with the copy machine over a paper jam.

"So, what is your next assignment?" Marc asked, wiping a bit of ketchup from the corner of his mouth.

"Well, I'm trying to get an assignment about weekend getaways, and I'm hoping it will mean my having to spend a weekend at St. Simons Island, visiting local restaurants and staying at a hotel – at a reduced rate."

"That sounds glamorous to me!"

"That assignment will be nice, if I can get it, but the other assignments are pretty run of the mill. A story on retail shopping for an in-flight magazine, and some writing for a couple of internal publications at a local real estate firm."

"Oh, you do writing for businesses?"

"I'm pretty much a for-hire writer. So, I end up writing for a lot of different companies, not just newspapers and magazines. And I have a blog that I write, but I don't get paid for it. I just sort of do it for me. I get invited to some nice places here in Atlanta, and then I write about the event, or the restaurant, or whatever."

"Could I hire you to help me write a prospectus for my investors, and some other publicity material I need for LindMark? Would the work you do for me be entirely confidential? What I tell you would not end up in the article?"

"Well, certainly. But don't you have Laura Lucas to do all that for you?"

"Not anymore," Marc said.

"Oh. So that day I saw you and Laura at the restaurant, you were firing her?"

"Something like that," Marc said, hesitantly. "But I could hire you?"

"Sure. How much work do you have for me to do? Do you have a set fee in mind, or do you want me to bill by the hour?"

Marc looked at his watch. "I've got to get back to the office. Why don't we discuss this further later tonight? Can you meet for drinks after work?"

"Yes, of course."

"I'll call you when I'm wrapping up at the office tonight and we can decide where to meet."

Once again the check never came, and Ravyn realized Marc had already taken care of lunch.

"Am I ever going to get to pay for a meal with you?"

"Not if I can help it," Marc said smiling as they left Murphy's.

Ravyn paced the floor of her condo waiting for her cell phone to ring, or at least indicate she had a text from Marc. It was already past 7 p.m. and if he didn't call soon, she was going to presume something had come up and he wasn't going to call for that drink.

Ravyn realized she would be very disappointed if he didn't call. But she was also hungry.

She looked over to see Felix licking his paws and washing his face after finishing up his dinner. "Lucky cat. You've already gotten your grub."

Ravyn went to the refrigerator and looked inside. Nothing much was in there, and what was there didn't think appetizing. She was torn between ordering some Chinese food and running down to Marlow's Tavern for a quick bite. Ravyn decided on the Chinese food, since the leftovers might very well be her breakfast in the morning.

When the phone rang 30 minutes later, Ravyn was sure it was the take-out delivery person needing to be buzzed up to her condo, but it was Marc instead.

"Are you ready for that drink?" he asked.

"Oh! I didn't think you were going to call. I've ordered Chinese. I thought you were the delivery guy."

"Oh, OK," Marc said. "Sorry. The day kind of got away from me. We can do it another time."

"Have you eaten? I've got enough coming for two. And we could discuss my working for you."

"That would be great. Where do you live?"

Ravyn gave Marc her address and hung up, and then felt panicked. She looked around her condo and realized how messy it was. She began racing around, doing a quick cleaning job, throwing a lot of her mess into her bedroom and shutting the door. Even Felix got exiled to the bedroom.

Ravyn was running the vacuum cleaner when the delivery man called, and 15 minutes later, Marc buzzed to be let up as well.

Ravyn felt nervous to have Marc see her home.

He came to the door wearing a charcoal gray sweater under a black leather jacket and dark khaki pants. Standing in the doorway, Marc looked incredibly handsome, Ravyn thought and felt her entire body tingle. She felt rooted to the spot and felt herself begin to feel flush.

"Everything alright?" Marc asked, looking a little perplexed.

"Fine, fine," Ravyn stammered. "I was just trying to clean up a bit before you got here."

"You didn't have to clean up for me," he said. But Ravyn noticed he was giving her place the once over.

Ravyn's condo wasn't that big, just 850 square feet. The living room was small, but one entire wall was glassed and looked south toward Atlanta's downtown skyline. With that kind of view, the room actually felt much larger.

The living room and kitchen were separated by a little breakfast bar that had two bar stools, and off to the right was a small bistro table and two chairs. It passed as Ravyn's dining room space. She had set up the Chinese food there.

Marc handed her a paper bag that contained a bottle of sauvignon blanc. "I wasn't sure what we were having. I hope white wine is OK."

"Perfect. I've got spicy garlic pork and hot and sour soup. I hope you like spicy food."

"Love it. You've got a great view," Marc said, motioning toward the glass wall.

"I know," Ravyn said as she pulled out two wine glasses. "I love this place. I love this view."

From her living room, Ravyn could sit on her couch and see the downtown skyline, including the 73-story Westin Peachtree Plaza, the tallest hotel in the Western hemisphere and Atlanta's fifth tallest building. She'd been on a couple of dates up at the Sun Dial restaurant at the top of the hotel, which rotated once every hour. She remembered how difficult it can be to maneuver around the restaurant, whose floors move, when you are tipsy, and even when you are not.

"How long have you lived here?" Marc asked, breaking Ravyn's reverie.

"I've been here about five years," Ravyn said as she began to spoon out the food into nicer bowls from the take-away boxes. "I'm really lucky. I had planned to buy a condo, but everything in Midtown was so expensive. Dave, the guy who owned this place, moved to Chicago for a job, but thought he would be coming back to Atlanta and he didn't want to sell. I rented it from him for the first year, and his job got extended for another year, so I rented for another year. Then the economy went south and I got laid off. I thought I was going to have to move."

"What happened?" Mark asked, as they started to eat.

"Dave, the owner, realized the job he thought he was coming back to in Atlanta was being eliminated and he decided to stay in Chicago."

"So, you are still renting?" Mark asked between bites.

"Still renting. The condo went back to the bank, but an investor bought it and I'm steady income, so I'm still here. I love this place, but I'm glad I never did buy the place from Dave. He offered to let me buy him out, but he was upside down in his mortgage. That's why the condo went into foreclosure. If I'd bought it at his rate, I'd have gone into foreclosure, too."

Ravyn and Marc ate in silence for a short while, the heaviness of Ravyn's discussion hanging in the air.

Marc reached for the wine bottle to pour each of them another glass.

"This is really good food," Marc said. "Where did you get it?"

Ravyn smiled. "I can't give away all of my secrets."

"But I want to know all of your secrets," Marc smiled back and they locked eyes.

Ravyn blushed and looked down. She could feel her whole body tingle and she suddenly felt very warm.

She picked up her wine glass and motioned toward the balcony of the living room.

Marc picked up his wine glass and followed Ravyn out onto the balcony.

It was a cool, crisp night in Atlanta and Ravyn gave a little shiver as she put her wine glass down on the small table out on the balcony.

"Are you cold?" Marc asked. He stepped back into the condo to get his leather jacket, which he then wrapped around her shoulders.

Ravyn could feel its warmth and smelled his scent on the jacket.

"Thank you. It's a little chillier than I thought."

"Finally fall in Atlanta."

Marc was standing right behind her and she could feel his warmth. She could smell his cologne. He smelled good.

She stood at the balcony railing looking out toward the downtown skyline, but was afraid to turn around and face Marc. She wanted to kiss him. She wanted to take him in her arms and cover him with kisses.

But she was trying to be professional. After all, Marc said he wanted to hire her. It was hardly appropriate to want to make out with her potential boss.

Ravyn shivered again.

Marc put his arms around her. Ravyn sank back into his body and let out a sigh. He turned her body to face him.

Marc leaned in, kissing Ravyn. She put her arms around his neck and they kissed again, this time longer, harder.

"Maybe we should go inside," Marc murmured.

Almost as one, they re-entered the condo and collapsed onto the couch, continuing to kiss.

Ravyn ran her hands through Marc's dark wavy hair, nuzzling his neck, smelling his spicy cologne. Marc ran his hands down Ravyn, who felt as though her whole insides would melt.

Ravyn felt so aroused, and she knew Marc was too. She could feel his arousal as he lay on top of her.

Marc suddenly stopped and sat up, licking his lips, as if to taste the last of Ravyn's kisses, and running his hand through his mussed hair.

"Maybe we should stop," he said.

"Yeah," Ravyn said, trying to catch her breath and trying to collect herself. "Maybe we should."

Marc got up from the couch, collected his jacket and stood at the front door. Ravyn sat up, too, and then ran her hand through her mussed brunette hair. She looked down to see a couple of buttons of her blouse were undone. She quickly buttoned them up. They looked at each other awkwardly.

"Thank you for dinner tonight," Marc said. "I had a nice evening."

"Me too."

"Good night."

Ravyn closed the door and wondered what in the world had just happened.

# Chapter 3

At 9 a.m. the next morning, Ravyn dialed her friend Julie Montgomery's number.

"Emergency lunch appointment! Emergency lunch appointment!" Ravyn practically shouted into the phone when Julie answered.

"Ravyn, what is the matter?"

"I made out like a teenager with Marc Linder last night!"

"What?! How the hell did *that* happen?"

"He came over for Chinese. We were drinking wine. We went out onto my balcony. We started kissing. Oh my God, Julie. I keep thinking I've made a big mistake, but it sure didn't feel like it last night. It felt so right."

"OK, I'm going to need lots of details. Where are we having lunch?"

"In the mood for sushi? Meet me at Twist."

"Oh good. Then I can get some shopping in, too."

Ravyn got to the restaurant, Twist, located in Phipps Plaza, one of Atlanta's upscale shopping centers, and got a table toward the back, where it would be only slightly quieter.

Even for the middle of the week, Twist was busy. But then, this was Atlanta's ritzy Buckhead area, and many of the stay-at-home moms or retired women had been shopping all morning at Phipps Plaza and were ready for lunch, too.

Julie arrived about 15 minutes late, several shopping bags in hand.

Ravyn spied her friend's Teavanna, Macy's and Nordstrom bags with envy.

"Sorry. I was at Nordies and wasn't keeping track of time. But I did get some cute shoes," she said, smiling, as she raised her shopping bag from Nordstrom. "OK. What happened last night? She asked as she slid into her chair.

"Marc Linder came over for dinner…"

"Why did Marc Linder come over for dinner at your place?"

"Well, we were supposed to meet for drinks, but he never called…"

"Why were you supposed to meet for drinks?" Julie interrupted.

"He asked me to work for him…"

"You're working for him?" Julie interrupted again.

"Jules! Stop!"

"I'm confused! I thought you were doing a profile story on him for Atlanta Trend."

"I did. That's over. I turned it in two weeks ago. But we met for lunch, and he offered to hire me for his company's communications needs. Not full-time, just as a freelancer. We were supposed to meet for drinks to talk about it, but he never called."

"You were going to meet over drinks? Isn't that a date?"

"It wasn't a date. It was business."

"Right. Business," Julie said as she rolled her eyes.

"Then when he did call, I had already ordered take-out Chinese and invited him over."

Ravyn had barely taken a breath as she rushed to explain.

"He came over, we started kissing…"

"And?!"

"And then he said he thought we should stop and he left!"

"He left?" Julie said, blinking.

"He left. Now I'm confused," Ravyn said, as she put her head in her hands. "I'm so confused."

"Did he say why he had to leave?"

"No. Just that he thought we should stop. And then he left."

"That's not good."

"No," Ravyn said, shaking her head, which was still in her hands. "That's not good."

"Ravyn, did you like kissing him?"

"Very much. I liked it very much."

"Well, then, you need to call him," Julie said, pragmatically, as she dropped her napkin in her lap.

Ravyn's head shot up and she looked at Julie. "And say what? 'Hey, really enjoyed making out with you like we were a couple of teenagers, but why the hell did you run out on me?'"

"No," Julie said, quite calmly. "Call him and ask about the job."

"What job?"

"The job he's hiring you for!" Julie said, exasperated. "Didn't you say he was hiring you?"

"We actually never talked about the job."

"I thought you said that was why he came over for dinner."

"It *was* why he was coming for dinner. But the kissing part got in the way."

"Oh," Julie deadpanned. "I hate when the kissing part gets in the way."

"Stop it, Julie. I really like him and I shouldn't. I want him to pay me money, but I also want him to kiss me. I want him to do more than kiss me."

"For money? I think that's illegal in this state."

Ravyn burst out laughing, startling the waitress who arrived to take their order.

"Let me in on the joke," the waitress said.

Both Julie and Ravyn started laughing. "Wish we could," Ravyn said.

Once they ordered, Julie asked Ravyn what she really wanted from Marc, a job or a toss in the sheets.

"If you don't want to play with fire, you've got to decide if it's the job or the man you want," Julie said.

"I know. I know you are right, but I want both."

"Who are you? Laura Lucas?"

That shocked Ravyn. "I'm nothing like Laura!"

"No, you aren't, which is why you have to decide if it is the job or the man you want."

"Why can't it be like all the romance novels and movies and be both?"

"Why indeed."

The food arrived and the friends enjoyed sharing spicy tuna rolls and a rainbow roll.

"You are so lucky, Julie. You have it all – the love of your life, two great kids. I envy your life."

"Don't, Ravyn," Julie said, putting up her hand. "There are many days I envy your life. You don't have to answer to anyone. If you want to watch all of the holiday movies on the Lifetime Channel, you don't have to fight anyone for the remote. If you want to take a nice long bubble bath, no one comes in needing you to get gum out of their hair. If you want to go out on a Friday night, you don't have to find a babysitter. God, there are days I just want five minutes of silence."

"I know you are right," Ravyn sighed. "We do think the grass is greener on the other side."

"I love my husband and my kids, don't get me wrong," Julie said with a bit of a sad smile. "But there are days I want to run away and be a single woman again."

Then Julie seemed to pull herself together and put on a smile. "Since I can't, I just have to live vicariously through you."

"Live vicariously through me? I'm boring!"

"I know. So, hurry and up and do something naughty with Marc Linder so I can enjoy it!"

Both women laughed.

Julie suddenly looked stricken.

"What time is it?" she said, sounding panicked.

"One thirty. Why?"

"Oh my God!" Julie practically shouted. "I've got to go!"

Julie stood up, rummaging through her large black handbag until she found a $20 bill and a $10 bill and threw both on the table. "Here, let me know if I owe you any money for lunch."

She grabbed her shopping bags. "I've got to be in the pick-up lane at the girls' school in 15 minutes, or it will take forever to get them, and we have soccer and piano lessons today."

"Do your daughters sleep? Do you?" Ravyn joked.

"Ha! What's sleep?" Julie said over her shoulder as she headed toward the restaurant's front door. "See you soon! Let me know how it goes with Marc!"

Ravyn waited at the table for the waitress to bring the bill.

"I'd like to know how it goes with Marc myself," she thought.

Ravyn kept herself busy the next few days, going to the gym, attending an art gallery opening and writing the event up in her blog, and working on some stories for other publications. But she hadn't heard anything from Marc and she was more than a little worried.

She knew she could, and should, just pick up the phone and call him, but she waited, thinking he would make the first move. He didn't.

Ravyn replayed that night they had dinner at her place over and over in her head. What had she done wrong? Why did he get up and leave? She thought he was really into her. She knew she was really into him.

She was starting to think naughty thoughts about him.

Just the night before she had woken up from the most erotic dream involving Marc. She could feel his touch, his hands strong, yet gentle. She could feel him kissing her, just like that night at her place.

But in the dream, Marc continued on, and he made love to her. She could feel the weight of him on her. She could feel him enter her. When Ravyn awoke, her whole body was sweaty, but she felt somehow satisfied.

Ravyn shook her head, trying to clear all the thoughts of Marc.

Across town in his small office, Marc was pacing the gray carpeted floor. Absentmindedly, he picked up manila folders and moved them around his desk.

Several times he had picked up his office phone to call Ravyn, but then put the receiver down. He didn't know what to say to her.

He knew he should call, to try to explain his behavior the other night. But he was angry with himself and embarrassed.

Marc was very attracted to Ravyn, but he knew from experience mixing work with romance was a bad idea. He thought of Laura Lucas and winced.

In hindsight, Marc knew he should have seen that train wreck coming.

Laura started working for him as a public relations and marketing consultant nearly a year ago.

Laura had called him out of the blue after their first meeting and made a business proposal. Wearing a low-cut dark red dress, she walked into his office and exuded sexuality. She seemed to weave a web that pulled him in.

He hadn't intended on hiring her. That was an expense he didn't think LindMark could afford.

But she was alluring and she explained how he needed to promote the company, which would increase the company's profile, and get venture capital interested in LindMark.

At the end of the meeting, he had hired Laura.

For the first few months, they kept everything professional between them.

But Laura was something of a vixen. She'd arrive at Marc's office to discuss marketing strategies in low-cut blouses and short skirts. Marc learned that was Laura's style, but soon she began flirting with him.

He was flattered, then tempted, then in over his head.

With Laura, romance, if that is what it was, was hot or cold.

One day she'd call him up during a meeting, telling his assistant it was an emergency and to ring her through, and then she'd have the hottest phone sex with him, knowing he couldn't respond.

The next day she'd be angry with him and threaten to stop working with him and stop having sex with him.

Within hours, she was back in his arms and his king-sized bed.

And the sex with Laura was good, Marc remembered. Really good.

He almost ached thinking about her.

Laura, with her jet-black hair that came just beyond her shoulders, her petite athletic body, her ample breasts, was an uninhibited and experienced lover. She knew what she wanted in bed and she got it.

Half the time, they never even got to the bed.

Marc had sex with Laura in places he never imagined – behind a nightclub; in Piedmont Park; in a dark alley behind the High Museum; on a hiking trail in Stone Mountain.

Laura liked the thrill of public sex and nearly being caught, and Marc got swept away by her dangerous nature. He could feel himself getting hard just thinking about her.

It was a heady six months for Marc, who had only dated casually after his divorce. Laura had taken control at a time when Marc was happy to let her do it.

Then he began to realize she wasn't helping his business. The whole Atlanta Trend interview with Ravyn Shaw pointed that out very clearly. Laura seemed to keep Ravyn from meeting with him.

Why? Was she jealous of Ravyn?

The ugly truth began to dawn on him. Marc wasn't paying Laura for public relations help. Essentially, he was paying Laura for sex.

So, he fired her.

But firing Laura wasn't easy.

He tried to let her down gently that afternoon in the restaurant.

For a few days afterward, there were angry, profane voicemails from Laura on his phone, but thankfully, those had stopped. At least he hoped they had. He worried it might be the calm before another storm.

Marc had not expected to be so attracted to Ravyn.

But she seemed to be so opposite of Laura. More like the girl next door than an experienced sexpot.

He found himself making excuses to meet with Ravyn, inviting her to dinner, wanting to talk to her, be with her.

When he found himself at her condo, his desire for her overwhelmed him and he found himself kissing her, wanting her. But then a sudden vision of Laura popped into his head.

Marc did not want to make the same mistake twice, so he made some lame excuse and got out of Ravyn's condo as fast as he could.

Now he stood in his office wondering what to do. He felt lost. He wondered what Ravyn thought of him; if she thought of him at all.

"She probably thinks I'm the biggest asshole there is in Atlanta," Marc muttered to himself.

Ravyn got up mid-morning and put on her running clothes, deciding to get in a quick jog at Piedmont Park.

She didn't have any assignments due right away and that time between assignments was usually when she recommitted herself to exercise.

Her yoga instructor would be happy to see her tomorrow, she knew, but would rag her about not keeping up with her practice. Ravyn wasn't sure she would be able to get into crow pose without tipping over.

A three-mile jog around the park left Ravyn feeling energized. But with no assignments ahead of her, she started to feel restless in the condo. What would she do with the rest of her day?

She went down to get her mail and wished she hadn't. There she found her credit card bill and one overdue notice on her gym membership.

She knew she could usually be late on her gym membership. Unlike the cable and power companies, which tended to cut off service rather quickly when a bill was late, the gym would let her go at least one month before she couldn't show up for a yoga class.

But the notice indicated she had overextended their generosity. They were going to cancel her membership unless she paid the overdue payment and next month's membership fee within five business days. If there was no payment, she would be turned over to a collection agency.

Ravyn knew it would be tough to pay that overdue bill. She had very little savings.

Her frequent lunches with Julie would have to be curtailed. A few other bills would probably be late in getting paid.

She really did need that job that Marc had offered. A steady contract job would give her a little financial security, at least in the short term.

As much as she wanted the man, Ravyn knew she needed the job more. The threat of being turned over to a collection agency made that point very clear.

Ravyn was going to have to swallow her pride, call Marc and get that job. She took a deep breath and dialed his number.

"Hello," Marc's baritone voice said.

"Hi, Marc, it's Ravyn. I wanted to call to talk to you more about the communications job you offered."

"The job?"

"Yes, you mentioned you needed help with some marketing and communications materials for LindMark. Do you still need help?"

"Yes," he said, hesitating. "I still need help."

"Well, I'd like to be considered for that work. Do you want me to submit a formal proposal? I could do that, but I would need to know a little more about the scope of the material your company needs. We could discuss it whenever you have time."

Ravyn's mouth had gone dry and her hands were sweaty just hearing Marc's voice. She felt like she was talking too fast.

"Are you there?" she asked, waiting for him to respond.

"Yes, I'm here. Sorry. I'm here."

"Do you want me to call back later?" Ravyn asked. "I can call back later, if now is not a good time."

"Why don't you stop by the office later this afternoon and we can discuss it," Marc said. "I can explain some of the materials my company needs."

"That sounds fine. I'll be there. Around two?"

"Two o'clock is fine. I'll see you then."

Ravyn hung up and her heart was pounding. This was going to be more difficult than she thought. If just hearing Marc's voice made her feel weak, how was she going to manage being near him in his office?

. Marc hung up the phone with Ravyn and wondered what he had just gotten himself into.

Why had he asked Ravyn to come by the office? "Because I want to see her," he thought. "I need to see her."

If he offered her the job, he could see her more often. But Laura Lucas's face kept haunting him. He did not want to make the same mistake with Ravyn that he had made with Laura.

Could he keep their relationship strictly professional? It seemed that's what Ravyn wanted. Why else would she call to ask about the job?

Well, if that's the way she wanted it, he would have to respect that.

Marc pulled out a legal note pad and began to write down some of the projects he'd need Ravyn to do for LindMark.

When Ravyn got to LindMark's offices, the receptionist led her straight back to Marc's office.

Marc stood up to shake her hand, but the gesture felt awkward.

"I'm glad you could see me today," he said, taking her hand, and then quickly dropping it. Her touch felt like electricity.

"Of course," said Ravyn, her mouth feeling dry again. "I wanted to learn more about the job opportunity."

"Sure. Let's see," Marc said, reaching for the note pad and starting to read off some of the materials he needed. "The company will need a prospectus that I can take to potential investors. That's probably the biggest project I need done and that will take some time. It will need to contain some financial data, and I would have to ask you to sign a confidentiality agreement that you would not disclose my company's financial situation with anyone outside of this office."

"Understood," Ravyn said. "I can agree to that."

"I'm not sure how much time that would take you, so we can discuss the compensation on that later. I may also need some press releases written from time to time, and if I get venture capital, I may need some more materials that are specific to the companies that are investing in my firm. We can discuss that at a later time, too. What are your initial thoughts?"

Ravyn was trying hard to concentrate on what he was saying, when all she wanted to do was reach over his desk and touch him.

But he seemed to be all business, so maybe the incident in the condo didn't mean anything to him. Maybe she'd read him wrong.

"Miss Shaw? What are your initial thoughts?" Marc asked.

Ravyn heard him address her formally, and realized it would be just business between them.

"Mar…, Mr. Linder, I can either draw up a proposal to be a temporary contract worker for you," Ravyn responded. "Or I can offer my writing services on a per hour basis, turning in an invoice to you every other week, whichever you prefer."

"I leave it to your judgment and I'll review your proposal, say, in a week? Is that enough time?"

"That's plenty of time," Ravyn said. "I'll send it to your office next week."

Ravyn left LindMark's office disheartened.

She had hoped there might be some spark between her and Marc, but after the meeting in his office, she felt perhaps her feelings weren't reciprocated. Maybe the night in her condo was just his way of seeing how far he could go with her, she thought. Maybe he was a player. He had, after all, been with Laura.

"Figures," Ravyn muttered.

Ravyn was glad she had plans for dinner that night with some single girlfriends. She did not want to spend the evening at her Midtown condo thinking about Marc.

She arrived at Danica Martinez's Reynoldstown home before the rest of the girlfriends arrived. Danica was a single mother of three who worked at the veterinary clinic where Ravyn took Felix. The two women had met when Ravyn first adopted Felix from a local rescue shelter and they had hit it off.

Danica had recently started renting the small three-bedroom home, and although it had been in rough shape when she got it, she had decorated it in white, cream, dark brown and terra cotta hues, making it warm and inviting.

Danica's children were with their father for the next four days, which is why Danica had pulled together the informal dinner at her house.

Although Danica always struggled to make ends meet, she was an incredible cook and could pull together a meal with just a few ingredients and a crock pot.

Ravyn walked into the house to the smell of a pot roast and fresh baked bread.

"Oh my God, that smells incredible," she said, giving Danica a big hug and handing over a bottle of red wine.

As she took off her jacket, Ravyn asked how Danica had been doing and how the children were.

"The same," Danica said. "And their father is still being an ass. He wants to lower the support payments again. He says he's not making as much money in the bad economy and he can't afford the child support. He sure could afford that bitch he was fucking when we were married."

Danica's eyes began to fill with tears.

"They are living together now," she said. "That's why he can't afford his own kids. He's spending all his money on her. I think we may end up in court again."

"I'm sorry, Danica," Ravyn said, sincerely, and gave her another hug.

"Thanks," she sighed as she wiped away her tears on a kitchen towel. "I don't want to talk about it tonight. I just want to get caught up with everyone."

"Fair enough. Who all is coming?"

"Tanya's coming. I think you met her at my last dinner party. She works at The Weather Channel. Jamie is coming. I don't think you've met her. She works at the hair salon I go to. And Sandy said she may come. She's the mother of McKenzie's best friend at school."

McKenzie, 7, was Danica's oldest daughter.

Just then the doorbell rang and Jamie arrived, bringing a decadent looking double chocolate cake, with Tanya close behind, who brought another bottle of wine.

The women gathered in the kitchen, each drinking a glass of wine and nibbling on cheese, crackers and fruit while Danica sliced tomatoes and a cucumber to go in the tossed salad for dinner.

Ravyn made small talk with Tanya and Jamie, immediately liking both women.

Tanya was thin and tall and had a young son, A.J. Jamie was short and heavier and also had a young son, Kody. She and Tanya talked about their boys and Ravyn smiled to hear their stories.

Danica gave the women another short update on her ex-husband and his latest tactic to get out of child support as she put the pot roast on a serving platter.

"My brother Adam is a lawyer," Tanya said. "Do you want to talk to him to see what you need to do?"

"I can't afford a lawyer," Danica said as she got the last of the salad together and brought it to the table.

"He won't charge you just to talk to him," Tanya said. "Plus, he's my baby brother. He'll do what I say."

They laughed and sat at the table to dig into dinner.

Two hours later the dinner party was winding down. Chocolate cake and coffee cups were the only things left on the table. Tanya and Ravyn were clearing the last of the dishes while Danica loaded the dishwasher.

"Where do you want me to put the wine glasses?" Tanya asked.

"I'll put them in the dishwasher," Danica said. "They aren't my grandmother's crystal, so I don't worry if they chip."

"What? We aren't classy enough for the good crystal?" Ravyn teased.

Danica's face fell, and suddenly she began to cry into her kitchen towel.

"I'm sorry, Danica, I was only kidding," Ravyn said, worried that she had said something to hurt her friend.

"No, no, it's not you," Danica said, wiping her tears with the towel. "I had to hock my grandmother's crystal to pay some bills. I don't think I'll be able to get it back before it gets sold at the pawn shop."

Now she was really sobbing.

"What pawn shop is it at?" Jamie asked. "I'll go get it tomorrow. And you can pay me back whenever you can. Don't go to a pawn shop for that stuff. Come to me. Let me help you."

"We'll all try to help you, Danica," Tanya said.

Ravyn was digging through her purse looking for what few dollars she had in there.

"Here, Danica," Ravyn said, giving her friend a crumpled $10 bill and a $5 bill. "I haven't had better food at a restaurant lately. Let's think of tonight as a kind of supper club. I got the blue plate special!"

"I can't take your money for tonight's dinner," Danica said, shaking her head. "I was hosting you. This was a party."

"You aren't taking my money, I'm giving it. Here," Ravyn said as she pressed the money into Danica's hand.

Tanya and Jamie were doing the same, grabbing some cash from their purse. Among the three women, they pulled together $86.

"Is that enough for the pawn shop?" Tanya asked.

Danica, crying again into the towel, shook her head "No."

"Well, I'll go tomorrow and get the crystal," Jamie said. "Is there anything else there I need to get?"

Danica began to cry harder. "My grandmother's wedding ring is there, too," she said between sobs.

"OK, OK, we'll take care of it tomorrow," Jamie said, as she hugged Danica hard. "It will be OK."

"I'm just so scared," Danica said. "I rented this house, thinking I'd have a fresh start for me and my kids. But now I need money for a lawyer over the child support again. This was all supposed to be over. It was supposed to be *over*. It just isn't fair."

"I'll talk to my brother," Tanya said, softly, trying to soothe Danica. "Let's see what he can help you with. It's going to be OK."

Ravyn got home that night and felt emotionally drained. Dropping her keys on the kitchen table, she went into her bedroom and sat down on the side of her bed, taking off her shoes and rubbing her feet.

She got up and walked into the kitchen, pouring herself a glass of wine as a nightcap.

She was worried about her friend, Danica, and she realized she was worried about herself, too.

Ravyn often worried that she might be one major medical bill – or one major veterinary bill or car repair bill – away from having real money troubles, too. She always managed to pay her bills, albeit sometimes late. But what if there came a time when she couldn't?

Would she be pawning her "good" jewelry, such as it was?

Ravyn, glass of wine in her hand, gave a little snort thinking about how little "good" jewelry she had. She put the wine glass down and looked down at her hands at her two sapphire rings and realized she would truly hate to part with them. She had her grandmother's diamond ring, too, but Ravyn would never be able to part with that. Or would she?

Ravyn quickly checked her emails, hoping to find offers of some freelance work, but only found spam and other junk mail. She drained her glass of wine and sighed again.

She went to bed in a foul mood.

Early the next week, Ravyn called LindMark, hoping to talk to Marc to tell him she had finished her proposal and would drop it off that afternoon. But mostly, Ravyn just wanted to hear his voice.

Ravyn had proposed a monthly contract, which could be terminated by either she or Marc, which would cover half of her rent and most of her utility bills each month. She thought the proposal was probably very conservative, but she was still nervous Marc would say no to it. She'd drop her price if she had to, but she hoped it wouldn't come to that.

The receptionist said Marc was out of town, but that Ravyn could drop the proposal off with her and she'd make sure Marc would receive it.

Ravyn was disappointed she wouldn't get to see or talk to Marc, but was glad to get the proposal dropped off and said a little prayer that she would get the contract.

Her evening at Danica's house had left her with lingering anxiety about her financial situation. Just yesterday two more bills had arrived in the mail.

Marc's receptionist called back two days later. Ravyn sighed with relief when the receptionist said Marc had accepted her proposal and would be sending her some financial material so she could get started on the projects for LindMark.

With some of her other freelance work, Ravyn would be able to pay her bills on time very soon.

She called her friend Julie Montgomery to tell her the good news.

"I got the contract job!" Ravyn said.

"That's great, Ravyn. So, no regrets about giving up the man?"

"Well, I am disappointed about not getting the man, too, but I am so happy to have the job. I think I'll sleep better at night now."

"I'm so happy to hear that," Julie said. Ravyn could hear the shouts of young girls in the background.

"Whoops! Gotta go. Ashley and Lexie are fighting again over a teen magazine."

"A teen magazine? They aren't teenagers yet. They aren't even 10 yet."

"Haven't you heard? The teen years start at 8. And you have no idea of the power of Justin Bieber."

The women laughed and then Julie rang off.

Ravyn ran a few errands that afternoon and then got home in time for a quick shower. She was heading out that night to a new restaurant opening in Midtown. That was one of the perks of her blog. Even though she didn't get paid for blogging, she did get invited to events, which meant she would have a glass of wine and some heavy appetizers tonight. In other words, she would have a free dinner.

Ravyn got to Cucina Asellina at 7 p.m. and the party was already started. The new restaurant had removed all of the tables for the evening, leaving a large open area in the center. Around the four walls, the restaurant had set up tasting stations with heavy hors d'oeuvres and wine pairings.

Ravyn filled a plate with some wild mushroom flatbread pizza and veal meatballs and got a glass of Chianti. She looked around the room to see if she recognized anyone.

She saw fellow blogger James Davidson and went over to say hello. He was deep in conversation with another woman, but he saw Ravyn and motioned her over to join them.

"Ravyn, how are you?" he asked, giving her a little air kiss.

"Good, James, how about you?"

"The same. I didn't see you at the Latitude opening," said James, mentioning a new Buckhead restaurant that opened the week before.

"I had other plans that night with girlfriends, so I missed it. How was the food?"

"About the same as any other new restaurant," James said. "I'll go back in a couple of weeks to try it out when they aren't putting out all the best stuff for us bloggers. Ravyn, have you met Avi Gates? She's the new retail reporter over at your old line of work," James said, introducing the two women. "Avi, this is Ravyn Shaw, freelancer extraordinaire."

"Abby is it?" Ravyn asked.

"No, Avi. I'm named for my grandmother," Avi said. "You used to work at the Atlanta Trib?"

"I did. I got laid off three years ago. Went into business for myself after that."

"Oh," Avi said, her voice trailing off. "Well, I just started there."

Ravyn could sense the awkward moment and made a motion that she wanted to freshen her drink and walked back across the room, politely saying "Nice to meet you" as she did. Ravyn hoped it sounded sincerer than it really was. She rather resented that the paper hired new, younger reporters, knowing the Trib was paying them half of what reporters used to make. And those new reporters took those jobs at that pay and were glad to have a job in journalism.

As she crossed the room, Ravyn felt a hand on her elbow and she turned, coming face to face with an ex-boyfriend, Shane Thomas.

"Oh!" she said, so surprised she nearly dropped her cocktail plate. "Hi, Shane. What are you doing here?"

"Same as you, I think, enjoying wine and appetizers," he said, laughing.

"Sorry, I just meant I get invited to these things because I blog about them, or have written about the restaurant for a freelance article," Ravyn said.

"I know the owner."

"Oh."

"It's getting crowded in here. Want to go out to the patio?"

"Sure, let me just refill this plate and glass."

Ravyn went over to the station serving calamari and shrimp and then got a glass of pinot grigio and then followed Shane outside.

Atlanta was having another warm fall night and several people were outside on the patio. Shane had found a table near the sidewalk.

Ravyn sat down and put her plate between them. "I'll share."

"Thanks. I should go get a plate, too. I'll be right back."

Ravyn sat at the table wondering why the universe was torturing her so. Shane, at six-foot, two-inches, deep green eyes and a swimmer's body, was a real estate agent and they had dated briefly about a year ago. It wasn't all that serious, but it was a lovely distraction while it had lasted, which wasn't long.

Honestly, they hadn't had a big blow up or anything like that. They just stopped calling each other. The brief affair had run its course.

Ravyn was interested in Marc, but she couldn't be while he was her boss. And now here was Shane again, looking incredibly handsome. Was she being tested in some way? It sure felt like it.

Shane returned with three plates loaded with appetizers and a full glass of wine.

"Wow. Were you a waiter in college? Nice job carrying all those plates."

"I was, actually. I worked at the Olive Garden my senior year of high school and a burger joint all through college to make a little money."

Ravyn and Shane made small talk for the next two hours, alternating who would go in to refill the plates with appetizers and the glasses with wine.

When the party began to wind down, Ravyn realized she was a little tipsy, and very horny. They stood at the valet stand waiting for their cars when Shane turned to her and kissed her.

"I've wanted to do that all night," he said.

"Really? I was hoping you would kiss me."

"Don't you live around here?" Shane asked.

"I'm just a few blocks down, actually. I could have walked here tonight, but I didn't want to do it in these heels," Ravyn said, pointing to her shoes.

Shane put his arm around Ravyn's waist and pulled her close. "Let's go over to your place."

"OK. Follow me when I get my car."

A few minutes later, Ravyn was unlocking her front door with Shane right behind her. She could feel his hard-on as he pressed against her. Shane wasted no time when they got through the door. He kicked it closed behind him and began kissing Ravyn urgently. Ravyn was kissing him right back.

She felt his hands pulling at her shirt, then felt his hands on her back and unhooking her bra.

Ravyn began undoing her shirt buttons and walking backward, leading him to her bedroom.

Shane was removing his shoes and undoing his fly as they fell onto the queen-sized bed, startling Felix, who leapt from the bed, giving a little yowl.

Shane was pulling at Ravyn's skirt and then her panties. She could feel his fingers begin to play with her, all wet and hot. She let out a moan as his fingers began to work their magic.

Shane quickly put on a condom and entered Ravyn, who let out another, longer moan. Ravyn clung to Shane's back and as she reached orgasm she moaned again. "Marc," she said. "Oh, Marc."

Shane climaxed and fell on top of Ravyn. "I'm Shane, Ravyn."

Ravyn's eyes flew open. "Oh my God. I'm so sorry, Shane."

Shane rolled over onto his back, smiling. "I don't know who Marc is, but I'm glad I was here tonight and not him."

Ravyn curled onto her side, away from Shane, and blinked back tears. She wished with all her heart Marc was here, and not Shane.

Ravyn woke up the next morning with a headache and a sense of dread.

"What have I done?" she asked herself, feeling the warm body, and hearing slight snores, next to her.

Shane stirred next to her and rolled over, throwing an arm over her. Then he grunted and opened his eyes.

"Good morning, beautiful," he said, with a soft smile.

"Good morning, Shane."

"What time is it? Do we have time for some fun this morning?"

"It's late, Shane. I've got to get up and get to work."

"You work from home," he said as he pulled her close.

"No, I'm doing some contract work and I've got to be at the office this morning," Ravyn said, trying to pull away. She just wanted last night to end. She didn't want to see Shane right now.

"OK, Ravyn," Shane said sitting up on her bed, looking around for is shorts and then pulling on his cargo pants. "I can take a hint."

Ravyn got up, grabbing her purple silk robe she'd gotten on a long-ago trip to San Francisco's Chinatown, and followed Shane to the front door.

"Do I at least get a cup of coffee?" Shane asked. He saw the look on Ravyn's face and realized he'd be stopping at Starbucks on his way home.

"I'll call you later," he said as he walked out the front door.

Ravyn closed it behind him, hoping he wouldn't.

Ravyn liked Shane. She liked the time they had spent together, but she remembered why they had broken up. Shane was a player and they hadn't been going out long when she found out he was seeing several other women, too. Ravyn needed a man who would be hers and hers alone. Shane was not that man.

Ravyn started a pot of coffee and got in the shower. The warm water felt good and she almost felt like she could wash away the events of last night. Not that she hadn't enjoyed the sex, but that's all it was. Sex. She wanted more than that.

Ravyn hadn't really lied to Shane. She intended to go to LindMark's offices today to drop off the first of the documents she had produced. She knew she could just email them in, but she was hoping she could see Marc as well.

Ravyn drank her coffee and ate a sesame seed bagel as she got dressed and put on her make up. She looked in the mirror, checking her profile on both the left and right side to make sure her make up looked just right. She wanted to look just right when she saw Marc today.

"*If* I see Marc today," she reminded herself.

She made sure to give Felix an extra pat on the head, since he hadn't been able to sleep on the bed last night. "Sorry, buddy," she said as she stroked his neck. "Won't happen again. At least not for a while."

Ravyn checked her email before she set out for LindMark's office and saw a message that the Atlanta Trend piece on Marc

Linder would be out by the end of the week. A PDF copy of the article was attached, something she always requested from her freelance assignments so she would have good clips to show to any other potential employer.

She read over the article and thought it looked good. The photo of Marc that accompanied the article also looked good. Ravyn printed off a color copy on her printer.

She knew it was a bit juvenile, but she wanted to be able to look at his face. She sighed. "Wish it was you last night."

# Chapter 4

Ravyn parked in the office building's parking deck and collected her things. She took a couple of deep breaths before she got out of her car. She knew why she felt a little nervous about seeing Marc, but she shook her head and tried to put her growing feelings for him out of her mind.

"What is this?" she asked herself. "A school girl crush? Get a grip, Ravyn."

When the elevator got to the sixth floor and she turned toward his office, Ravyn smiled and put her best professional face on.

"Good morning," she said to the receptionist. "I know I don't have an appointment with Mr. Linder, but I have some preliminary documents he'd asked me to create. Is he available?"

"Let me see," was the no-nonsense response.

Just a few minutes later, Marc walked into the reception area.

"What a nice surprise, Ravyn. I wasn't expecting you."

"I know, Mr. Lind–, Marc. But I have some preliminary documents for you and I wanted to be sure I was capturing exactly what you wanted. If you have a few moments, I'd like to go over them with you. If you are busy, I can drop them off and you can call me when you get a chance to look at them."

"I have some time now, why don't you come back to my office."

Ravyn followed him down the hall, inhaling, smelling his cologne. Just the smell of it reminded her of their night of aborted passion and it nearly made her weak in the knees.

"Calm down," she thought to herself. "He's just not that in to you."

Marc motioned for her to enter his office first and closed the door. He then offered her a chair and pulled a second chair up next to her, his knee brushing hers and setting off a spark of static electricity. Ravyn felt as if she'd been shocked by lightning. "Oh!" she exclaimed.

Marc smiled. "Sorry about that. Now, let me see what you have."

Ravyn handed over three color brochures she'd printed out on her little Canon home printer. The quality wasn't all that good, but it would give Marc an idea of what a professional brochure would look like.

The first one was fairly general, simply stating brief information about the company and how it had grown over the past three years. It was the kind of tri-fold brochure that might be handed out to potential vendors or clients at a tradeshow, she explained.

The second was more detailed, with some growth projections and soft revenue numbers. It was a brochure that would be given to clients and vendors who were more serious about doing business with LindMark, but weren't quite ready to sign a contract.

The final piece wasn't really a brochure as much as a one sheeter that had even more detailed revenue numbers and growth projection graphics. The real nitty gritty of LindMark, if you will, she explained.

It had two color pie charts and a blank space where she would place a professional head shot of Marc. This was the kind of material that could be given to prospective investors and clients who had signed on the dotted line.

Marc read each item silently, his black rimmed reading glasses propped on his Roman nose.

"This is the right track, but I'd like to see more detail in the one sheeter," he said. "This is the one I give to investors, right?"

"Yes. I am still working on the prospectus, which is the one you'd use for venture capital investors. I really see this piece," she said as she held the one sheeter "as something you give to the level right below the venture capitalist, or to the venture capitalist initially to get him or her to bite. And I need to get a professional head shot of you to put in the blank space."

"I've got a head shot somewhere on my computer."

"When was that head shot taken? If it was more than a year ago, let's go ahead and get a new one. I know a photographer who would do it fairly inexpensively. I used to work with her at the newspaper and she does some freelance on the side. I can call her to set that up."

"No, Laura Lucas had one taken just a few months ago. It's not that old. We can use that."

Ravyn felt her back straighten and bristled at the sound of Laura's name but hoped Marc didn't see her reaction.

"OK. That sounds fine," she said, trying to sound cool. "Is there anything you see that you want me to change on any of the material I've brought today?"

Marc began scratching out some things on each brochure and scribbling some notes in the small margins.

"Can you read my writing?" he said over his reading glasses as he showed Ravyn the papers.

"I think so," she said as she squinted at the writing. She realized she probably needed reading glasses, too. "If I can't make it out, I'll call you or text you."

"When do you think you'll have the prospectus done? I've got another meeting in California in a couple of weeks and I'd like to bring that new material with me."

"I can make the changes to these brochures today and drop them off at a print shop tomorrow. That should only take a day, or two, at the very latest. I can work on the prospectus the rest of the week and have that to you first thing on Monday. If you can look at it right away, we can get that to the printer on Tuesday, rush it, and have it by the end of that week. Will that work?"

"That works. Do I need to write you a check for the printed stuff? And what about this work? Shall I pay you now?"

"That would be fine," Ravyn said, but inwardly she sighed with relief. She needed to pay more than a few bills. "Let's see if the printer will invoice the company, and if you could pay me today, that would be great."

"I'll get your check to you tomorrow, is that OK?" Marc said as he stood up, signaling the meeting was over.

"That would be fine," Ravyn said as she stood up, too.

Marc and Ravyn stood facing each other. Suddenly it felt rather awkward. Ravyn quickly looked down.

"Great," Marc finally said. He walked to his door, opening it, leading Ravyn out of his office, placing his hand at the small of her back, an intimate gesture. "Get me the prospectus on Monday so I can look over it. I'd really like to take it to investors when I head to California."

"I will. I'll see you Monday then."

As they neared the reception area, Ravyn turned toward Marc.

"I forgot to tell you," she said. "The Atlanta Trend piece will be out next week. You can use that in your investor materials as well. You should put every piece of positive publicity you can in front of potential investors."

"Great," Marc said. "So, it's positive publicity, then? I can't wait to read it."

Ravyn left Marc's office and he could still smell her perfume, which smelled a little like vanilla. Marc could not stop thinking about Ravyn, and he wished he could.

Marc felt like he was doing some kind of dance, trying to keep the investors interested in LindMark. He needed the materials Ravyn was working on quickly, but he knew once that work was completed, he would not have an excuse to see her again. And he wanted an excuse to see her again.

Marc went back to his office and began making notes on the new software, what it would do and how much money he estimated it would take to get it developed and through initial beta testing. Conservatively, he thought it would take about $5 million, if everything went right. Unfortunately, he didn't have a single investor that was willing to fork over the entire $5 million.

He was trying to schedule meetings with several investors in California, hoping he could convince two or three of them to kick in at least $1 million. Marc hoped he wasn't going to have to do this song and dance for five individual investors, or more.

Marc nearly filled a sheet of yellow legal paper with his ideas and notes. He knew he would have to transcribe the notes onto his computer, but he liked writing things down first. He thought it helped him think better.

Marc inhaled deeply and could still smell the faint scent of Ravyn's vanilla perfume.

Why did he keep thinking of her? What was it about her?

Marc's divorce had left him rather gun shy of dating, initially. Then for a few months after his divorce, he began dating, if one could call it that, several women at a time, never connecting deeply with any of them. He never considered himself a "player," but in looking back, Marc realized that's really what he was during that time.

Eventually, he met Laura Lucas at a networking event. He needed public relations help for LindMark and Laura's dark beauty was an added benefit. He hadn't meant for them to become lovers, but one night, over maybe one too many Old-Fashioneds, he found himself in bed with Laura, who was as aggressive and energetic in the sack as she was in her career.

Now it was Ravyn he kept thinking about. Her blue eyes, her soft smile, her athletic body. He picked up his phone, wanting to call her, to hear her voice.

Instead, Marc put down the phone and sighed again.

Bradford Cunningham read the advanced digital copy of Atlanta Trend and then slammed his fist down hard on his desk. It paid to have friends that could get him what he wanted in Atlanta, but he was disgusted as he read the profile on Marc Linder.

"What an ass-wipe article," he said to himself. "That prick doesn't deserve this ink. I want an article on *me*, dammit. My company is better than his."

Cunningham also knew that Linder was trying to put together some capital for his company, and Cunningham knew which companies Linder was going after. Cunningham was going after the same money at those same companies. He knew he would have to work fast to make sure his company got the money.

Cunningham picked up his cell and called his new publicist, Laura Lucas.

"Laura, Bradford here. Have you gotten any responses yet from the VCs out in California? I want to know we've got money coming in."

"Bradford, you are going to have to be just a little more patient. I've got two calls in with ATC Capital, and I've talked to the director of business development at BlacKat Angels. And we should hear back next week from Star Bridge Capital."

"Why is this taking so long? I need the money for my company. I need to be sure I get it. I don't want money that should come to my company to go to Linder. Make sure I get the money."

"I'm working on it. I've got some ideas that will show LindMark isn't the best company to invest in."

Cunningham hung up the phone and rubbed his temples.

His head hurt as he pored over the cash flow charts his chief financial officer had sent over. BC Enterprises was sound but was very cash poor.

Cunningham, if he were being honest with himself, knew he was partly to blame. He'd invested heavily in the company on equipment and other capital improvements that really should have waited until the company had better revenue stream.

He looked around at the office equipment he'd bought rather than leased. What a mistake, he thought.

And now he'd hired Laura Lucas to help give his company a little sizzle.

Well, Bradford smiled to himself, thinking of Laura's dark hair and curvy figure. He rather hoped Laura would give him a little sizzle, too.

Ravyn got back to her condo with some take-out from Farm Burger. Felix yowled loudly as she walked in.

Ravyn wasn't so sure Felix was saying hello, or just making a hungry comment on the hamburger he could smell in the bag.

She poured a Diet Coke, sat at her little breakfast bar and started up her laptop computer. She wanted to finish making the changes to the brochures for LindMark so she could drop them off tomorrow at FedEx Office. Felix was making things difficult as he rubbed himself on her legs, meowing, begging for some of the bleu cheese burger.

Ravyn finally relented and dropped a small piece of the burger on the floor next to Felix. "Alright you little beggar. Here you go." Felix gulped it down greedily and looked up, as if asking for more. "No sir, that's all you get."

Ravyn finished the burger and started in on the sweet potato fries when she checked her email and saw a message from Atlanta Trend, with a PDF of the profile story on Marc. She moved the PDF file into her projects completed folder on her computer. Ravyn would likely use that story as a clip when she sought out other profile pieces for other publications.

The Atlanta Trend editor also wanted to know if she wanted to write a 900-word story on a new economic development initiative in North Fulton County called Progress Partners. The story was due in two weeks.

Ravyn quickly responded that she'd love to write it. What she'd love even better was the $300 paycheck she'd get for a couple of days work. She looked over the assignment, made some quick emails to the sources she'd need to interview to set up a time when she could call them.

Another email confirmed acceptance of a story idea she'd pitched about a new set of restaurants that had opened recently in Atlanta. In reality, Ravyn would simply rework some of the blog posts she'd done about these restaurants and turn it in to one of the in-flight magazines she occasionally wrote for, but it would be another $200 for a short story. Suddenly, Ravyn felt much better about her finances for the month.

She sent out a couple more emails to the restaurant owners to set up interviews, and she knew she'd probably get a couple of invites to come in and sample the menu. That was always such a fun part of her work. She'd met many of Atlanta's top chefs and restaurant owners. She realized she should try to capitalize on that. Maybe there could be some revenue in that.

About an hour later, Ravyn got an email from the owner of Meehan's Public House, a locally-owned chain of taverns, which had just opened its newest location in Midtown. The owner,

Phil, offered to have her come over to sample the new menu and take a tour of the new space.

"This is more like it," Ravyn thought. She made an appointment to be there later that evening. She checked her digital camera and noticed the battery was a little low, so she started to charge it. She'd probably bring her camera and take a few photos at the restaurant tonight. Maybe the in-flight magazine would accept a few of her photos. Maybe she could manage to get a few more dollars for the assignment.

Ravyn showed up around 7 p.m., and Meehan's was pretty full of the after-work crowd, even for a Tuesday night. Ravyn waited by the dark wood bar for Phil.

Meehan's was an Irish pub and the bar made of wood stretched across the length of the left side of the restaurant.

"Can I get you a Guinness?" asked the bartender in a slight Irish accent.

"No thanks, I'm waiting on the owner," she replied. "Now why is every bartender in this town incredibly handsome?" she wondered. "Must be a pre-requisite for the job."

Phil showed up about 10 minutes later, extending his hand and apologizing for making her wait.

"Do you want a Guinness? A glass of wine?" he asked.

"Let me take the tour first," she replied. "It's hard to take notes with a glass of wine in my hand."

"Fair enough. Are you ready?"

"Sure, lead the way."

Phil pointed toward the dark wood bar, which had a mirror nearly the length of the wall behind it. Most of the bar, with its intricate carvings along the top above the mirror, came over from Ireland, he explained. They walked over to the front door, which looked like it came from an ancient mansion.

Turns out, it did, he said.

"Over there is stained glass from a church in Spain," Phil said, pointing to a window.

The pub even had a small stage for local bands, an outside patio, and a private room for events or parties.

As they walked toward the back of the pub, Phil stopped at what looked like a phone booth.

"I'm very excited about this," he said, looking like a boy who just got a much sought-after birthday present. "This is a confessional from a church in Paris. It cost us $10,000. I know I was crazy to get it, but it is so cool."

Ravyn stepped up into the confessional and closed the door, turning toward the small, grated window. "Forgive me, Father, for I would love to sin," she said and let out a little giggle.

Phil laughed on the other side of the door.

"What are you going to use this for?" Ravyn asked, stepping out of the confessional. The space was so small; it would be hard to put even a tiny bistro table and chairs in it.

"I'm not sure. But you have to admit it's cool."

Ravyn hastily scribbled some notes about the confessional in her notebook. "Oh, it sure is."

They ended up back at the bar and Ravyn took a seat.

"Let me get you a menu," Phil said. "I'll have the kitchen send out a few things on small plates. Is that OK?"

"Perfect. I'd like to try a few things, but I don't want a full meal, OK?"

Ravyn ordered a glass of white wine and waited at the bar for some of the food to arrive. The bar was noisy, but not overly so. The restaurant had high ceilings and the wood seemed to help absorb some of the noise.

All of these observations she kept scribbling in her notebook.

"You a reporter?" the bartender asked.

"I am," Ravyn said, before she realized she really wasn't anymore.

"Who do you write for?" he asked.

"I write for a lot of different magazines. I'm working on a story about some of the new restaurants in Atlanta for an in-flight magazine, like the ones you read on a Delta flight."

Just then Ravyn realized she'd forgotten to take any photos for the story. She reached into her purse, pulling out her little digital camera.

"I've got to take a few photos for the story," she said. "Can I get a shot of you at the bar?"

"Sure," said the bartender, with that light brogue.

"What is your name?" she asked, poised to write it into her notebook.

"Sean McGinty," he said.

"Of course," Ravyn thought to herself. "Well, Sean, say cheese!"

Ravyn backed up so she could get Sean centered in the photo. She took several to be sure she'd get something that might be usable for the story. The bar had flat screen TVs on either side, and she tried to keep those out of the photos. She wanted to get the wooden bar with its intricate details in the photo, however.

"Thanks, Sean. Don't take my wine, will you? I want to get a few other photos."

She walked around the restaurant, following the path Phil had shown her, taking a photo of the front door, the stained glass, and that funky confessional.

When she got back to the bar, the first of her menu tasting plates had arrived.

She started with the lobster bisque, then had feta stuffed dates. Pretzel bites and bangers with homemade Guinness mustard followed. Lastly, she had some shrimp cocktail.

Phil stopped by as Ravyn was finishing up.

"This is really good, Phil," she said. "Not what I expected for pub grub."

"No, we're really proud of that," he said. "We do have some fried food, but it's not all fried food. We like to think this is really a step above what you'd find at a pub. More what you would find at a true Atlanta restaurant, which is really what we are."

Ravyn finished writing down Phil's comments, and then thanked him for the dinner. The story would likely run in the next issue of the in-flight magazine and she'd call Phil before it ran to double check his quotes, she said.

The next morning, Ravyn got an email from Bill Lang, a former co-worker at the Atlanta Trib. Bill had covered politics at the daily paper for years before taking a buy-out when times began to get tough at the paper. Ravyn wished she had gotten such an offer, but she didn't have the tenure Bill did.

Now Bill was the spokesman for the Atlanta City Council president, but they had kept in touch over the years. Bill invited her to meet him for drinks after work and she was delighted.

They agreed to meet at the bar at Baraonda, an Italian restaurant near the Fox Theatre in Midtown.

Ravyn got there first and took a seat, placing her purse on the seat next to her. Bill arrived only a few minutes late, apologizing about the traffic.

"How've you been?" he asked, as he gave Ravyn a little hug and kissed her on the cheek.

Bill was incredibly handsome, dressed in khaki pants and a maroon polo shirt. But Bill was gay, so Ravyn could only admire from afar.

"I'm doing OK," she replied, honestly.

The bartender appeared and they each ordered a glass of wine, along with two appetizers they'd split.

"How about you?" she asked.

"I've been really busy with the upcoming referendum on the water/sewer improvement tax," Bill replied. "It's hard for Councilman Sands to come out in support of the tax, but he knows that's about the only way to pay for the needed upgrades to the infrastructure. Just about every day there is a new major water line break or sewer break in the city and we just can't keep up with patching everything. We need to have a plan to really fix the problems."

"You sound like you are campaigning, Bill."

He smiled. "Well, it's different being on this side of the fence. It seems so long ago that I was the one grilling someone like me about the need for a tax. Now I'm answering reporters' calls trying to relay information that doesn't sound like a rehearsed sound bite."

"And?"

"And it all sounds like a rehearsed sound bite."

Their wine arrived and they clinked glasses. "To former reporters," Bill said.

"To former reporters," Ravyn replied.

"So, what are you up to these days?" he asked. "Are you getting enough freelance work?"

"I'm doing OK, not great. So far, I've been able to pay the bills, but some months it gets a little scary. But I just did get a contract job with LindMark Enterprises – you know, Marc Linder's company. I'm doing some media materials for him."

"You are? I thought Laura Lucas was doing his PR work."

"She was, when I met him to do a profile piece on him for Atlanta Trend, but she's no longer working for him. Marc fired her."

"You know they were an item," Bill said, rather than asked.

Ravyn shook her head to acknowledge she did. She wished she didn't know that, but she did.

"I'd be careful if I were you," Bill said.

"Careful? Of who? Marc?"

"No, Laura. She can be a real snake in the grass. Just because she's not working for him anymore doesn't mean she wants someone else working for him."

"Oh, I know she can be difficult."

"I'm not talking about her being difficult to work with. Just be careful. She can cause trouble that's hard to deal with."

"That sounds like the voice of experience, Bill."

"I'm afraid it is," he said. "She's not above spreading lies to get what she wants. I'm very certain she started a whisper campaign against Councilman Sands over a development deal on the south side of town that nearly led to a grand jury investigation. I don't have any proof that she's the one who started it, but she was working for the developer that didn't get the contract on that deal. She's trouble."

"I won't argue with you there."

"What's Linder like?"

"He's smart, driven. He's trying to get some investor money for his company to jump-start some growth, but he's having trouble finding it. I'm on board to work up some materials he'll give to investors to make them want to spend money on his company."

"Now that sounds like a rehearsed sound bite," Bill said, smiling.

"Ha! Maybe just a little bit. Maybe I'm getting the hang of this freelance gig."

The food arrived and they chatted about mutual friends between bites. Most of their mutual friends were former co-workers. Few were still working journalists. Those who were often had to leave Atlanta to find other jobs, usually at smaller newspapers. It was a great way to catch up on where everyone was and what they were doing.

When the check arrived, Bill quickly grabbed it. "My treat," he said.

Ravyn began to protest. "Let's just split it," she said.

"No, I invited you," Bill responded. "Besides, I'm the one with steady income."

"I can't argue there," Ravyn said. "Thanks, Bill. I appreciate it."

"Hey, what are friends for?"

Ravyn got back to her condo and tossed her purse and keys on the breakfast bar. Even though she and Bill had shared only appetizers, she felt pretty full.

It was still early in the evening, so Ravyn decided to put on her work out clothes and go down to the fitness center in her condo complex, rather than over to her gym, now that her membership was paid up. She wished it were still light enough out to go for a run in Piedmont Park, but since it was fall, the daylight disappeared earlier and earlier. She didn't feel comfortable running in the park alone at night, even though she felt Atlanta was a safe city.

She walked in the fitness center and glanced over at the three treadmills in a row along the front. She lucked out and found an empty treadmill at the far end and plugged her headphones into the small television attached to it. Ravyn flipped through the limited TV channels and stopped when she saw Bradford Cunningham being interviewed on a local news program.

"Investors have got to support small businesses," he was saying. "The financial community is not doing its part, so businesses have to turn to private investors."

He looked rather dashing, dressed in a suit and tie, appearing very confident and authoritative. He probably does know what he's talking about, Ravyn thought.

"But so many small businesses are chasing the same private investors, some that really have no business chasing those investors," Cunningham said. "Businesses like BC Enterprises have a shot at great growth with the right capital and investment, whereas other firms – weaker firms – are out there chasing the same dollars. And if they get those dollars they are just going to squander them."

What the hell was he talking about? Ravyn wondered. Was he talking about LindMark and its pursuit of venture capital? Was he calling LindMark a weak company?

"Maybe I'm just being overly sensitive," she thought. "Surely he's not talking about LindMark."

The program then switched to a professor of finance from Georgia State University, who began discussing global investment firms and the difficulty in access to capital. The program concluded shortly thereafter.

Ravyn finished her 30-minute run and went back up to her condo. She looked at her cell phone and saw she'd missed three calls from Marc.

"Hmm… Wonder what he wants."

She took a quick drink of water as she dialed his number.

"Did you see Bradford Cunningham?!" Marc shouted at her through the phone. "That bastard!"

Ravyn had never heard him so angry.

"I caught just the very end of the program, but I couldn't figure out what he was talking about," she answered. "I was at the gym, on the treadmill. I missed part of the news segment."

"He was talking about *me*! My company!" Marc continued to shout. "I want a retraction! Get me a retraction!"

"Did he say LindMark's name or your name on the program?"

"No, but he was talking about me."

"Marc, if he didn't say your name or the company's name, I can't ask for a retraction."

"Why not? He was defaming me and my company! He was talking about me!"

"Unless he specifically said your name or your company's name, he can't be called out on it. But let me call the program producer tomorrow and see if we can get you on the program to give your views. I'll work up a pitch to them tonight and call tomorrow. If they accept, I'll give you some talking points and you can be on the program. What topics would you be comfortable talking about? Or do you want me to send you a list of topics and you can pick one?"

"Send me a list," Marc said, somewhat calmer.

There was a long silence on the phone. Ravyn felt she could barely breathe and he wasn't sure Marc was still there.

"I'm sorry I yelled at you," he said quietly.

"It's OK. I understand your being angry. I wondered what he was talking about as well. I wondered if he *was* talking about LindMark, but I didn't hear the first part of the program, so I couldn't be sure."

"I think he was. I know he's been talking to ATC Capital and BlacKat Angels as well. I'm not supposed to know that, but I've heard that through the grapevine."

"I take it the venture capital world is a small club," Ravyn said. "A lot of firms are probably talking to the same guys for funding."

"It's true," Marc said, sounding tired. "It's just so frustrating. I know we have a good product. I truly believe we do, or I'd have thrown in the towel a long time ago. That's the lawyer training in me. I know when you need to cut your losses and settle a civil case. But I don't think I should settle on this. There is no need to cut my losses."

"Then you shouldn't," Ravyn said, sincerely.

Marc sighed a deep sigh.

"You sound really tired," Ravyn said, then wishing she hadn't said that. It sounded too personal, considering he was her boss, not her boyfriend.

"I am tired," he said. "I haven't been sleeping well."

"What's keeping you up at night?" Ravyn asked, quietly thinking, "I wish it was me."

"Oh," Marc said flatly, "Just worried about getting this financing. And this thing with Bradford Cunningham doesn't help."

"Well, let me work up some ideas for some positive publicity for LindMark and get them to you tomorrow."

There was a long pause between them again on the phone.

"What time is it? Have you eaten?" Marc asked. He sounded so tired.

"I had a small bite earlier tonight, before my run on the treadmill," Ravyn said.

"Oh. OK," Marc said.

Was he asking her out to dinner? Ravyn wondered, half hoping.

"Well, get those ideas to me tomorrow, will you? I'll talk to you then."

"I'll call you in the morning," she said, as she hung up.

Damn, she thought. What just happened?

Marc hung up the phone and felt lonely. Ravyn had asked him why he wasn't sleeping at night and he'd told her he was worried about the finances of his company, but that was only half of it. He was thinking about her.

He didn't want to. He cursed himself for thinking about her in that way. But he couldn't help it. He was attracted to her. He had hoped he could see her tonight, even if it was over a burger at The Vortex. But then he sighed a long sigh. Maybe it was better if he didn't see her.

Although he knew he would lie awake all night tonight thinking of her, but trying not to think about her.

Shit, he thought. This is bad.

Ravyn spent the next two hours that evening working on some story ideas to pitch to the local TV newsmagazine and then drawing up some talking points for Marc, should he like any of her ideas.

She decided to quit when Felix began yowling for food and rubbing his body all over the bar stool she was sitting on.

"OK, King Felix. Let's get you fed, and then let's go to bed." Ravyn glanced over at the digital clock in her kitchen. It read 11:20 p.m. She'd worked longer than she'd intended.

She got off the bar stool, shut down her laptop and stretched.

"Well", she thought, "at least I'll be in bed at a decent hour – for me, anyway."

Ravyn's cell phone rang early the next morning. She reached over to see it was Julie Montgomery calling. She hadn't heard from her friend in a while, so it was a nice surprise.

"Hello, stranger," Ravyn said sleepily into the phone.

"Hello, stranger, yourself. Where have you been?"

"Here. Just busy with work, which is nice."

"Is work the only thing you are busy with? Not busy smooching on your couch with a certain CEO?"

"No," Ravyn said with a little sigh. "No smooching with the CEO. What's up?" she asked quickly to change the subject.

"What are you doing next weekend? Specifically, what are you doing next Friday through Sunday? Please, please, please tell me you are free."

"I think I can be free. Why?"

"Yay!" Julie said, sounding giddy. "Rob's co-worker gave us the use of his lake house up at Lake Lanier for the weekend and Rob told me to take some girlfriends. He'll watch the girls. I'm putting together a girls weekend at the lake!"

Ravyn hadn't heard her friend sound so happy in a long time.

"Wow! That sounds great. But won't it be too cold for the lake?" Ravyn asked, knowing it was October.

"Well, the lake water should still be pretty warm, and it looks like we'll have nice weather, in the low to mid 70s. Plus, it will be all about relaxing, drinking wine and playing cards – mostly it's about not having kids for the weekend! Heaven!"

"Well, then, I'm in!"

Ravyn was glad she'd be able to spend some time with Julie. With the work she'd been doing for LindMark and with her other freelance work, she hadn't seen her friend in about a month.

Ravyn spent the rest of the week reaching out to local television news producers, trying to get them interested in using Marc in some of their business stories. She didn't have any success, but she knew it was a process. She just needed to keep getting his name in front of them.

# Chapter 5

Ravyn drove her little Honda Civic north on I-85 and then merged onto I-985 toward Lake Lanier mid-morning on the Friday she was to meet Julie and two of Julie's friends at the lake house.

The morning was mild enough that she opened the sunroof. Twice she caught herself singing to the radio. She blushed thinking someone might have heard her singing the latest pop tune at the top of her lungs.

Ravyn was really looking forward to the get-away. She was caught up with most of her freelance work. Her neighbor Jack Parker was going to feed and water Felix over the weekend. She felt the stress melt away as she set her cruise control and motored north.

Thank goodness for the navigation application on her cell phone, or Ravyn would have missed the cut off road to the lake house, which went two miles down a road that was not well marked.

But as she pulled up to the house, she heard herself say, "Wow."

It wasn't so much a little lake house, as a lake mansion.

She parked on the driveway near the front door, behind Julie's minivan, and walked up the gray slate stone steps, and then knocked on the heavy wooden door.

Julie opened it with a drink in her hand, even though it was not quite noon.

"Ravyn!" Julie exclaimed. "You're here! What can I get you to drink?"

"Julie, it's not even lunch yet."

"Oh, Ravyn, you know what they say; 'It's five o'clock somewhere!' This is my vacation!"

Julie poured Ravyn something out of the blender that tasted like it had way too much rum in it.

"Let me show you your bedroom and then give you the tour," Julie said, as she led Ravyn down a hallway to the left of the front door.

They walked all the way to the end and Julie opened a door. The bedroom had a queen-sized bed with a Southwestern motif bedspread. A flat screen TV hung from the wall opposite the bed. Julie opened the bathroom door, which led into a full bath, including a jetted tub and separate shower.

"Is this the master suite? I can't take this."

"No, this isn't the master suite," Julie said. "All of the bedrooms are like this."

Ravyn put her overnight bag on the bed, which was tall, like it was set on a platform. The bed also had about a half dozen throw pillows on it. She wondered if there would be room for her on the bed.

"Whose house is this?"

"Oh, one of Rob's co-workers. And the wife is a decorator, so every room is pretty much straight out of a fashion magazine."

"I'm going to be afraid to sleep on the bed or spill anything on the floor. Maybe I should just sleep out in my car," Ravyn said, only half joking.

"We'll be fine," Julie said, grabbing Ravyn's hand and almost sloshing her cocktail in her other hand. "Let me show you the place. It's incredible."

Julie led Ravyn through the rest of the house, taking her through the two other bedrooms on the first floor, including the true master suite, which had a double shower. Ravyn had a sudden flash of her and Marc taking a shower together in it, and blushed.

"Why am I still thinking of him?" she asked herself. She shook her head and took another sip of her rum drink. I need to chill out, she thought and took another sip, getting a strong taste of rum.

Then Julie led Ravyn upstairs to the loft area, which had two more bedrooms, one decorated in soft greens and turquoise, the other in oranges and dark maroon. The loft bedrooms shared a bathroom.

"This house is incredible," Ravyn said as they came back down the stairs to the first floor.

The majority of the lake house was its great room, which had windows all along its length, overlooking Lake Lanier. The great room was also all open. A fireplace was on the right, with the kitchen and dining room, with a large wooden table, to the left. The kitchen had a large, tall island, covered in gray granite with flecks of blue. Around the outside of the island stood leather bar stools, with the plastic coverings still on the seats and plastic wrapping covering the legs.

"Don't they trust the company?" Ravyn asked, laughing.

"I think this furniture was just delivered," Julie said, putting her hand on one of the bar stools. "I guess we have to be careful."

The floors were tiled, but the great room had large faux fur area rugs over the tile. Comfortable leather couches curved around the fireplace, and a very large flat screen TV was mounted on a pivoting arm just to the left of the fireplace. This lake house was clearly a guy's get away, too, Ravyn thought.

The doorbell chimed and two more women arrived, Julie's friends Lynne and Celia, who were sisters.

Introductions were made, and more rum drinks were poured. Julie led the other women to their bedrooms, while Ravyn stepped out onto the back deck of the house, which faced the lake.

The house was set up a little bit on a bluff, so it overlooked the lake, which looked deep blue. The sky was clear, with hardly any clouds, and although the day was warm, it was not too hot. A warm breeze stirred and Ravyn turned her face toward it and smiled.

But by the time the sun goes down, Ravyn thought, it will be cool out here tonight. She was glad she had brought a heavier sweater at the last minute.

The deck ran the length of the house, and had stairs going down toward a boat dock on the left, about where her bedroom was located. Ravyn noticed a door by the end of the deck and realized her bedroom probably was on the other side of that door, so she could go out onto the deck from her room.

She stood at the deck railing and looked out over the lake. There was hardly a boat out there. But it was early October and it was early in the weekend. It would probably be more crowded on Lake Lanier once people started getting off work in Atlanta and heading up to their weekend homes.

Ravyn pulled open the sliding glass door along the deck and stepped back into the great room. Lynne, Celia and Julie were laughing and clinking glasses.

"Where's your glass?" Julie asked Ravyn. Ravyn looked around and found it. "Here's to good friends and a good girls weekend."

"Here, here," the women said, and clinked their glasses again.

After the women had lunch, they wandered down to the boat dock, which had a little bit of a steep climb, since the house was up so high on the bluff.

"Watch your step," Julie called back to the others as she led the way down.

When they stepped on to the dock, they found a couple of personal water craft with the covers still on.

Julie had a set of keys in her hand and began unlocking a storage bin, and then began pulling out life vests and a couple of floating chairs. Lynne and Celia began to take off the coverings to the water craft.

"Here," she said as she handed off the vests. "I'm looking for the keys to the SeaDoos."

"They'll let us ride these?" Ravyn asked.

"Sure. We'll just leave them some gas money for them," Julie said. "I saw a jar in the master bedroom that said 'gas money,' so I'm guessing that's what it's for."

"Do you know how to ride one?"

"I do," Julie said. Celia and Lynne shook their heads yes, as well.

"Well, I'll just ride along on the back," Ravyn said.

"Oh, Ravyn, by the end of the weekend we'll have you driving one all over this lake. If we're going to go out, we ought to go out soon, before it starts to get too crowded. Did everyone bring a bathing suit?

The women trudged back up the steep stone steps to the house to change. Ravyn, who worked out often, took a break half way up, trying to catch her breath.

"Geez, this is a workout in itself," she thought. She saw Julie was stopped, too.

"I'm getting my exercise today, that's for sure," Julie said.

The women got to the house, quickly changed and headed back down to the boat dock. Julie and Celia got on the yellow

SeaDoo. Lynne checked Ravyn's life vest to be sure it was snug before they both got on the silver and black one.

The women pulled out of the cove, mindful to observe the no wake zone, but once they hit the buoy marker, both Lynne and Julie opened up the throttle. Ravyn felt herself starting to slide off the back as the SeaDoo roared to life.

"Hang on!" Lynne shouted, but her voice was mostly lost to the wind. Ravyn quickly grabbed Lynne's life vest and hung on tightly.

The SeaDoos jetted across the lake, the wind stinging Ravyn's eyes, making them water.

But the speed was thrilling. Ravyn felt a rush go through her whole body. She found herself laughing, even though as she did, her mouth filled with wind and the sound of her laugh could not be heard.

Julie and Lynne seemed to race each other along the lake, before cutting back and speeding back the other way. They bounced along the lake, sometimes jumping over the wakes of the few boats that were out on Lake Lanier and jumping each other's wakes.

Ravyn grinned from ear to ear, watching the lake shore zip by. She would not have been able to recognize the cove they came out of if her life depended on it. She was glad she was with someone who knew the way. At least she hoped the drivers knew the way.

After about a half hour, the women pulled back into the cove, cutting the speed down to no wake as they gently came back to the dock.

"How'd you like that?" Lynne asked Ravyn over her shoulder.

"That was great. But I'm glad you were driving," she replied.

"Oh, we'll have you driving this thing by tomorrow. You'll see."

Ravyn started to protest, but Julie was taking off her vest and collecting those of the other women.

Lynne and Celia quickly put the SeaDoos up on their platforms and locked them.

"Hey, let's see how warm the water is," Julie said. "Anyone up for a buoy swim?"

"What's a buoy swim?" Ravyn asked.

"Remember that buoy we passed on the way in? The no-wake buoy marker? Let's swim out to it and back. Last one in fixes dinner!"

Ravyn hesitated just a second too long and was the last girl in the water. She wasn't all that strong a swimmer, so hers was mostly some breast stroke, freestyle and dog paddle, but she made it around the buoy and back.

The water was still warm, but when the women climbed out of the water, all felt slightly chilled. Thankfully, Celia had thought to bring towels down when they first came down to ride the SeaDoos.

"I guess I'm fixing dinner tonight," Ravyn said as she dried off and wrapped the big green towel around her body. "What ingredients do we have? Do we need to go to the store?"

"No, I brought some chicken and pasta and rice," Julie said. "And I brought some salad fixings. We might have to be a little creative with those ingredients. I think they have staples already in the house, so we can scrounge and see what else we can find. If we need to make a grocery run, we can do it tomorrow. I think we'll be OK for tonight. I think it's time for cocktails again, girls. Let's get this party started!"

Then all four trudged up the steep steps to the house. A cocktail seemed to be an appropriate reward after that climb, Ravyn thought.

The women scattered to their bedrooms to shower and change.

Ravyn got into the shower, which had one of those newer rain shower heads and felt the warm water caress her body. It felt good after the swim.

She got out, dried her hair and changed into some khaki capri pants and a hot pink top. It was still warm enough to put her sandals back on.

She came out into the kitchen and Julie was once again blending something alcoholic in the blender.

"Ready for another?" she asked, handing Ravyn a glass.

"I guess so, but I think I should get dinner started."

"Fine, but you can still do it with a drink in your hand," Julie said, handing off a hurricane glass with pink frothy contents.

Ravyn took a sip and it was just as strong as the first one from this morning. She put the glass down and looked through the refrigerator, which seemed bigger than her entire condo kitchen.

She pulled out some chicken tenderloins. She looked in the pantry and found some Italian bread crumbs and Parmesan cheese. That would be a coating for the chicken, she thought. She found chicken broth and rice, and knew that would be her starchy side dish, but she was looking for a vegetable to add.

Better try the freezer, she thought.

Ravyn opened the freezer and found a vegetable medley of carrots, broccoli and cauliflower. Well, this will have to do, she thought.

Within the hour, the women were sitting down to eat.

Julie opened a bottle of white wine for dinner and poured liberally.

The ladies began to chatter about work and families, and recent books read. Ravyn felt a little left out on the talk about families but added something to the work and books read discussions.

"OK, who's reading the mommy porn book?" Lynne asked. "Fifty Shades of Grey?"

"I have!" Julie blurted out.

Ravyn looked at her friend. Ravyn had heard all the hoopla about the book, which had been flying off the shelves and been discussed ad nauseam on every TV news show, but she was surprised Julie had time to read the book.

"When do you have time to read?" Ravyn asked.

"Oh, I didn't read it. I listened to it on books on tape," Julie said. "Thank God for Audible."

"With the girls in the house?" Ravyn asked, surprised.

"Of course not! But I've got to tell you, Rob seems to like the book, too."

The three other women turned and looked at Julie. Julie giggled and then blushed a deep pink. "I may be married, but I'm not dead, girls."

Once dinner dishes were cleared and washed or put in the dishwasher, the women headed out onto the deck. Julie found the stereo system and managed, after several tries with the buttons, to get it to play from the speakers on the deck, which had a string of white lights all along the railing.

The Drifters began playing "Save the Last Dance for Me," and then The Tams started in with "Be Young, Be Foolish, But Be Happy." The Catalinas then crooned "Summertime's Calling Me."

Ravyn found herself teaching Celia and Lynne how to shag, the state dance of South Carolina, a dance her parents had taught her.

"One and two, three and four, five, six," she counted out.

Julie just seemed to be keeping the beat, rather than actually following the steps to the shag.

Julie went back in a couple of times and came out with another full pitcher of blender drinks. Evening became night and a waxing sliver of a moon came out. With no city lights, the stars looked clear and crisp.

By about 2 a.m., the women finally stumbled off to their bedrooms.

Ravyn knew she had had too much to drink and her calves were starting to hurt from all the dancing on the wooden deck, but she couldn't remember when she'd had so much fun.

Ravyn woke up Saturday morning with the sun streaming through the windows and a pounding headache. Clearly the back of the lake house faced east. Ravyn groaned and pulled two pillows over her head. She didn't hear anyone else up, so she rolled over and tried to go back to sleep. But the pounding in her head and the need for water to begin rehydrating forced her to get up.

She lopped into her bathroom, found her aspirin in her purse and her water bottle on the bathroom countertop and swallowed the medicine and the water down. Then she refilled her water bottle and drank the whole contents again before laying back down on the bed.

Ravyn dozed off for another hour, only to be awakened by the sound of coffee beans being ground. Someone else was up and making coffee. There might be hope for her pounding head yet.

Ravyn got up, pulled on some shorts and a T-shirt and padded down the tile floor to the great room. Lynne was working the Cuisinart coffee maker.

"How strong do you like your coffee?" Lynne asked.

"This morning, as strong as you can make it," was Ravyn's reply, as she pulled her hand through her brunette hair, trying to untangle her tresses.

"I'm a little hung over, too. I think Celia and Julie are still down for the count. Want to take our cups out on the deck? It looks nice out."

Ravyn and Lynne slid open the sliding glass door and stepped out into the cool morning air. Ravyn gave a little shiver but decided not to go back in for her sweater. The coffee will warm me up, she figured.

They settled down on two deck chairs and watched the steam come off the lake. The water this morning was warmer than the air, making little wisps of steam rise. The sun was up already, but Ravyn thought it would have been a beautiful sunrise, had she managed to wake up that early.

"How do you know Julie?" Lynne asked.

"She and I used to work at the Atlanta Daily Tribune together, back when we were both reporters," Ravyn answered. "How about you? How do you know her?"

"Julie knows my sister Celia," Lynne said. "They were on the same tennis team two years ago. Celia still plays, but I don't think Julie has played much now that her girls are in all those activities."

"I think you are right. She keeps pretty busy through her daughters, which is why I'm so glad her hubby suggested she do a girls weekend. I know she could use it. My coffee's gone lukewarm. Shall I get us a refill?"

Lynne nodded as she took another long sip of her coffee.

Ravyn stepped back into the lake house and brought the pot back out, refilling their cups.

"I didn't ask if you take yours with cream or anything."

"I'll go get the creamer," Lynne said.

Minutes later they were back out sitting on the deck watching the water, listening to the birds.

"It's so peaceful here," Ravyn said.

Just then the sound of a motor boat began to roar.

"I think you spoke too soon," Lynne said, laughing.

The sliding glass door slid open again and Julie and Celia stepped out. Julie's hair was unbrushed and dark circles were under her eyes. She's had a rough night, too, Ravyn thought.

"Hey where's the coffee pot?" she whined.

"Oh, sorry, we've got it out here. Let me make you girls a fresh pot."

Julie, wrapped in a thick white bath robe, slumped down in a deck chair. "Now I remember why I don't drink a pitcher of rum runners."

"They were kind of lethal," Lynne said. "But they sure were good."

"And my calves ache this morning," Celia said, reaching down and rubbing her legs. "I think it was from all that dancing. My old body isn't used to that much movement."

"Celia, you are two years younger than me," Lynne chided. "You are not that old!"

Ravyn came back out on the deck with a fresh pot of coffee and two more coffee cups for her new friends. She had checked the fridge before she came out, and saw they had eggs and bacon.

"Anyone up for breakfast?" she asked. "I can whip up some scrambled eggs or make some French toast."

"That would be wonderful, Ravyn."

Ravyn went back into the house and back into her bedroom to check her cell phone before she got started on making breakfast. It's not that she expected any calls or needed to make any. She just wanted to check it.

She was pleasantly surprised to see a text from Marc.

"Where are you?" the text read.

"Lake Lanier," she answered back, as she walked down the hall and back to the kitchen.

"Nice. Romantic getaway?"

"Girls weekend."

"Have fun."

"Will do."

There was no response after that.

"That was odd," Ravyn thought. "Marc never texts me."

She put her phone down on the kitchen counter and began to rummage through the pantry again until she found some maple syrup. With that, she knew she was going to make French toast for breakfast. She got the griddle hot and put on the bacon, careful that she didn't get splattered with hot grease, and then laid down the egg-soaked bread. All the while she kept glancing at her phone, as if Marc would suddenly start communicating with her again. It was just odd that he had in the first place.

She hadn't told him she was going to the lake this weekend, but then she never told him her weekend plans. Why should she? They were just employer and employee, not boyfriend and girlfriend.

Still, the messages gave her heart a little start.

Ravyn pulled out four white plates from the cupboard and set them on the counter top and then looked for two serving plates. She stepped back out onto the deck where Julie, Lynne and Celia sat chatting and drinking their coffee.

"Do we want to eat breakfast inside or out here?" Ravyn asked.

"Oh, let's eat out here," Julie said. "When do we ever get to eat outside?"

"It's almost ready," Ravyn said. "I just need some help bringing out the food."

Celia stood up and followed Ravyn back inside. They gathered the serving plates filled with bacon and French toast, another pot of coffee and some creamer.

Lynne and Julie got the breakfast plates, paper napkins and cutlery and brought those out to the patio table.

The women tucked into the breakfast food, making small talk between bites.

Ravyn finished her French toast and pushed the plate away, curling her legs under her on her chair and looking out over the lake. It was so beautiful. She wished she could be sharing it with a man. She wished she could be sharing it with Marc.

"Penny for your thoughts," Julie said.

Ravyn looked up from her reverie. She hadn't realized she had drifted off with her thoughts of Marc.

"Oh, just thinking … um, how lovely it is here."

Julie smiled with a knowing smile. "Yes, lovely."

The women lingered a little while longer before going back into the house. Julie and Lynne washed and put away the dishes.

Ravyn headed back to her bedroom to take a shower. The rain shower head hissed as she turned it on and she waited for the water to get warm before she stepped in.

She could not stop thinking of Marc and his text. It just seemed so odd. She wondered if she should call. Did he need something?

Ravyn soaped up her wash cloth and felt the warm water caress her. She started daydreaming of Marc caressing her. She started to remember their one ill-fated make-out session on her couch. She could almost feel his breath on her neck, his lips on hers. Ravyn quickly opened her eyes, shook her head as if to chase away those thoughts and finished her shower. "I must not think of him."

The women met up an hour later and decided to head into Gainesville for some shopping and provisions. Coming back hours later, loaded down with bottles of wine, food stuffs and one or two new clothing items, the friends milled around the great room and kitchen.

Ravyn plated some hummus, pita chips, Kalamata olives, carrot sticks and cucumber slices for a light snack. Julie reached for a bottle of pinot grigio. "This should help wash that down," she said, with a big grin.

The women kicked off their shoes and sat down in the overstuffed leather chairs and couches that surrounded the enormous stone fireplace along the wall of the great room. Above the stone fireplace was an equally enormous buffalo head, which Ravyn had noticed the night before and meant to ask about. She looked up at its blank glass eyes. "That thing is a bit creepy," she said to the group. "It almost looks like it is staring at me."

The three other women looked up.

"Maybe that's where they keep the video camera, to spy on the house guests," Lynne said. "It's our own Peeping Tom."

"Oh my God!" shrieked Julie. "Don't even say things like that. I came out here naked last night to get some water!"

"Well, Tom saw you," Lynne deadpanned.

"You are freaking me out," Julie said, standing up, her wine sloshing out of her glass. "Now I need to see if there is a camera in that stupid bison head."

Julie was standing at the stone fireplace, looking up. She put down her wine glass, and grabbed onto some of the flagstone pieces, attempting to climb it like a rock wall.

"Give me a boost, somebody!"

Celia and Lynne got up and stood behind her, as she gingerly climbed a few feet up. But the bison was a good 10 feet above the floor, and Julie could only just touch the underside of the bison's bearded chin.

"I can't see, I can't see. Can anyone get me up higher?"

Celia, who was probably about 5-foot, 8-inches tall, stood behind Julie and bent down, putting Julie on her shoulders.

"Oh Lord," Ravyn groaned. "This has disaster written all over it."

Julie could just reach the bison's eye on its left side. She tapped the side of its face hard to see if it was hollow when suddenly the left eyeball popped out, dropping to the ground with a loud crack, like a marble hitting a cement floor, and then rolled away.

"Holy shit!" Julie exclaimed, wobbling as Celia tried to ease her off her shoulders. "Did anyone see where that thing went?"

All four women got down on their hands and knees to search for the errant eyeball, which Lynne found under one of the end tables.

"Oh shit, oh shit, oh shit!" Julie said, holding the brown eyeball in her hand, then putting it up to her own eye. "How do I look?"

"Julie!" Lynne said. "That thing gives me the creeps. Put it back."

"How do I get this thing back up there?" Julie asked.

"Let's see if we can find a ladder," Ravyn said. "They had to get ol' Tom up there somehow, and there are light bulbs in all those recessed lights, so there has to be one around here somewhere."

The women fanned out in the house, and the sound of opening and closing doors could be heard. Ravyn walked outside looking for a crawlspace or outside storage area. She walked around the house, finding a garden hose, a rake and one garden glove against the right side of the house.

She climbed the steps up to the back deck and looked around, not seeing anything. Then she thought to look under the deck, since it was slightly raised. Ravyn peered under the deck, but no luck.

The four women met back inside the house, clearly disappointed.

"I have no idea where a ladder is, so I guess we've got to figure out how to get this back into Tom," Julie said, holding up the eyeball. "OK. I'm going up."

She began to climb the flagstone fireplace again, much as before. She got close, but had to stretch up to push the eyeball back in. Then Julie climbed back down.

The four women looked up.

"Ummm. His eye is crooked," Lynne said.

Sure enough, the left eye was not looking forward, but off to the side.

"Well, I'm not climbing back up there," Julie said. "Maybe no one will notice. I'm sure they won't. Whew. I'm ready for more wine. All that climbing made me thirsty."

"Julie, everything makes you thirsty!" Ravyn said.

"Why yes, yes it does!"

The rest of Saturday night was spent cooking up dinner, drinking wine and laughing at silly jokes, mostly at the expense of Tom the bison.

Ravyn couldn't remember a time when she had had so much fun, especially with two new-found friends.

And she loved that Julie was having such a good time. She knew her friend didn't have much free time with her two young daughters.

Ravyn sat in one of the chairs in the great room, drinking a lovely pinot noir, and smiling at Julie, who was dancing wildly to a Jimmy Buffett song on Pandora radio.

"Fins to the left, fins to the right, and you're the only bait in town," Julie sang at the top of her voice.

Ravyn was thankful for Julie's husband, Rob, at that moment, for being so aware that she needed this weekend.

Why can't all guys be like Rob? Ravyn wondered. She took a deep breath and sighed.

Then her thoughts turned to Marc. What kind of guy was Marc, anyway? she wondered. Was he like Rob? An understanding man? Or was he a player, like Shane. Just out for a quick screw and selfish?

Ravyn frowned. She really didn't know anything about Marc. Yet she was attracted to him. Why did she have to feel this way? He was making her life feel more complicated than it should.

"Penny for your thoughts," Julie said, as she flopped down next to Ravyn, nearly knocking her wine glass over.

"Oh, Julie, I was just thinking about Marc, and wondering if he could possibly be as wonderful as your husband."

Julie's eyes grew wide.

"Ravyn, Rob is no saint. Let's remember that. And are you still thinking about Marc in a boyfriend way? You sly, vixen, you."

"This isn't funny, Julie. I can't stop thinking about him, and I need to stop thinking about him. He's my main meal ticket. I don't want to screw that up."

"Does he have feelings for you?"

"I don't know. But this morning he texted me, asking what I was doing up here. Maybe I should have lied and said I was up here with Bradley Cooper, or some other gorgeous celebrity. Make him jealous."

"Ravyn, you aren't that kind of woman, and you know it. You aren't a Laura Lucas."

"Aren't I? When it comes to Marc Linder I wonder. Why does it have to be so hard, Julie?"

"Ravyn, my life isn't all that easy, either."

"But you and Rob are so perfect. Your girls are perfect," Ravyn said, as she poured each of them another glass of wine.

Julie frowned and then sighed. She took a deep drink of wine and pushed her blonde hair back.

"Rob cheated on me," she said quietly.

"What!" Ravyn shouted. Celia and Lynne looked over.

"Hush, hush!" Julie chided. "It's true." Julie's eyes began to well with tears. "It was last year. I opened our Marriott rewards notice from the mail. He used Marriott points to get a hotel in Washington, D.C., for a weekend. He told me it was for work, but he was there with one of his co-workers – Amy. I don't know her last name."

Ravyn felt like she was in a bad dream. Not Rob. Surely, not Rob. Julie must be mistaken.

"How do you know he cheated?"

. "He told me when I confronted him with the Marriott notice. Why would he have used points to go for a work trip? He would have charged that back to work. I suspected something anyway. He had been acting distant and odd for weeks before that. We hadn't had sex in a long time. I confronted him. He confessed. I threatened to leave him. We've been in therapy ever since."

"Oh, Julie. I'm so sorry," Ravyn said, her voice cracking.

Julie started to cry. "I thought he loved me."

"He does love you, and he loves those girls. You know that."

"I know he loves his daughters. That I know," Julie said with conviction. "But we've drifted apart. I don't know if we'll get back to where we were."

"Do you still love him?" Ravyn asked, quietly.

"I think I do," Julie said, taking another gulp of wine. She smiled a wan smile. "Hell, it's why he let me come on this weekend. He's still trying to make up for his indiscretion. At least I'm getting something out of this humiliation."

"Oh, Julie, don't think that way."

Julie wiped tears from her eyes. "I try not to, but it's hard. He slept with another woman. He saw another woman naked! He put his dick in another woman! I've never cheated. I've never even thought about another man. Why would he do this to me?"

Julie started to sob softly again. Ravyn moved toward her friend sitting on the leather couch and put her arm around her.

"I don't know why he would cheat. I would never have thought he would. I'm so sorry." Ravyn was sorry that her friend was hurting. It wasn't fair that she was feeling this way. She didn't deserve this. Stupid Rob!

Julie wiped her eyes again and breathed out a long breath.

"I didn't come here to be unhappy. I came here to have fun!" she practically shouted, standing up and holding up her wine glass in a kind of boozy toast. "I came to forget about my shit husband! I came to get drunk, and dance, and have a good time!"

Julie walked a little unevenly over to the stereo and cranked up the volume on Pandora radio. Alan Jackson crooned "It's Five o'clock Somewhere" and Julie started singing loudly along with the song, swinging her empty wine glass in her hand.

Lynne and Celia got up to dance, too.

Well, if you can't beat them, join them, Ravyn thought, and got up as well. She got the bottle of pinot noir, which was nearly empty and refilled her glass, as well as poured the rest of the bottle into Julie's glass.

Lynne reached over for another bottle of wine and popped the cork.

After another hour of dancing around the great room and out onto the back deck, Ravyn walked back to her bedroom to use the bathroom. She grabbed her phone to check it.

There was a text message from Marc. "How's the girls weekend?" it read.

"Having a great time. Lots of wine and laughs," she wrote back. "Back tomorrow. Need anything?"

She stared at her phone, but there was no answer.

She put her phone down and went into the bathroom. When she came out, she checked her phone again. Still nothing.

Ravyn put her phone down and went back to the deck, where the party had moved.

The women were curled up in outdoor lounge furniture. Big wicker furniture with plush cream-colored cushions surrounded a small fire pit, which Lynne was attempting to light with some small pieces of wood that had been stacked near the back deck of the house. The flame flickered slowly, then caught.

Ravyn sat down in a chair and pulled her feet under her to keep them warm. The flames snapped and licked and almost seemed hypnotic. She took another sip of red wine. It seemed to warm her in the chill early October air. She took a deep breath. The air was crisp and cool. She looked up and saw hundreds of stars, all but invisible in Midtown Atlanta, where city lights hid the winking diamonds.

She felt so content at that moment, even though it had been an emotional night.

The party broke up about an hour later. Ravyn put the wine glasses near the sink. She'd wash them in the morning. She was too tired to do it that night.

She gave Julie a big hug goodnight and walked down to her bedroom. A text message from Marc lit up her phone. Ravyn's heart leapt.

"Glad you are having good time. When are you back?"

"Having fun. Back tomorrow. After lunch. You need me?"

Ravyn realized that was a loaded question. She hoped the answer was yes. She waited a few moments to see if there would be a reply. There was none. She went to bed.

Ravyn awoke Sunday morning with the sun streaming through her bedroom window again. She rolled over and pulled the pillow over her head, feeling slightly hung over again. Not nearly as bad as Saturday morning, thank goodness. She got up for a glass of water and more aspirin and laid back down, smiling.

She awoke again about an hour later. She listened for any sounds in the kitchen. Everyone must be slow this morning, as well.

Ravyn got up, went to the bathroom, and then checked her phone. No message from Marc.

She grabbed her robe and padded into the kitchen to make coffee and toast. It was chilly in the great room that morning. She wrapped the robe tightly around her and sat down at the breakfast bar, flipping through an old issue of People magazine that had been in the great room.

Celia padded in, pulling her hair up into a pony tail. "I thought I smelled coffee."

"Yep. I hope I didn't wake you."

"No, I was up. I think Lynne and Julie are still asleep though. I think they had more to drink that I did."

"Yeah, I think you are right."

"Want to go for a quick walk? I'm guessing we will be packing up this morning to head back."

"Sure, I'd love to walk. I feel like I haven't gotten any exercise this weekend. Well, other than bending my elbow."

Celia laughed. "I know what you mean."

Ravyn quickly pulled on some jeans, her sneakers and a sweater and met Celia back at the front door. They stepped out into the cool morning.

"Oooh! Much cooler than I thought!" Ravyn said. "Funny how it can be so much cooler here than in Atlanta."

The women began a brisk walk down along the road that lead to the lake house. They passed a few other houses, all still this Sunday morning.

Celia walked at a good pace, swinging her arms to get a good workout. Ravyn and Celia made small talk along the route, which went down to the edge to the main road and then back. Ravyn estimated they'd walked about two to two and a half miles.

When they got back, both Lynne and Julie were in the kitchen.

"Hey, we wondered where you two had gone," Lynne said. "I'm going to scramble up some eggs for breakfast. Want some?"

"Sounds great," Ravyn said. "Need some help?"

"Nope, I got it."

"I'll just go wash my hands," Ravyn said as she walked to her bedroom. She picked up her phone and saw a text message from Marc.

"You interested in dinner tonight?" it read. "Seven p.m.?"

Ravyn had to read the message twice. She quickly replied yes.

"I should be back by late afternoon. Let me know where to meet you."

"You pick" was the immediate response.

Marc was online!

"Somewhere in Midtown?"

"Sure. You are in Midtown, right?"

Ravyn wondered why he asked that. He had been to her condo. He'd made out with her on her couch. "Yes," she replied. "But I can do Buckhead. Are you in Buckhead?"

"I'm in Buckhead. But I can come to Midtown."

"What about Portofino in Buckhead? I've only eaten there for lunch."

"Good choice. I'll make a reservation. See you at seven."

Ravyn realized her heart was racing. She was going to see Marc tonight. It felt like a date.

She was smiling when she walked back into the kitchen.

"What happened to you?" Julie asked, noticing Ravyn's perma-grin.

"Oh, just got a good email."

"Marc?"

"Oh, oh no," Ravyn lied. "A new freelance job."

Julie looked hard at Ravyn, smirking. "Sure. A new freelance job. Be careful, Ravyn."

Ravyn walked over to her friend and gave her a long hug. "I will. Promise."

The women ate breakfast, lingering over the final pot of coffee before they started packing up for the 45-minute drive back to Atlanta. It was early enough in the day that the drive should be easy, but when it comes to Atlanta traffic, one never knew.

Ravyn bagged up the trash, sorting out the glass and other materials to be recycled. She winced as she looked at all of the wine bottles and the empty bottle of rum in the recycle bin.

She walked to the back deck for one last look over Lake Lanier. It was a calm morning. The water looked like glass. The air smelled fresh and crisp. "Won't smell like that back in Atlanta," she thought.

Ravyn met up with the others as they loaded up their cars.

"Why does it feel like I'm going back with more stuff than I came with?" Julie asked.

"Probably because you are," Ravyn said. "Did you grab the rest of the wine and food out of the fridge?"

"There were only two bottles we didn't open. I've got those. And some of the food I tossed. I didn't think Ashley or Lexie would eat the leftover paté. If they do, I've got daughters with very expensive taste. I'm sure the raccoons up here will love me for leaving them paté. But I did pack up the cold cuts and bread. My girls will eat sandwiches."

Ravyn hugged her friend. "You know your girls love you more than anything. And I hope you and Rob can work things out."

"I know Lexie and Ashley love me. I love them so much. And I still love Rob. I just don't know if he…" Julie let her voice trail off. "Now listen, Ravyn, you behave yourself tonight with Marc."

Ravyn started to protest, but realized her friend knew her too well.

"I will," Ravyn said. "And if I don't, I'll be sure to tell you about it."

Julie laughed. "I'm counting on it!"

# Chapter 6

Ravyn got back to her condo in the early afternoon, with enough time to take a quick nap before her dinner with Marc.

She woke up, showered and then spent the next 45 minutes trying to figure out what to wear. Eventually she opted for her black mini skirt and her black and cobalt blue top. A black tuxedo blazer, black tights and black boots finished out the ensemble.

Ravyn then attempted something elegant, but natural, with her hair. It didn't work.

"Gah! Why won't my hair cooperate?" She asked her reflection in the mirror. She was tempted to just put her hair up in a ponytail, but that would look too casual, she thought. Instead, she swept her part to one side and tried to get her hair to look fuller.

She bent over and brushed it out, then flipped her head back and finger combed her hair, then quickly put on some hairspray and hoped it stayed looking presentable.

A bit of lipstick and mascara and she was ready. An hour too early.

Ravyn paced her condo, straightening up magazines and fluffing couch cushions. She never fluffed couch cushions. "Ugh! I can't get all sweaty!"

She sat down and tried to read one of the magazines she'd just straightened. She flipped through the issue of Runner's World, then realized it was from four months ago. She'd read it already, four months ago. She got up to throw it in her recycle bin when her phone rang. It was Marc.

"Hello, Marc. Not canceling out on me are you?" she said, trying to sound casual and not panicked.

"Hi Ravyn. Just wondered if you'd like to come by my house in Buckhead first. I need to give you some material and then we could just drive up to Portofino together. Or I could come get you. I'm happy to do that, as well."

He sounded so professional. Ravyn suddenly felt very overdressed and foolish. This was not a date, she thought inwardly. This is a business dinner.

"I, ah, I can come by your place. It's on my way, I think. Where do you live?" Ravyn asked, trying not to sound disappointed. She felt like such a fool. She could feel tears beginning to well in her eyes, but she dared not cry or her mascara would run. She tipped her head up so the few tears would not roll down her face. She then dabbed the corners of her eyes with her fingers and fished for a pen and piece of paper.

"I'm ready," she said. "What's the address?"

Marc gave her the address to his home, which was in an older neighborhood in south Buckhead, a ritzier part of the city of Atlanta. It wasn't all that far from her condo, actually.

After hanging up with Marc, Ravyn went into the bathroom to dab her eyes again and make sure her makeup still looked OK. She considered changing clothes, but then she would be late. She grabbed her purse and phone and left.

Ravyn drove north on Peachtree Street from Midtown, crossing into Buckhead. She turned into the Garden Hills neighborhood and slowed on the street where Marc lived. It was starting to get dark and she was having trouble seeing the house numbers. Her phone suddenly rang. It was Marc.

"I think you just passed my house. Turn around and pull up next to my driveway. My house is the one with the BMW in the driveway."

Ravyn turned her Honda Civic around and pulled up next to Marc's bungalow-style house. He was standing at the front door and waved.

"Sorry," he called out. "I should have come to get you."

"No, no, that is alright. It was on my way."

Marc had on a cream-colored V-neck sweater and khaki pants and loafers. Ravyn now knew she was overdressed.

She walked up the steps to the small front porch and Marc extended his hand in greeting. His hand felt warm when she took it. She could smell his spicy cologne and inhaled deeply.

"Good to see you," he said, drawing her into the house. "Do you want a glass of wine before we go?"

"Sure."

She walked into his home. It was warm and inviting, but certainly looked like the home of a bachelor.

A dark brown leather couch ran along one wall of the living room, which had a small fireplace on a far wall, painted neutral light beige. A matching leather chair was at an angle from the couch, and a solid wood coffee table centered the furniture. Several newspapers and business magazines, including the Atlanta Trend issue with Marc's profile, were scattered on the coffee table. A bookshelf was to the right of the fireplace. It was filled with books, but, oddly, a few sports trophies – the kind that looked like they belonged to a child – were also on one of the shelves.

Marc led Ravyn through the living room and through a small den. A computer desk stood against one wall with a laptop sitting on it. Manila folders and papers were stacked neatly at the side of the laptop. A treadmill, with a sweatshirt draped over it, was also in the room.

They walked into a large kitchen, filled with stainless steel appliances and light beige granite counter tops. The granite was flaked with green. Ravyn ran her hand along the cold stone. Her little condo kitchen was spartan compared to Marc's kitchen. She longed for some granite counters. She longed for real kitchen counters, not the two postage-stamp-sized counters she had.

"What would you like? Red or white?" Marc asked. "Or would you prefer a different drink? I can make a martini or an Old-Fashioned."

"Wine is fine. Whatever you have opened is fine by me."

"Let's see," Marc said as he opened his wine fridge, which was tucked under one part of the counter. "I have a white grenache, a pinot noir, or a chardonnay."

Then he reached up, above the counter, and a built-in wine rack held some more bottles, pulling out a few to glimpse at the labels.

"I have a zinfandel or a cabernet, if you want either of those. Oh, here's a Malbec, too."

"The pinot noir sounds good."

Marc pulled two large-bowled wine glasses from under the wine rack. She noticed fluted glasses and small-bowled glasses hanging under the wine rack as well.

He deftly pulled out the half-stopped cork and filled both glasses before handing Ravyn her glass. "Cheers," he said, clinking her glass.

Ravyn took a sip, then a longer sip.

"This is good," she said.

"I'm glad. It's been open a while, I wasn't sure it would still be good. But I have another bottle in the rack."

"You said you had some material for me?" Ravyn asked.

"Oh, yes," Marc said, setting down his wine glass and moving back into the den. Ravyn followed him with her wine glass. He took one of the manila folders, briefly looked through its contents, and started to hand it to her, then pulled the folder back.

"Well, you don't have to take this right now, but here are the new financial numbers for the company. I'd like you to update the prospectus for serious investors. I've got a meeting with some interested VCs in a couple of weeks and I want current material."

"Of course. No problem. I'll have that to you in just a few days." Ravyn took another drink of her wine. It was nearly gone. She hadn't meant to drink it so fast. She didn't want to be tipsy.

"Can I top you off?" Marc asked.

"Oh, I don't know. I haven't eaten anything yet."

"Here, just a little more. Why don't I drive us to the restaurant? Then we can come back and you can get the folder."

"Oh, OK. That's fine," Ravyn said, as Marc poured a little more wine in her glass. He found his glass and poured a bit more in his, as well.

They drank in awkward silence for a moment, before Marc asked, "How was your weekend at the lake?"

"It was great. It was a girls weekend. I ate too much. I drank too much." Ravyn suddenly stopped talking. She winced thinking she shouldn't have told him she drank too much at the lake. She didn't want him to think she was a lush. "I got to ride a jet ski," she said quickly.

"You've never ridden one before?"

"Not before Friday. It was fun."

"It wasn't too cold?"

"Not really. It got chilly later in the evening, but we were off the water by then."

Ravyn looked down and her wine glass was nearly empty again. She was going to have to slow down or she would be drunk before they got to the restaurant. She put her wine glass down on the counter and pushed it toward the backsplash.

"Should we head to the restaurant?" Marc asked. "I'm hungry."

"Me, too. I'm ready."

Marc walked to the living room and took a set of car keys out of a small bowl by the front door and put on a light brown sports jacket.

He led the way down the front porch steps and walked to the passenger side of the car, opening the door for Ravyn.

"Thank you," she said.

She climbed into the older-model BMW, sliding into a leather seat.

Marc got in and started the car. "Shall I put on the heated seats?"

"Heated seats? I'd love my buns toasted."

Marc laughed. Ravyn loved the sound.

"Sorry, that's kind of a family joke," she explained. "Whenever my dad grills hamburgers, he always asks 'Anyone want their buns toasted?' Kind of lame, but it always makes me laugh."

Marc smiled, pushing a button on the dashboard. "OK. Toasted buns on the way."

Marc drove north on Peachtree Street until he reached the heart of Buckhead. Retail stores lined the road, a mix of boutique stores and national chain stores.

Buckhead proper once had a notorious entertainment district, where bar crawling and seedy clubs often provided the front-page headlines of the weekend newspapers and TV stations. Shootings were not uncommon, which was an odd juxtaposition for the tony residential areas just beyond the Buckhead bar district.

Right as the recession hit, a developer bought up the Buckhead bar district properties, knocking it all down with plans for the "Rodeo Drive of the South." High-end jewelry stores, luxury hand bag retailers and ultra clothiers were rumored to take space in the proposed development.

Unfortunately, plans for upscale retail, condos and hotels fell apart as the recession deepened. All of the property ended up in foreclosure, and the giant 8-acre dirt hole, where the bars once stood, now was an eyesore in the community. Construction fencing, plastered with peeling posters touting once-prospective retailers like Prada, Gucci and Van Cleef & Arpel, barely hid the blight.

Ravyn had written many of the stories about the plans for the new development, called Uptown Buckhead. She even attended the groundbreaking in August 2006, remembering the large white tents, shrimp cocktail and flutes of champagne. She remembered the enthusiasm and optimism for the development.

That all changed in the following years. Uptown Buckhead slid slowly into foreclosure, stories Ravyn wrote for the Atlanta Daily Tribune before she, herself, fell victim to the recession.

Marc turned left onto West Paces Ferry Road, then right on Paces Ferry Place, which was lined with not only quaint restaurants in former houses, but also art galleries and other businesses. He parked on the side of the road not far from the restaurant.

"You've got good parking karma tonight," Ravyn said.

"Good parking karma?"

"That's what I say when I find a great parking spot in Atlanta. I say I've got good parking karma that day."

"Ah," Marc said.

Ravyn suddenly felt dumb for saying that. Parking karma indeed, she thought to herself. I need good conversation karma tonight.

Ravyn and Marc got out of his BMW and took the short walk to Portofino, an Italian restaurant. They walked up the steep driveway to the front heavy wooden door. Upon entering, Ravyn remembered why she so enjoyed the restaurant. It had such an intimate feel. It had an outside patio terrace, covered with large vines. In the summer, it provided some shade that made eating out there, even in August, tolerable.

Ravyn had only ever eaten at Portofino for lunch, and mostly when she had an expense account at the newspaper. It was months since she had dined here. Dinner tonight was going to be a treat.

The owner, who acted as the maître d', showed them to their table, which was in one corner of the main room of the house. Ravyn was a little disappointed they weren't outside on the terraced patio, but as they walked up, she noticed it looked full.

The maître d' held Ravyn's chair for her, then laid a black napkin across her lap. He then handed the wine list to Marc and a dinner menu to each of them.

"Sparkling or still water tonight?" the maître d' asked.

"Ravyn, what is your pleasure?"

"Sparkling, with a wedge of lemon, please."

"Sparkling for the lady. And you, sir?"

"Still for me, please."

"Very good. I'll have your waiter right over."

Within seconds, a waiter appeared with a bottle of sparkling water and poured some in Ravyn's glass. He left and returned with a small plate of lemon slices and a water pitcher to fill Marc's glass.

"My name is Jason. I'll be your server tonight. May I start you off with some wine this evening? Maybe an appetizer?"

"Give us just a moment," Marc said, studying the wine list.

"Very good, sir," and Jason deftly disappeared.

"Do you want to stick with the pinot noir, or are you thinking of having fish tonight?" Marc asked.

"Hmm. I usually get the lamb Bolognese when I come here for lunch, and I see it is on the dinner menu. I may get that, so the pinot noir would be perfect. What are you thinking of getting?"

"I think I'll get the braised short ribs, so a bottle of the pinot noir would be fine."

Jason returned. "Have you decided?"

"I think we'll have a bottle of the Domaine Alfred pinot noir," Marc said.

"Very good choice, sir. Would you like to hear the specials?"

Jason then rattled off a list of the specials that evening, and although the trout dish sounded good, Ravyn knew she still wanted her lamb.

"Do you need a few moments or are you ready to order?" Jason asked.

"I think we're ready. Ravyn?"

"I'll have the lamb Bolognese."

"And you, sir?"

"I'll have the braised short ribs," Marc said, handing off his menu.

"Any salad or appetizer with that?"

"Ravyn, do you want an appetizer?"

Ravyn studied the menu. "The fried artichokes look good."

"We'll have an order of those, please," Marc said.

"Very good, I'll put in your order." And with that, Jason again disappeared.

Ravyn took one of the lemon slices and squeezed it into her water before taking a sip. She was feeling a little light-headed from the wine she drank before dinner. She was hoping the food came quickly.

Jason returned with the bottle of wine, presenting the label to Marc, who nodded. Jason uncorked the wine, handing the cork to Marc for inspection. Marc sniffed at it, then put it down.

Jason poured a small amount of wine into Marc's glass. Marc took a sip and nodded. Jason then poured a full glass for Ravyn and then Marc.

"Enjoy," Jason said. "Your appetizer should be out shortly."

Marc raised his wine glass to Ravyn. "To venture capital."

Ravyn took her glass and toasted to Marc. "To venture capital."

The appetizer arrived and Marc and Ravyn found themselves mired in small talk.

Marc played tennis last week for the first time in ages with an old friend. Ravyn met two deadlines for a travel magazine. Ravyn thought privately that this felt like a really bad first date, which was so stupid since she and Marc actually knew one another.

"Tell me about the meeting with the new venture capitalists," Ravyn said before taking another bite of the fried artichokes.

"They aren't new," Marc said. "I talked to them several weeks ago when I was in California. They passed me over then, but they are willing to take a look at me again. I hope the new financial statements will convince them to help fund the project."

"I hope so, too."

"But I don't really want to talk about business tonight," Marc said. "Tell me about your college years. You went to Montana, right?"

"Missouri."

"Oh, right, Missouri. What was it like?"

"I loved it. I applied and got accepted without ever visiting the campus. It was, and still is, the No. 1 journalism school in the nation, and I wanted to be a journalist. I've known that since I was in the eighth grade and worked on the school newspaper. So, I applied to the No. 1 journalism school. I don't know what I would have done if I hadn't been accepted. But I got in and flew out to Columbia, Missouri. The first time I stepped off the plane at Columbia Regional Airport, which was out in the country, I wondered what I had gotten myself into. Imagine! A New York girl landing in a cow field! I looked around and had some serious doubts. But the campus was wonderful. When I was there, the campus had about 25,000 students total. I went to football games, basketball games, theater…"

"When did you have time to study?" Marc teased.

"Oh, I studied, and graduated with honors. Even now I have such fond memories of my time there."

"I admire that in you. You are a risk-taker."

"Risk-taker? I don't think of myself as a risk-taker."

"No? Deciding to go to a college you've never seen because you know it's what you wanted? That's taking a risk. Maybe a calculated risk, but still a risk. I went to the University of Georgia because all of my friends were going there, and it was close to home. That's not taking a risk. You are a risk-taker."

"I've never really thought of it that way, but I guess you are right."

"I am right."

"Are you always right?" Ravyn teased.

"Oh, not always. I was really wrong about my marriage."

Ravyn didn't know how to respond to that. Suddenly, there was an uncomfortable silence.

"Sorry," Marc finally said. "I really don't want to talk about my failed marriage."

"Neither do I," Ravyn blurted.

Marc laughed nervously.

"To dodging emotional dynamite," he said, raising his glass again. "Cheers."

"I'll drink to that."

Jason appeared with their meals. Ravyn was grateful for the break in the conversation. It had taken such an odd turn.

"Wow. This looks really good," Ravyn said. "So does yours."

"Do you want a bite?"

"I do. Do you want a little of mine?"

"I'm not a big fan of lamb, but I'll try it."

Ravyn put a little of the broad noodles, sauce and shredded lamb on her bread plate and slid it over to Marc. Marc did the same with his ribs.

Ravyn bit into Marc's dish and made a low moan. "Wow, that is good."

Marc took a bite of the lamb Bolognese. "Hmm. Not as good as my ribs, but not bad. Not enough to make me a fan of lamb, though."

"Fair enough," Ravyn said. "More for me then."

Marc refilled Ravyn's wine glass, then his. "Were you in a sorority at college?"

"No. It never appealed to me. The sorority girls always seemed to be so cliquish. It wasn't my thing. I did, however, get invited to frat parties. Some of them were pretty wild. They used to make this stuff they called spolioli. It was lethal."

"What's spolioli?"

"Near as I can tell, it was fruit punch and PGA. Pure grain alcohol," Ravyn said. "After drinking that stuff, it's a wonder we're not all blind."

"Oh, we called that stuff joy juice," Marc said. "We called it something else, too, but it's pretty offensive. The idea was the joy juice would bring down the defenses of fine young Georgia co-eds."

"Oh, I'm sure it did," Ravyn said, laughing. "I got invited to frat parties, and I know they were trying hard to bring down the defenses of fine young co-eds at Missouri, too. My senior year I lived in a house behind the Sig Chi house. I saw some wild, wacky stuff. But that frat house is where lots of guys from the university swim team lived, so there was lots of eye candy, as well."

"I bet."

"Were you in a fraternity in college?"

"I was a P.A.D. at Georgia."

"A what?"

"Phi Alpha Delta," Marc explained. "It was the pre-law fraternity, since I was determined to get a law degree. It was OK. I still have a few frat brother friends here in Atlanta. Mostly, it's a great networking tool, except I'm not a lawyer anymore."

"Maybe it could be, though, if they were investors," Ravyn said.

"I don't want to talk about business tonight," Marc said, his brow furling. "I've been so consumed lately with business. I just need a night when I don't think of how I need money for LindMark."

"OK. I won't bring it up again tonight," Ravyn said.

"I'm sorry. I don't mean to snap. I'm just tired."

"I can understand that. For me, being a freelancer means I never know if I'll have money to pay the rent month-to-month. I like being my own boss, but sometimes it's really scary."

Marc stared at Ravyn. "I never thought of it that way. You are an entrepreneur just like me."

"In a way, I guess I really am. I hate having to worry about bills and clients who don't pay on time and not having health insurance…"

"You don't have health insurance?" Marc interrupted.

"I had it. When I was first laid off, I had COBRA, but that runs out after 18 months. And when I started looking for health insurance on my own, it was more expensive than what I was paying for COBRA. There were a couple of months when I was late on my rent. Paying for health insurance didn't make financial sense if I was going to be homeless."

"I've got to get you on our coverage," Marc said, turning serious. "Why didn't you tell me that? You have to have health insurance."

"I know. But I'm 33. It's not like I'm 65 with high blood pressure and a bum knee."

"Ravyn, you can't think like that. My friend Jenny was 32 when she was diagnosed with breast cancer. She didn't have health insurance and relied on Medicaid for her treatment. It was awful. She's not here today, and I'm convinced it was because she got sub-par treatment."

Ravyn fell silent. She didn't like to think about stuff like that. It was exactly what she felt when she thought of her friend Danica, with three children and trying to keep a roof over their heads.

"Sorry, how did we get so serious?" Marc said, pouring more wine. "See, this business with *my* business is making me too uptight. But I do want to talk to you about getting on our health policy. I need to check how I could do it, since you are a contract employee, but my administrative assistant Rachael is sharp and if anyone can find a way, she can."

Ravyn smiled. "That would certainly ease my mind about that."

Both Marc and Ravyn had finished their meals. Ravyn hadn't eaten all of hers, but planned to box the rest.

"Not hungry?" Marc asked.

"No, I'm nearly full, but I wanted to take some home for lunch tomorrow. It's how I keep my girlish figure," she giggled.

"Your figure looks fine to me."

Ravyn blushed. Everything about this night was starting to feel so wonderful. Here she was at Portofino with Marc! He was complimenting her, he was interested in her life. It felt like a real date and she was enjoying his company.

"It's no use," she thought to herself. "I really like him. I wish he liked me the way I like him."

Jason appeared to clear their plates. "Would you care for a box for that?" he asked Ravyn, who nodded yes. "Did you save room for dessert?" he then asked.

"I leave that to the lady," Marc said, pointing to Ravyn.

"Care for some tiramisu or gelato?" Jason asked.

"Well, will you split something with me, Marc?"

"Let's see the menu. I'm not much of a dessert eater."

Jason produced the dessert menu, and Ravyn studied it hard. Everything looked good. The tiramisu, the warm chocolate cake, the panna cotta, the gelato.

"Will you split some chocolate cake with me?" she asked Marc.

"Sure. And I'd like a coffee, black," Marc said to the waiter.

"How about you, Madame? Coffee? Cappuccino?"

"Do you have decaf cappuccino?"

"Yes," Jason replied.

"I'll have that, please."

Jason placed new forks and small plates on the table, then disappeared.

An awkward silence fell between Ravyn and Marc again. Ravyn began to fidget with her fork, then realized Marc was staring at her and put it down. She sat on her hands to still them.

The dessert and coffee arrived and Ravyn's eyes got wide. The piece of cake was larger than she expected.

"Oh boy, I hope you are planning to have some," Ravyn said.

"Maybe a bite," Marc said.

"Oh sure, leave all those calories to me."

But she took a forkful and ate the first bite. She felt bliss at what touched her taste buds.

"Oh wow," Ravyn said with her mouth still full.

Marc took a stab at the cake and ate a small bite. "Very rich," he said.

"Rich and chocolate-y," she said, taking another big bite. She ended up eating about half the slice, far more than she intended. She was starting to feel the waistband expand on her mini skirt.

"Oof," Ravyn said, pushing the dessert plate away from her. "I am definitely going back on a diet tomorrow. I have overindulged this weekend."

"You don't need to diet," Marc said. "You look fine."

"Well, thank you. I was not fishing for compliments, but I'll take it. But I do need to dial it back. We were a little heavy with the wine and food and snacks at the lake. What time do I have to be at work tomorrow? Because I'm going to have to go for a run tomorrow morning."

Jason arrived with the check and Marc put down his credit card.

"May I help pay?" Ravyn asked.

"Of course not."

OK. Now it did feel like a real date, Ravyn thought, as she stood up.

As they turned to leave, Marc put his hand in the small of Ravyn's back to guide her out. Ravyn felt a current of excitement run down her spine.

Marc opened her door and guided her in his BMW. They barely talked as they drove back to his Buckhead home.

They pulled into the driveway, and Marc broke the silence.

"I've got those financial statements for you in the house. Do you want to come in for a moment?"

"Oh, sure. I can come in for a minute."

Marc opened the front door and walked back to the small den where he'd left the manila folder.

Ravyn walked into the living room and stood there, waiting, with her takeout box from Portofino in her hands.

"Can I offer you something to drink?" he asked, taking the leftovers. "Let me put that in the fridge for you."

"I'd love a glass of water," Ravyn said. "And where is your bathroom?"

"Down that hall and to the right."

When Ravyn returned, Marc had placed a glass of water on the coffee table, along with two glasses of wine.

"There wasn't much left in the bottle," he said. "Just these two glasses." He handed one of them to Ravyn.

"You aren't helping with my plan to dial it back on the food and drink!"

"You said you were starting tomorrow," Marc teased. "You have ... two more hours," he said, looking over at the clock on one of the bookshelves. "You should make the most of it."

Ravyn giggled. "Well, then, where are the chocolate chip cookies?"

"No cookies in this house, sorry. Sit, please."

Ravyn sat on the leather couch while Marc walked over to the fireplace and started the gas logs. Then he turned on some music, a smooth jazz station on Pandora, and sat at the other end of the couch.

"The fire feels nice," she said.

"It does. I only need it a couple of months out of the year, but it's nice to have." Marc's leg brushed against Ravyn's, but he didn't pull it away. Ravyn didn't move hers, either.

"I certainly don't have a fireplace in my condo. My folks have one at their house in South Carolina. It's always nice when I visit them at Thanksgiving or Christmas and they have it going."

"Do you visit your parents often?" Marc asked.

"At the holidays, and I usually go in the spring to help my mom with some spring plantings. They have a big front yard and mom likes to have her flowers in."

"I wouldn't know a thing about flowers. I have a brown thumb when it comes to plants."

Ravyn could believe that, as she took another sip of wine. There wasn't a single plant anywhere that she could see in Marc's house. His house definitely needed a woman's touch, she thought. Her touch.

"What are you thinking?" Marc asked.

"Oh, just that you could use some houseplants, and which ones I'd recommend," she said, blushing.

Ravyn wasn't sure if it was the wine, the fire or Marc, but she was starting to feel warm all over. She stood up.

"I should be getting home. It's late and my boss will want me to start working on his financials early tomorrow," she teased.

"Can't have you be in trouble with your boss," Marc laughed back. "He sounds like an asshole. I'll walk you out."

Marc helped Ravyn put on her jacket as they stood at the front door.

"I had such a nice evening, Marc," Ravyn said, standing close to him. She could smell his cologne and feel his body heat. "Thank you."

She turned her head slightly, meaning to give Marc a peck on the cheek. But he turned his head and the pair kissed, tentatively.

Ravyn felt an electric current run through her entire body. She dropped the manila folder and put her hands on Marc's muscular arms.

They continued to kiss, with a kind of hunger and intensity she had not felt in a long while. Marc wrapped his arms around the nape of Ravyn's neck. His tongue found hers.

Marc's hands slid down Ravyn's shoulders and continued to her waist. He gently began to walk her down the hall toward his bedroom. Ravyn let herself be guided. Marc didn't turn on the light, but deftly began to remove his sweater and her blouse. He unhooked her bra with one move.

Ravyn felt her breasts crush against Marc's warm, slightly hairy chest. His hands moved down her back, undoing the zipper of her mini skirt.

Ravyn reached for Marc's belt, undoing it. She then began tugging at her tights and boots before she and Marc both fell onto his bed.

Marc supported himself on one arm as he removed his pants. Ravyn felt the heat of his bare skin.

Marc began to kiss her neck, gently sucking as he did so. He moved down her chest and began sucking at her nipples. Ravyn groaned. Marc's hands moved down her waist again, to her hips.

He continued kissing down to her navel, then the top of her pubic bone. Ravyn moaned, loudly.

"Marc, Marc," she said.

"I want you," he said.

"I want you, too," she answered.

Marc continued kissing her inner thighs, then began moving back up until he was on top of her. Ravyn felt the weight of him. It felt good.

Ravyn ran her hands down Marc's back, grabbing his tight buttocks, before reaching for his balls, gently caressing them. Marc let out a moan of his own.

"Ravyn, Ravyn, you are so beautiful," he whispered, caressing her cheek. "You are so beautiful." He began kissing her again, gently. Ravyn continued to stroke him on his thigh. It had the desired effect. Marc began to kiss her more ardently. He's breathing deepened and grew quicker. Ravyn's breath quickened as well.

Marc moved back down to Ravyn's breasts, flicking her nipples with his tongue. His fingers caressed her soft center. Ravyn thought she might explode.

He began to move back on top of Ravyn, then stopped.

"What's the matter?" Ravyn asked, suddenly worried he was going to run out on her again.

"Just a moment," he said, reaching for his bedside table.

Marc then moved back on top of Ravyn, and the lovemaking began in earnest.

Ravyn seemed to lose sense of time as their bodies intertwined. She gasped with pleasure and called out Marc's name. Marc moaned and shuddered before collapsing on top of her, spent.

Ravyn could feel tears in the corner of her eyes as she gasped with pleasure. Marc rolled over, wrapping Ravyn in his arms. She sighed and heard his breathing become soft and even. He was asleep. She smiled and closed her eyes. She never wanted this evening to end.

Ravyn awoke disoriented. It took her a moment to realize she wasn't in her bed. In the dim bedroom light she could see Marc sound asleep.

Marc, she thought. It really happened. Last night really happened. She almost felt giddy.

Then she felt a pang of dread.

What does this mean now? Was this just a one-night stand? He's her boss! Would that mean he would fire her? Could they continue seeing each other? Or would it be too awkward?

Ravyn felt herself getting anxious. She knew she was being ridiculous, but she'd never slept with her boss before. Her dating life consisted of meeting men through friends or at parties. They hooked up for a while, then it ended. She didn't want it to end with Marc. She wanted it to last and last.

Marc stirred next to her. "Are you up? What time is it?" he asked in a sleepy tone.

"I'm awake. I don't know what time it is. I don't see a clock in here."

Marc rolled over and looked on the nightstand at his phone. "It's 2 a.m. Just about the time a pesky reporter should be calling me. You won't mind if I take it, would you?" he teased as he rolled over toward her.

"I'm really sorry about that. I didn't realize the time when I called you."

"Well, now I am very glad you did."

"You are? You were pretty mad."

"I'm not mad now," he said, pulling Ravyn close.

"What happened before?" Ravyn blurted. "At my condo?" She hadn't meant to ask him why he had left her condo that evening, but it bothered her.

"Oh, that," Marc stammered, releasing Ravyn. "I just, I just wasn't ready."

"Oh," Ravyn said, quietly.

"But I'm ready now," he said, hugging her again. "Ravyn, you are so smart, and funny, and beautiful. I just wanted to be sure this is something you wanted too. I've made mistakes before. I wanted to be sure this wasn't a mistake."

"Marc, I do want this."

"Good, then we are agreed," he said as his hand slid up her body. Ravyn felt electricity again when he caressed her and let out another low moan.

They slipped into an easy lovemaking, matching each other's rhythms before climaxing nearly in sync.

As she fell asleep for the second time that night, Ravyn didn't think she could ever feel this blissful again.

Marc's phone chimed a morning alarm and both he and Ravyn shook the fog of sleep from their heads.

Although she hadn't gotten much sleep the night before, Ravyn couldn't remember when she'd woken up feeling so rested. Then she remembered. She always slept like a baby after making love. It was like a sleep tonic.

"Good morning, sunshine," Marc said, getting out of bed and pulling on some pajama bottoms. "How do you like your coffee?"

"With a little cream and sugar," she said, pulling herself up on one elbow as she held the covers around her. "Umm, do you have a T-shirt I can borrow? I don't know where my clothes are exactly."

"Oh sure," he said, reaching into a dresser drawer. "Catch."

Ravyn grabbed the shirt he tossed and quickly pulled it over her head. She was looking on the floor for her underwear, spotting them in a small pile by the bed. She let out a groan when she spotted them.

"What's the matter?" Marc asked.

"Oh, nothing," Ravyn said, slipping on her panties. "Just that if I knew I was going to spend the night here, I would not have worn some old granny panties. I would have at least worn a thong."

"How do you women wear those things? They don't look comfortable. They are sexy, but they don't look comfortable."

"They aren't comfortable. We wear them because we know you men find them sexy. If it were up to us, we would only wear comfortable underwear."

It struck Ravyn this was the oddest morning after sex conversation she had ever had with a man. Why in the hell were they talking about her underwear?

Ravyn followed Marc into the kitchen, where he set up the coffee maker and then began pulling out some eggs.

"Scrambled or fried?"

"You're going to fix me breakfast?"

"I can't send you home hungry. I don't know about you, but I'm famished," he said with an impish grin. "I seem to have gotten a workout last night."

Ravyn blushed and smiled. "Scrambled."

Marc whipped up the eggs with a little milk and made some toast. In just a few minutes they were eating breakfast on a little bistro table in the kitchen.

"This tastes great. Thanks."

"Well, I can't have you going into work hungry. You said your boss was kind of an ass."

"No, YOU said my boss was an ass, not me," Ravyn laughed. "I'd never say that about my boss. He's smart and charming and incredibly handsome. And he's a good scrambled eggs maker, too."

"Sounds like a guy I'd like to meet."

"I'll be sure to introduce you."

"Speaking of work, I've got to get going," Marc said, collecting their breakfast plates.

"Oh sure, me too." Ravyn went back into the bedroom and found her clothes, putting on everything but the tights, which she wadded up and stuffed into her purse.

"I'll see you later," Marc said, kissing her at the front door with the Portofino takeout bag and manila folder with the company financials in his hands. "Don't forget these."

Ravyn felt the spell of the evening was suddenly broken.

Ravyn got home to face an angry tomcat.

"Sorry, Felix. I thought I was coming home last night. I know you are hungry." She put cat food in the bowl and put fresh water in another bowl. She'd have to see to the litter box later. Right now, she needed to hurry up and shower and get started on the financial material for LindMark.

An hour later she was poring over the statements, jotting down notes and writing a rough draft of the new brochure.

LindMark had a healthy third quarter. It was in the black, but only by the slimmest of margins. Ravyn realized why Marc was so worried about getting the venture capital. She saw from the statements his income was only just covering his expenses. She wondered how long the company could survive if he had a couple of down quarters. She'd written enough stories about small-business owners to know they operated usually without much in the way of reserves. How many restaurant openings had she written about only to write about their closings eight months later?

But the financial statements also made it clear LindMark could not grow or expand without some cash infusion. The company could likely continue just as it was, but it would be stagnant. And once that happened in any business, it was just a matter of time before it closed.

Ravyn sighed. She didn't like to think of Marc's company closing. What would that do to Marc? What would it do to her? What would that do to them?

Ravyn's phone rang. It was Julie.

"Hey girl, what's up?" Ravyn asked her friend.

"I was calling to see how dinner went last night."

"Oh, it went fine. Really fine. It lasted all night long."

"Ravyn! You didn't!"

"I did. We did. Oh, Julie, I really, really like him."

"Tell me everything!"

Ravyn began to recount the evening and found herself getting aroused just talking about it. She left out the sordid bedroom details but did tell her friend what a good and considerate lover Marc was. She even told Julie about her embarrassment over the ratty underwear.

"Well, you'll just have to wear something sexy next time. But it sounds like he only needs you to get his heart racing, not some frilly black lace lingerie. When are you seeing him again? Tonight?"

"I don't know," Ravyn said, suddenly concerned. "We didn't make another date. I don't know when I'm seeing him next."

"Well, he'll call today, don't you think?"

"I hope so," Ravyn said, her voice trailing off. She wasn't so sure. "Julie, did I make a mistake?"

"Does it feel like a mistake?"

"No."

"Then it wasn't. You'd know if it was."

"Thanks, Julie. I know you are right. What's on your agenda today?"

"Oh, the usual. Soccer practice for the girls. Couples therapy for me and Rob."

"Julie, you will get through this. I know you will. And you both will come out stronger for it."

"I hope you are right."

"I am right. I love you too much for it not to be right."

The friends said their goodbyes and Ravyn looked up to see it was after lunch. Good thing Marc had thought to give her the lamb Bolognese leftovers this morning. She'd have something to warm up in the microwave.

Another two hours later and she was finishing up the new brochure for LindMark. She'd have to ask Marc how to proceed to get it printed. She wasn't sure he'd want the employees at FedEx Office to know his company's financial business.

Ravyn smiled. "I guess that means I do have a reason to call him today."

# Chapter 7

Marc had a hard time concentrating at the office that day. His mind kept drifting back to the night with Ravyn.

He kept thinking of her soft skin, her warm places, and her moans of passion. It made him aroused just to remember last night.

He knew he probably shouldn't have slept with her, but he was so attracted to her. Dully, he remembered he'd also been attracted to Laura Lucas and slept with her.

"Look how that turned out, sport," Marc thought to himself. Laura was still a thorn in his side.

Several times during the day, he'd nearly called Ravyn, just to hear her voice. But he stopped himself. He wasn't sure why, except that he didn't want to seem like a lovesick puppy.

Marc kept looking over the third quarter numbers. He was hoping they would be good enough for the VC big wigs. He was tired of fighting every inch for his business. He wanted, just for once, for it to be easy.

He knew, in his heart, this is what he wanted to do – be his own boss and own his own business. But lately he was weary of the everyday fight to keep his head above water. The adrenaline rush of being an entrepreneur was starting to wear thin.

And what possessed him to tell Ravyn he could get her on his company's health-care policy? That was the most expensive part of his business. He was wondering how he was going to keep that for his current employees, few as they were.

Marc rubbed his eyes and pulled his hands down his face. He felt so tired, like he could sleep for hours and hours. He took a deep breath and tried to clear his mind. Maybe I should go to the gym, he thought.

He grabbed his gym bag, which he kept at the office, and left for the L.A. Fitness in Midtown. Maybe a good run on the treadmill, or a series of reps on the Smith machine, would get him focused again.

Marc pulled into the parking deck, which was attached to an office building. Both shared the parking, so it took him a few floors before he found an open spot and eased his BMW into a parking space.

He walked in, saying hello to the young 20 somethings working the front desk. The blonde wearing a tight hot pink tank top gave him a big, enhanced-whitening smile.

"Easy cowboy," he thought to himself. "That's nothing but trouble."

He grabbed a towel in the locker room and began working out on the weight machines before he moved to the cardio machines.

He started the treadmill and tried to concentrate on the Fox News broadcast on the TV screen before him. It wasn't working. He began to look around him and noticed Bradford Cunningham two machines down. Cunningham didn't seem to notice Marc.

Marc punched it up to 6 mph and ran hard for the next 30 minutes. When he finished, his legs were quivering and his heart was pounding. Sweat beaded across his body. He had never felt better.

He grabbed his towel and headed for the showers.

"Hey Marc. How's business?"

Marc turned to see Bradford walking toward the showers as well.

"Fine, Brad. How's business with you?"

"Better. I hear you're still looking for some VC. Any luck?"

Marc's face darkened. "Not yet, but I have some good feelers out." He did not want to talk to Bradford about business or venture capital or even the weather.

"I hear you are meeting with Mike Pollock next week. Good luck."

Bradford turned and headed toward one shower stall and Marc walked to the opposite end. He showered quickly and left the gym. Marc did not want to run into Bradford again and he wanted to find out how he knew about his upcoming meeting with the venture capitalists.

Marc weaved up Peachtree Road in the BMW and returned to his office in a foul mood.

Ravyn worked on LindMark's brochure for the better part of the day, then sent out invoices for two articles she'd written for an airline travel magazine. Those tended to pay a decent rate. She was hoping she would get a couple more. Then she searched online for some more freelance jobs available. Most of the online freelance jobs she found were hardly worth inquiring about, the pay was so low. It was a simple case of supply and demand: too many folks doing freelance work to support themselves and not enough jobs out there. Job posters could ask for rock bottom fees because they knew so many were hungry for the work. Ravyn was one of them.

She found five prospects where the pay wasn't too low and sent three queries and two proposals. Ravyn always felt that for every 10 proposals she sent out, she'd get one back that turned into a job.

Ravyn finally looked up at her kitchen clock and saw the time.

"How did it get to be five o'clock?" she wondered. "And why haven't I heard from Marc?"

She tried to tell herself he was probably busy with work. He was the boss, after all. But inwardly she was worried. She hated the first few days after a new relationship. While she felt giddy with that rush of being with a new man, doubts always managed to creep in.

Ravyn didn't like that about herself. She didn't want to be one of those clingy women who obsessed about the man in her life. But she wished she had heard from Marc. She would have felt more confident about the budding relationship.

Ravyn picked up her cell phone and pulled up Marc's number. Then she hesitated to call. Instead, she sent a text. "Finished the brochure. Need guidance on printing."

Then she texted her fellow blogger James Davidson to see if there was a restaurant opening tonight. Maybe she could get a free glass of wine and appetizers for dinner, as well as catch up with a friend.

James texted back that there wasn't an opening tonight, but he was going to review the new menu at the restaurant 4th & Downs and invited her to be his guest. He'd be able to expense her meal as well, as long as she ordered different items from the menu, so he could try those as well. It was a favor she was glad to provide.

Ravyn met James at 7 p.m. at the restaurant, owned by its chef Jay Downs, in Atlanta's Old Fourth Ward. The restaurant, which had exposed brick walls and exposed pipes, was busy in the bar area when Ravyn walked in. James was seated at a high table and waved her over.

"I thought I'd try one of the cocktails while I waited," he said, nursing an amber-colored drink.

"What is it?"

"They call it 'A Modest Proposal.' It's whiskey, lime and bitters, basically. It's good. Want one?"

"Maybe not whiskey. What else do they have?"

James handed over the cocktail menu and Ravyn looked it over. She settled on a drink called "The Other Shore," a ginger-infused rum drink with lemons and pink peppercorns. It was spicy, but Ravyn liked spice, so decided to give it a try.

"What have you been up to? I haven't seen you at many events lately," James asked.

"I've been working for LindMark Enterprises, mostly," she said quickly. "I'm helping the company with some of its publicity."

"Nice. Didn't you do a profile on the owner?"

"Yes, that's how I got the job now." Ravyn really didn't want to talk about Marc. He hadn't called her all day and she was feeling uncomfortable about it. She just wanted to enjoy her dinner with James and talk about anything other than LindMark.

"What have you been doing?" she asked, hoping to change the subject.

"I picked up a job as a blogger for a fashion magazine," he said. "That makes two blogs I'm doing for different publications. I'm really happy with it, but it means I'm eating out a lot. I'm not sure my waistband is going to like those jobs."

"Oh James, you are funny. You look great. And I envy you. I'd love to have a steady job as a blogger. But I know you can't live off doing just one blog."

"That's the truth. I've got two blogs and all the other work I do," he said.

After about a half hour, James signaled for the bar tab and he and Ravyn were seated in the main dining room. The restaurant was very open, with art lining the exposed walls. Toward the back of the restaurant, the kitchen could be seen through a glass wall and the kitchen staff was working furiously.

Ravyn began to peruse the menu and swallowed hard. The prices were way more than she expected to spend.

"Are you sure you can expense all this?" Ravyn asked warily. She was considering ordering the soup as her meal. It would have been all she could have afforded.

"Ravyn, order what you want. I've got this."

"OK. What are you thinking of getting so I can order something different."

"I think we'll get the flank steak appetizer to start. Do you eat red meat?"

"I eat everything," she said, looking up from the menu.

"Good. Then I think I'll get the grouper," James said. "What about you?"

"There are a lot of things on the menu I've never eaten. I'm not sure."

"Do you like poultry? Try the pheasant, because I want to try it. If you hate it, you can eat my grouper."

"OK. That's fair. I've never had pheasant, so I'll try it."

They ordered some side dishes and wine and spent the next hour talking shop and finding out what was going on with mutual friends.

"I had no idea Richard was moving to California!" James exclaimed. "I can't believe he's moving there to be with a woman he met online."

"Well, he got a job out there, too," Ravyn said. "Let's hope both things work out."

"What have you heard from Julie Montgomery? You're friends with her, aren't you?"

"Yes. She's one of my best friends. She's a stay-at-home-mom to two girls. Although, I swear her social life is busier than mine. Well, her daughters' social lives are busier than mine."

"How is your social life? Dating anyone?"

"Um, not really," Ravyn lied. "What about you? Are you and Rick still dating?"

"Oh no," James said. "That's been over for a while. I'm kind of in a slump. I haven't met anyone in a while who really excites me. But that waiter over there looks cute. Maybe I'll slip him my number."

Ravyn turned to see who James was talking about, but only saw an older, balding man.

Ravyn turned to James with a shocked look on her face and James burst out laughing. "Got you."

Ravyn laughed then too. It's what she loved about James. He was an easy friend.

"Hey, I heard *Cleopatra* magazine might be looking for a managing editor," James said. "I don't think the position has been advertised yet. You should apply."

"James, I haven't been an editor for real. I mean, I was a part-time editor at that small paper in South Georgia, but not a full-time editor. There are far more qualified people out there that will get it."

"Don't sell yourself short, Ravyn. You are good at what you do. You are very organized and always meet deadlines. You've had daily newspaper experience and you'd get good references from all of your freelance clients. In fact, that is probably in your favor. You've worked for so many magazines and trade pubs."

"Wow. *Cleopatra*. I would love to work there. Aren't they headquartered in New York?"

"The parent company is in New York, but they have fashion magazines all over the country. I forget what the one in Los Angeles is called. They all have exotic names, like *Calliope*. Maybe that's the one in L.A. Let me see what my friend Craig says. He's a graphic designer over there. I'll find out when that job is supposed to be posted. Maybe Craig can get your resume in before the job gets posted."

"James, I'd really appreciate that. I would really like to work full-time again and have a steady paycheck. And health insurance. And a paid vacation. And a paid sick day!"

Ravyn started to feel giddy. *Cleopatra* was a high-end fashion magazine in Atlanta. She had written a couple of articles for it, but was not one of its regular freelancers. Articles included the hot restaurants that were opening or had new chefs, the latest trends in jewelry, makeup and fashion, and occasional interviews with celebrities, many of whom were filming movies or TV shows in Atlanta.

As Ravyn began to think about the job at *Cleopatra*, Chef Jay Downs came to the table.

"How is everything tonight?" he asked.

"Very good, Jay," James said. "The grouper was excellent. And you know Ravyn Shaw, don't you?"

Ravyn and Jay shook hands. "Have we met?" he asked.

"We have, but it was a long time ago. At a media tasting shortly after you opened."

"Oh, who do you work for?"

"Well, myself now, but I was with the Trib back then. I really enjoyed the pheasant tonight. I've never had it and it was really good."

"Thank you. If there's anything I can get you, let me know."

Ravyn and James looked over the dessert menu and decided to split some cake over coffee.

"James, thanks for letting me tag along tonight," she said as they were ready to leave. "I really appreciate it. And thanks for the job tip. Please let me know what you hear. The more I think about it, the more I'd like to apply for that job at *Cleopatra*."

"Glad I could be of help. I'll talk to Craig tomorrow and let you know."

The friends parted ways in the parking lot.

Ravyn headed back to her condo. She was thinking about the magazine job when her phone rang. It was Marc.

"Hi there," she answered.

"Well, hello. I tried texting you earlier and didn't hear from you. Everything OK?"

"Oh, yes, sorry, I was out to dinner with my friend James. I didn't hear the phone."

"Oh," Marc said flatly. "I didn't mean to disturb your dinner."

Ravyn cringed. Why had she said she was out with James? Now Marc is going to think she was out with another guy!

"Oh no, that's fine," Ravyn said quickly. "James is an old friend from my newspaper days. He was reviewing 4$^{th}$ & Downs and let me tag along to help him try some dishes."

"Sounds like a date," Marc said, almost angrily.

"I suppose it would have been if my name were Robert," Ravyn said, trying not to get angry herself.

"What? Oh. I'm sorry. It was kind of busy at the office today. Did you say you had the brochures ready?"

Ravyn's heart sank. Did Marc really just call to talk shop? He wasn't calling to talk to her about last night?

"I do have the brochures, but I didn't know if you wanted me to give them to the printer, or if you wanted to do them on your printer. I wasn't sure how sensitive the material was."

"You can take them to the printer. I think that will be fine. Can you wait on them while they are printed?"

"OK. I can do that tomorrow. I can have them to you in a day or two."

"Great. That's fine. Thanks. I'll talk to you later then."

"Bye," Ravyn said, but Marc had already hung up.

She could feel tears welling up in her eyes. She pulled into her parking deck, parked her car and ran to the elevators, hoping no one would see her. She got into her condo, threw her purse on the floor, sat on the couch and wept.

Marc poured himself another Scotch and remained in a foul mood. He had not meant to confront Ravyn about her evening with – what was his name, James? She said it was just dinner with a friend. That's all it probably was. But he instantly felt jealous.

Marc told himself he did not have a right to feel jealous. He and Ravyn were not really dating, although he wouldn't mind that. He wanted to get to know her better. He wanted to be with her.

Instead, he fumed at himself, fumed at Bradford Cunningham and continued to drink his Scotch. About an hour later, Marc was very buzzed. He normally didn't drink more than one Scotch a night and he'd had four, with less and less water.

He finally got out of his leather chair and picked up his phone. He held it in his hand and found Ravyn's contact page. All it had was her number. He didn't know her birthday, even.

"I'm sorry," he wrote in a text. "I didn't mean to be an asshole."

Marc stared at the message for a while before he sighed and finally hit send.

Ravyn heard the ping of her phone and picked up her purse, still down on the floor. Her eyes were swollen from crying. She'd cried so hard, one of her contact lenses had come out and she had a hard time looking at the message.

It was from Marc! "I'm sorry. I didn't mean to be an asshole" it read.

Ravyn wasn't quite sure how to respond. He had been an ass. At least he realized he was being an ass.

"James is just a friend. Really." she texted back.

"Let me make it up to you. Dinner tomorrow?"

"OK. Where?"

"My place. I'll cook."

"You cook?" she texted back.

"I can grill a steak. And bake a potato. Come at 7."

"See you tomorrow."

"Come hungry."

Ravyn felt better after she put her phone down. She was going to see Marc again and he said he was sorry for tonight. She went into her bathroom to wash her face. Her eyes still looked red, but less swollen.

She poured a glass of white wine and booted up her laptop.

"Time to work on the resume," she said to herself. She also did some research on *Cleopatra*, its parent company Horizon Publishing and its editor Samantha Hunt.

When she looked up from her laptop, it was nearly midnight. She shut down and started getting ready for bed. Felix slept curled up squarely in the middle of her queen-sized bed.

"Why is your half of the bed always the middle, my man?" Ravyn said as she nudged Felix out of the way and turned out the bedside light. She was asleep within minutes.

Marc awoke with a pounding headache. He had not meant to drink so much Scotch the night before. And had he really offered to fix dinner for Ravyn tonight? What a bad idea. He hadn't touched his grill in ages. He wasn't even sure he had propane. And he'd have to pick up a couple of steaks on his way home from work tonight, which meant he'd have to leave early. He hadn't planned on that.

Marc considered whether he should cancel on Ravyn and plan another night. No, that would probably send the wrong message, he thought.

As he drove to work, he realized he'd just have to push himself to get everything done early at work and get home in time to grill steaks.

Ravyn arrived at Marc's that evening unsure of their relationship, or even if there was one.

Ravyn had opted for blue jeans and a dark plum sweater. She did, however, remember to wear sexy underwear. Just in case.

Ravyn handed Marc a bottle of red wine as he escorted her in. "Smells good, what's in the oven?"

"The potatoes, but I just put them in. The steaks are marinating. It might be another hour before we eat. Is that OK?"

"That's fine. I had a late lunch."

"Can I get you a glass of wine?"

"Sure."

"What did you bring me? A pinot noir. Hmm. That's good to start, but we'll want something heavier for dinner. Do you want to start with the pinot?"

"It's fine."

Marc disappeared toward the back and Ravyn stood in the living room. Everything felt awkward.

Marc returned with the wine. "Sit, please."

Ravyn sat on the couch and Marc sat in the leather chair. They sipped their wine in awkward silence.

"I want to apologize for last night," Marc finally said. "It's not my business who you have dinner with."

"James is just a friend. A gay friend. But if he ever changes sides I'm all over him." Ravyn tried to give a little laugh, but it came out more as a snort.

Marc smiled. "Let's hope James never changes sides."

Ravyn then smiled, too.

"I should have asked this a long time ago, Ravyn," Marc asked. "Are we dating?"

"I hope so. I don't just sleep with anyone." Ravyn suddenly flushed.

"Good," Marc said. "I want to keep seeing you. I just need to know this isn't some fling."

"I don't want it to be. I want to see you exclusively, too."

"It's just I made a mistake with Laura Lucas and I don't want to repeat it."

"I am *not* Laura Lucas," Ravyn spat.

Marc looked over to see Ravyn's angry face. He got up and moved over to the couch. "I'm sorry. I'm not implying you *are*

Laura. She caught me at a vulnerable time in my life and took advantage of that."

Marc stood up and paced his living room.

"Once again, I feel like this is a vulnerable time in my life," he continued, "with my company needing capital to grow. I don't want to be taken advantage of again."

"Boy, you really don't know me, do you?"

"No, I don't," he said, turning back to Ravyn. "And you don't know much about me."

"But I'd like to," Ravyn said, sincerely.

"OK," Marc took a deep breath. "Let's consider this our first date. Let's just take it slow."

Ravyn gave an inward laugh." Guess I didn't need to wear the sexy underwear tonight," she thought to herself.

"To taking it slow," she said, and raised her wine glass.

The rest of the evening went smoothly. Marc and Ravyn chatted like a couple who were on a first date, finding out about each other's likes, family and childhood. Ravyn laughed when Marc recounted learning to ride a bike and suffering his first broken bone as a result.

"That was your *first* broken bone? What else have you broken?" she asked.

"A couple of toes when I attempted to kick a flower pot out of the way. I was wearing flip flops. I don't recommend doing that. What have you broken?"

"A couple of promises, but never a bone. Oh, but I once broke a window at our house in South Carolina. It wasn't really my fault, but my dad didn't see it that way."

"What happened?"

"I was mowing the yard and there was a gravel patch by the down spouts of the gutters. I ran over the gravel with the mower and it shot a pebble through the living room window. One of those pebbles also caught me in the leg. I had a knot on that leg for weeks! I was just glad it didn't hit me in the head. I'd have been knocked out."

"Why did your dad blame you for that?"

"Well, he told me never to run over the gravel with the mower."

"Aha! So it was your fault."

"No! No! I'll never admit it was my fault! But my dad made me pay for that window anyway. It was a long summer that year with no pocket money."

"Were your parents pretty strict with you?"

"Yes and no. They certainly put restrictions on what I could and could not do that were pretty age-appropriate. They did that with my sister, too. But they also let me and Jane make mistakes. I cringe when I see parents today who either give their children everything or try to protect them from everything. I had to do chores for an allowance and that was what I had to go to the movies or buy a new album or cassette. Remember vinyl albums?"

"Yes, I do! My folks were the same way. Since I have two younger siblings and my father worked for an insurance company, we didn't have a lot of extra money. Oh, we had a family vacation every year and there were Christmas presents under the tree, but we were not wealthy. But I would have never known that. My parents sacrificed for us kids, but we were so loved. I really thank my parents for that."

"Me too. Are you close to your family?"

Marc's face changed ever so slightly. "I'm close to my parents and my sister, but not my brother. He's... Well, he's a bit of a challenge."

Marc has a brother? Ravyn remembered him mentioning a sister for the profile, but not a brother. Not at all. Ravyn didn't push the subject since she sensed a shift in Marc when he talked about his family.

"What's your favorite childhood vacation memory?" Ravyn asked.

"We went to Jekyll Island almost every summer for a week. That was always great fun. We stayed at a shabby little motel with a kitchenette so my mother could fix meals and save money. But we always had one meal out, usually on the night before we left, and we kids could order whatever we wanted. I always ordered the shrimp. I still love shrimp."

Marc's eyes shone when he talked about the beach vacation memory.

"I love the beach, too. My family tries to go to Hilton Head Island in South Carolina every year, but we took some family vacations to Myrtle Beach, too."

"What's your favorite childhood vacation?"

"Well, it wasn't my favorite vacation when it was happening, but now that I think back on it, it was pretty hilarious. We took a cross-country trip to visit my grandparents in Nebraska when I was a teenager. Our car had no air conditioning and it was summer. That was back when you didn't have to keep kids in booster seats, or even seat belts! My sister and I were hot and miserable in the backseat and started fighting," Ravyn started laughing at the memory. "I kept yelling that Jane was on my side of the car and to make her stop. My dad pulled the car over on the side of the highway and just lost it. He got out of the car and just started yelling at the sky, shaking his fists, pounding the hood of the car."

Ravyn started laughing so hard she could barely tell the story.

"He broke his hand!" she gasped. "We had to find a hospital in the middle of nowhere and he got it all bandaged up. He had that bandage on for the rest of the trip, trying to drive with what looked like a giant catcher's mitt on his hand. My sister and I didn't make another peep on that trip!"

Ravyn wiped tears away from her eyes.

"I know it sounds awful, but we'd never seen him like that. Here was this mild-mannered college professor and he's just railing at the sky and pounding the car. I think we were all in awe and terrorized at the same time. It's one of our best family stories now. 'Remember the time your father broke his hand yelling at the sky?!'"

Marc was laughing too. "You are a good storyteller."

"Well, I guess I had better be if I'm in journalism."

"You still think of yourself as a journalist?"

"I guess I do. I didn't leave because I wanted to. I left because I was laid off."

"Would you go back to a reporter's job if you could?"

"In a heartbeat," Ravyn said more quickly than she expected. "In fact, my friend James told me about an opening at a magazine I want to look at. Oh, don't worry; I won't abandon my work for you. And this magazine job may be a long-shot anyway."

"No, Ravyn, you should pursue your dreams. You clearly have a passion for storytelling."

Ravyn smiled. She didn't know what to say. But what Marc was saying was true. She was a good storyteller and she wanted to tell stories again.

"Would you be a reference for me for the magazine job?"

"Of course! You've done a great job for LindMark, and me."

Both Marc and Ravyn suddenly got quiet, as if they had said all they could think to say that night. Ravyn smiled a shy smile at Marc, who looked uncomfortable in the silence.

"Well, let me help you clean up, and then I guess I should be going," she said.

The pair cleared the table and moved about the kitchen, clattering the dirty dishes before Ravyn began loading them into the dishwasher.

"Do you have a set way of putting dishes in?" she asked.

"In what?"

"The dishwasher. Do you have a set way of putting dishes in the dishwasher?

"No. Why?"

"Well, some people do, and I didn't want to load the dishwasher wrong if you had a specific way to put the dishes in."

"People really do that?" Marc asked incredulously.

"Yes. I have a way of loading the dishwasher that I like and I don't like it when dishes don't go in the right way."

Marc looked at Ravyn, puzzled, as he handed her another plate.

"I had no idea there was a right way."

Ravyn sighed, continuing to load the dishwasher. "I guess there is no right or wrong way, really, just the way people are set in the way they do things. I just don't know the way you like things."

"I like you," Marc said, taking Ravyn by the hands. "And I like the way you do things." He kissed her lightly on the lips. Ravyn kissed Marc back. Maybe she did need the sexy underwear after all.

But Marc broke it off, holding Ravyn by her arms.

"I want you, Ravyn, but I want to know you first. Is that OK?"

"It's OK."

Ravyn met Julie for lunch the next day at Twist, one of their favorite places. It was the first time in a couple of days the friends had been able to catch up, and Ravyn recounted her dates with Marc at his house.

"It has to be the first time in the history of the universe that a man has cold feet," she told her friend.

"You have completely buried the lead, how was he in bed?" Julie asked. "You only hinted before. I want the gory details!"

"Oh, he was great. I mean, *really* great. It's nice to sleep with a man who knows how to please a woman. Maybe that's where I went wrong all these years. I should have been sleeping with divorced men who know their way around a woman. I've been dating all these single guys who just don't get it," Ravyn said, biting into a piece of tuna roll.

"Oh, I don't think that's it. I've slept with plenty of single men who knew what they were doing. You just never found the right lover. And now you have," Julie said, pushing around her seaweed salad.

Ravyn was almost shocked at the conversation she was having with Julie. She'd never really talked to her friend about their prior sex lives and lovers. And here they were, back at Twist having sushi, and discussing just that.

"How are things with you and Rob?" Ravyn asked tentatively.

"About the same. No, that's not true. It's been OK lately. Our therapist has had us go out on dates. You know, like a date, when we were single. Without the girls. It's been nice. It feels like we are connecting with each other again."

"I'm happy to hear that. I'm glad it's been better between you two."

"We went out to the movies two nights ago and we held hands. Then we started getting a little frisky. I gave him a hand job in the theater! Geez, I haven't done that since I was 16!"

"Julie! You did that when you were 16?"

"C'mon, Ravyn. Don't be a prude. I did that with a lot of boys as a teenager. I wasn't going to sleep with them, but I wanted to have fun with them. I got some good head, too, you know, and my hymen was perfectly safe until I was 18."

Ravyn stared at her friend and felt like she was a completely repressed woman. She hadn't lost her virginity until she was a junior in college, and with a boy she thought she was going to marry. Ravyn smiled inwardly at her naïveté. She could not imagine herself married to Tom Stephens now. She wondered what ever happened to him.

"Where are you?" Julie demanded.

Ravyn shook herself from her reverie. "Oh, just thinking how you were *way* ahead of me in the sexual development department."

"Well, a lot of fat good it is doing me now. My husband cheated on me and you are the one having all the fun with a new man."

"I'm not having *that* much fun. We've only done it once, and I just can't read him. I'm into him, but I don't quite feel he's all that into me. What was that book from a few years back? 'He's Just Not That Into You.' Maybe I need to read that."

"Oh, he's into you," Julie said. "The fact he wants to slow it down just a little means he doesn't want to blow it with you."

"You think? I've never had a man want to slow it down. They always want to go, go, go. I'm worried his wanting to slow it down means he's not interested."

"I think he's interested. I think he's just scared."

"God, I wish I understood men," Ravyn said, sighing, before popping another bite of tuna roll in her mouth.

"Ravyn, men wish they understood women. It's a vicious cycle. I think he likes you, or he wouldn't be telling you he wants to slow it down. He'd just dump you. When men aren't interested, they move on. I should know."

"Oh, Julie. I'm sorry. I'm sorry I'm going on about myself and whining about my problems. Are you really OK?"

"I feel like I'm in limbo. I feel like Rob and I are just going through the motions. We're in therapy, but it feels wrong. It feels forced. Does that make sense? The date felt really nice, but then we got home and it all seemed to fall back into the old routine."

"Julie, I wish I could say I knew how it felt, but I don't. I just want you to be happy. If the therapy isn't working, can you go to another therapist? Maybe your therapist isn't working for you. Find another one. And if that one doesn't work, find another one after that. I want you to be happy, and I think you are happy with Rob."

Julie's eyes welled and tears began to roll down her cheeks. "I know you're right," she said, reaching for her purse and fishing for a tissue. "I love him. I can't help but loving him. But I don't understand why he slept with her."

"Julie, I'm not a psychologist or a psychiatrist or anything like that, but let me ask you: Have you asked him that? Have you asked him why he did it? Ask him. Talk to him."

Julie dabbed at her eyes then looked at Ravyn. She snuffled and her lower lip quivered, then stopped. "I've never asked him why he did it. A part of me doesn't want to know. But I know you are right. I should ask him."

"Julie, I'm not a professional. I don't mean to…"

"No, Ravyn. I've never asked him why he did it. I'm going to ask him," she said, nodding her head and looking determined. "I'm going to ask him."

Ravyn, inwardly, felt troubled. She wished she could just wave a magic wand and  make her friend's marriage be better. But she couldn't. Ravyn just worried that Julie's confrontation might backfire, and that would be devastating, for both Julie and Rob, and Ravyn.

Julie composed herself, wiped her eyes again, and tucked the snotty tissue back in her bag.

"Thank you, Ravyn," she said, tilting her chin up and smiling wanly. "Thank you for helping me see what I needed to see."

Ravyn reached over and took her friend's hand. "You know I would do anything for you. I just want to see you happy."

"I will be. I feel sure I will be happy."

Ravyn got back to her condo and once again booted up her laptop to go over her resume. She really wanted to impress the powers that be at *Cleopatra*.

About an hour later, she brought the brochure material for LindMark to the nearby FedEx Office to be printed. She waited for the material, then drove it over to LindMark's offices. She left it at the receptionist's desk, without even asking for Marc.

As she reached the parking deck of LindMark's building, she got a text from him.

"What gives? You don't even say hello?" the text read.

"Sorry," she wrote back. "Busy with resume. Talk tonight?"

"Call u later."

That evening Marc called.

"The brochure looks great. Thanks for doing that."

"Hey, it's part of my job. Did you hear anything about the venture capital today?"

"No. That's what is so frustrating. I feel like I'm close, but then I don't hear anything. I'm supposed to go to a reception in a couple of weeks to meet with some more money men. Hey, will you be my date?"

"You want me to go with you?"

"Yes, I'd like you to go. It will make me feel less nervous. Plus, I think some of the money men will have their wives with them. I don't want to go alone."

"So, I'm just arm candy, huh?" Ravyn teased.

"No, I didn't mean it like that."

"I'm just yanking your chain. I'm OK with being your arm candy. But do you know what the dress is? Business casual? Semi-formal? Women need to know these things."

"I have no idea. Do I need to ask someone?"

"No. I'll just wear an LBD. I'll be OK."

"LBD? What is that?"

"Little black dress. Every woman's friend."

"Mmm… I can't wait to see you in a little black dress. Then I'd like to see you out of it."

"Really. You sly dog, you. Is this where we have phone sex?"

"Phone sex? Ravyn! Do you want to have phone sex?"

"Are you alone?"

"Yes. Why?"

"Well, I wouldn't want to have you get a hard on in front of a crowd."

Marc felt his breath quicken. Ravyn hadn't said anything untoward, but the thought of having phone sex with her was making him excited.

"And what if I was in a crowd? What would you do to me?"

Ravyn felt herself flush. She could hardly believe how bold she felt, talking to Marc this way. She felt sexy and alluring and in control.

"Well, first I would run my hand down the front of your khaki pants."

Marc looked down. He was wearing khaki pants. How did Ravyn know that?

"I feel your hand," he said, his voice deepening.

"Next, I'd undo your zipper, slowly."

Marc closed his eyes. He almost *could* feel her hand pulling down his pants zipper.

"That feels nice. What's next?"

"I like your silk boxers. I rub my hand over the front of your boxers. You are starting to get hard."

Ravyn could feel herself getting wet talking to Marc. She squirmed on the breakfast bar stool she was sitting on in her condo.

"Starting to get hard. I *am* hard," Marc replied, his voice husky.

"Oh God," Ravyn said.

"I'm on my way over there," Marc said.

"Hurry," Ravyn replied.

Marc buzzed to be let into Ravyn's condo 20 minutes later.

Ravyn met him at the door and the couple began to devour each other instantly. The sex was hot and intense. Ravyn came twice before Marc collapsed on top of her in her bedroom.

"So much for taking it slow," Ravyn whispered in Marc's ear.

Marc grunted and rolled over in her bed.

Ravyn felt exhausted, but exhilarated. Marc was a good lover and at this very moment she felt truly content.

A few minutes passed and finally Marc spoke.

"You can't talk to men after sex," he said.

Ravyn rolled over to face him.

"What?"

"You can't talk to men after sex. We can't think."

"What, is all the blood in your little head and not your big head?" Ravyn giggled.

"Something like that," Marc said as he pulled Ravyn toward him, wrapping her in a bear hug. Within seconds, he was snoring softly.

Ravyn sighed. She wasn't really sleepy, but Marc's arms were heavy on her body, and she couldn't really move. She snuggled down in the bed and willed herself to sleep.

Ravyn woke with a start when she heard a loud thump in her bedroom and Marc cursing.

"What's the matter?" she asked, sleepily.

"Shit! I stubbed my toe! I have to use the bathroom. Where is it?"

Ravyn reached over and turned on the bedside light. "Through the door, on your left."

Ravyn heard Marc stumble through the door, saw the bathroom light flick on and heard the door shut. Then she heard the long steady stream of his pee.

She marveled at how long it seemed to go on. Damn, is he a camel?

She heard the toilet flush and the faucet run in the bathroom sink and realized she had to go, too. She jumped up, grabbing her robe and when Marc came out of her bathroom, she rushed in. "Next!" she said.

When she came out, Marc was getting dressed.

"Are you leaving?" she asked.

"Well, I hadn't planned on being here tonight."

"Oh," she said, trying not to hide her disappointment.

Marc finished buckling his pants and walked around the bed toward Ravyn. "Do you want me to stay?"

"Well, I don't want you to feel like you have to rush off," she said, sitting down on the side of the bed, pulling her robe tighter around her.

"Ravyn," Marc said, pulling her up from the bed and holding her to him. "Ravyn."

Ravyn pressed herself into him and felt him getting hard again. She felt her nipples get hard and begin to press against her robe and Marc's chest.

Marc reached down and began to kiss her again, softly at first, then earnestly.

They once again wrapped their arms against each other. Ravyn broke free for just a moment to turn off the bedside light, and their passion began anew.

Ravyn awoke the next morning with Marc slumbering softly next to her. Felix had planted himself in the small of her back. She wasn't quite sure if she could move without waking both of them. But her bladder felt full and she knew she would have to move soon.

Ravyn tried to slide Felix over, but he chirped, then yowled, annoyed.

"Move over, big guy," she whispered to her cat.

"What?" Marc said, rolling over. "What?"

He reached for Ravyn and tried to pull her to him.

"Just a minute," she said, escaping to the bathroom.

As she returned to the bedroom, Ravyn saw Felix was pacing in the kitchen, demanding food. "OK, you first." She filled his food bowl and scratched his head.

Marc tottered out of the bedroom sporting slight stubble on his face and mussed hair. Ravyn smiled at him and ran her hand through her hair, realizing it felt like a bird's nest.

"Morning," she said. "Coffee?"

"Yes, coffee."

Ravyn got the coffee pot going and searched her refrigerator, hoping she had something that might resemble a decent breakfast. Her fridge looked bare.

"I don't think there is much here in the way of breakfast."

"Is there something close by?" Marc said, running his hand over his stubbly chin.

"There's a Starbucks not far, or Highland Bakery. That's not far, either."

"Highland Bakery. Where is it? Can I walk there?"

"Yes, but let me go with you. Let me just put something on and fix my hair."

In a few minutes, Ravyn and Marc walked hand-in-hand the few blocks over to Highland Bakery in Midtown. The bakery and restaurant smelled wonderful when Marc opened the door for Ravyn. She could smell the fresh baked goods and her mouth immediately began to water.

They queued up and Ravyn ordered a chocolate croissant, while Marc got a bagel before they headed back to Ravyn's condo.

Once there, Ravyn poured the coffee. She took hers with cream and sugar but wasn't sure how Marc took his.

"Black," he said.

"I learned something about you this morning," she said.

"Oh?"

"You take your coffee black," she said, smiling at him. This is the part of every relationship she loved. Learning new things about a new man. She was still smiling when Marc asked her what she was thinking about.

"Last night," she fibbed, then smiled.

Marc smiled, too, before taking a bite of his bagel.

"What's on your agenda today?" he said, wiping a bit of cream cheese off his lip.

"Well, I'll scout for a few more freelance jobs, go for a run. What about you?"

"Run my business, look for capital, and go over that brochure. Send me an invoice for that, by the way."

"Sure. I will."

Marc finished his bagel and gulped down the last of his coffee. "See you later, OK?" Marc kissed Ravyn goodbye, not just a small kiss, but a hearty one. Ravyn kissed him back, deep.

"You are going to make me want to stay here all day," Marc said.

"Would that be bad?"

"Not bad for me, but bad for business. I've got to go."

"OK."

Ravyn shut the front door behind him, leaned against it and took a deep breath. "Damn, I wish he didn't have to go," she whispered.

Ravyn searched her usual freelance job sites and made inquiries to a couple of assignments. She got an email from Atlanta Trend about a short story they needed about a new project in South Georgia. She gladly replied that she could do it.

Then she thought about that little black dress she told Marc she could wear to the venture capital function.

"I'd better make sure that still fits," she thought.

Ravyn dug it out of her closet and tried it on. She turned several times in front of the mirror.

"Well, it will be OK, but I may need to get a girdle," she thought.

Ravyn knew she couldn't afford the really high-end shapewear, but she was hoping she could find something just as good, but less expensive, online.

She began looking through her jewelry to see what she might wear with it. She didn't have much good jewelry, but had some fun, funky pieces, as well as some more "classic" pieces.

In a conservative crowd, she decided she ought to go with the understated, classic pieces.

Ravyn then turned her attention to what shoes she would wear with the dress. She decided she might need to get a new pair of black or silver sling-backs for the event. She could probably find a good pair at T.J. Maxx or Marshall's.

She called Julie to see if she wanted to shop with her that afternoon in Buckhead.

"Hey, Julie, I need to find some sling-back shoes for an LBD-event. Want to come with me to shop this afternoon?"

"Where are you going? Phipps? The shoe department at Nordies? You can find great shoes there."

"Julie, I can't afford the mall, or Nordies. I was thinking about T.J. Maxx and Marshall's."

"Why don't you go to DSW? There's that discount area in the back. I've gotten some great shoes there. The store is right next to T.J. Maxx. And we could grab a bite at the Mexican place that's there. You know, chips, salsa and a margarita! They have those swirl margaritas with sangria in them. They are so good!"

"OK. Can you go today?"

"No, the girls have soccer this afternoon. Tomorrow's better. Can we do it tomorrow? I'm completely free until 2:30."

"Sure. Let's shop and then grab lunch."

"Don't want to eat first?"

"No way! I'm not going to have a margarita at lunch and then end up buying five pairs of shoes because you keep telling me how cute they are!"

Ravyn and Julie both laughed.

"OK. See you around 10:30?"

"Great. See you then."

Ravyn fixed a tuna sandwich for lunch, with Felix going nutty when she opened the can.

"Hold on! Hold on!" she told Felix, nudging him as he wove around her legs, meowing. She got the tuna and he got the tuna water.

Then she sorted through her mail, which consisted of two bills and no checks.

Ravyn shopped online for some shapewear and late that afternoon sent an invoice to LindMark for her recent work.

Around 7:30 p.m. she got a text from Marc.

"Still smiling about last night," it read.

"Me too. Want to come over tonight?"

"Can't. Still working."

"Bummer."

"Call you later tonight. OK?"

"OK," she texted back.

"Maybe there would be more phone sex tonight," Ravyn thought. "Sweet."

# Chapter 8

Ravyn checked her hair and makeup again in the bathroom mirror. She ran her hand down her little black dress, smoothing out the fabric under her fingers. She so wanted to look special for Marc's event tonight.

She found some stray strands of hair sticking up near her part and tried to make them stay flat. She spritzed a little more hairspray and tried again.

She didn't know why she felt so nervous, then thought, "Well, it is the first time Marc and I will be seen out in public as a couple. Maybe that's why I'm all nerves."

Ravyn took a deep breath, trying to calm down.

The past week and a half had been nearly perfect. She and Marc talked and texted several times during the day, and often saw each other at night, after he was finished with work. A few times, those meetings at night had become overnight stays. She loved waking up in his arms.

The November evening was mild, so Ravyn opted just to bring a shawl, which she could wad up into her purse, if needed. The only other items she put in her purse were her lipstick, some breath mints and a comb.

She was so glad she and Julie had gone shoe shopping early enough for her to break in the cute sling-backs she was wearing.

She knew she looked silly the past few days walking around her condo wearing heels, but she didn't want to chance getting blisters on her feet tonight and feeling miserable.

She checked her hair and makeup again.

"Stop!" she told herself. "It's as good as it's going to get."

Ravyn was ready a full hour before she was to drive up to Marc's house. They would go to the reception at the Atlanta History Center from there.

The Atlanta History Center was just off Paces Ferry Road in Buckhead, not that far from Marc's house, but in Friday evening traffic, it could take them an hour to get there. The reception was to start at 6 p.m., with a more formal program starting at 7 p.m. Marc told her there would be a couple of speakers and said he hoped she wouldn't be bored.

He doesn't realize I've covered run-of-the-mill planning and zoning meetings at City Hall, she thought and smiled at the memory. He doesn't know the meaning of the word bored.

Ravyn remembered covering one zoning meeting for the Trib where an "adult entertainment business," in other words a strip club, wanted to set up shop in town. Hundreds of neighbors from the proposed business area showed up to protest.

But the zoning commission proceeded with its regular items – routine variances and set-back requests – for the first two hours before taking up the strip club rezoning on the agenda, all the while allowing tensions to simmer in the audience. Then the fireworks began.

People shouted. People cursed. People started singing "We Shall Overcome." A fist fight broke out and one man got arrested for punching the owner of the strip club.

Ravyn got a front-page story, but readers would never know to get that story she felt like she had watched paint dry first.

She shook her head to dispel the long-ago memory and check the clock for what seemed like the $20^{th}$ time. She was close enough to the time she intended to leave for Marc's house. She just ought to go. At the last minute she put together an overnight bag to put in the trunk of her car – just in case night turned to morning at Marc's house tonight. She smiled inwardly. "I hope it does," she thought.

Peachtree Street was its typical Friday afternoon. Only in Atlanta could rush hour on a Friday in the fall start at 2 p.m. Then Ravyn remembered it was a home weekend for the Georgia Bulldogs, and scores of University of Georgia football faithful were headed to Athens, Georgia, about an hour and a half from Atlanta, to begin tailgating a day early.

She crawled the few miles to Marc's house, grateful she had left earlier than she had planned.

Marc answered the front door in a suit. Ravyn inhaled sharply.

"You look…," she started. "You look amazing."

She planted a light kiss on his lips and looked at him again. He looked incredible. She wished in that moment they were not headed out for the evening, so she could get him into the bedroom.

"You look great yourself," he said, pulling her close for another kiss. "I like the little black dress, LBD did you call it? Are you ready? I don't want to be late." Marc looked at his watch.

"We'd better go. Traffic is a mess."

"I was afraid of that. I really want to network at the reception before the speeches, so let's go."

They got into his BMW and made their way to the history center, where they found the small, two-story parking deck already full. The line for the valet was also backed up, with several attendees standing by their cars waiting impatiently.

Marc didn't want to wait in the valet line. It would take too long. He drove out of the deck, pulling as close as he could to the front door. "I'll let you out and find a place to park."

Ravyn got out and went inside to wait. About 15 minutes later Marc arrived, looking anxious.

"I had to park way over in the neighborhoods," he said, grabbing her elbow and moving her into the reception area. "Let's go."

Ravyn could see he was worked up about meeting the right people. Her job, tonight, she realized, was to be the silent arm candy.

"Why don't I go get us some drinks while you mingle," she said. "What would you like?"

"Scotch and soda, if they have it. If not, a Sweetwater or pale ale."

Sweetwater was a locally brewed beer. Ravyn wasn't much of a beer drinker. She preferred wine. She queued up to the bar while Marc disappeared into the crowd. She was glad she had thought to throw a few dollars into her purse. It would come in handy for tip for the bartenders tonight.

"Hello again. Miss Shaw, isn't it?"

Ravyn turned to see Bradford Cunningham behind her.

"Oh, yes, Mr. Cunningham. Good to see you this evening," Ravyn lied.

"Are you here for a story?"

"No, I'm the guest of Marc Linder," she said.

"*Interesting*," he replied, with what looked like a smirk on his lips.

Ravyn didn't like the way Bradford said the word, almost in an accusatory manner.

Just then, Ravyn was first in line, and turned to give her order.

"Two drinks?" Bradford asked, a bit too loudly. "Party starting early, eh?"

"Yes. It helps me deal with boring people."

Bradford's smile froze on his face, as Ravyn gave her most sweet smile and walked away.

Ravyn sidled up to Marc, handing him his Scotch and soda. Marc stopped to introduce her to Chad Allen.

"Chad's an angel investor for startup tech companies," Marc explained.

"Oh, are you interested in LindMark, Mr. Allen?" Ravyn asked.

"No, Miss Shaw. Angel investors are solo investors. I only pick about one or two small companies to help each year or every other year. Marc's company is too big for me. He's after venture capital, which is often a group of investors – with larger wallets – going after slightly larger companies."

Ravyn was grateful for the explanation, but she felt like an idiot. "Why didn't I know that before?" she asked herself. "I really should learn more about Marc's company and what its needs are."

"Oh," she said, her voice small.

"I'm sure you'll find some good resources here tonight, Marc," Chad said, turning to Marc and offering a handshake. "Good luck."

Chad walked away and Ravyn felt so stupid.

"I'm sorry, Marc. I didn't mean to interrupt and sound so idiotic."

"No, no. Chad's a good guy. He's trying to help me meet some new guys. What's the matter? You look upset."

"Sorry, sorry. I just met Bradford Cunningham in the bar line and he was just oily."

"Did he say something to you?" Marc asked, looking angry.

"No, he didn't say anything out of line, it was just his tone. He thinks very highly of himself, doesn't he?"

"He most certainly does," Marc said, peering over Ravyn's head to Kyle Martin, another venture capitalist he wanted to talk to. "Sorry, excuse me for a moment."

"Sure," Ravyn said, but Marc had already moved over and was talking to Kyle.

Ravyn moved back to the main entrance's foyer, where some of the new exhibit pieces at the Atlanta History Center were in glass cases. She sipped her red wine and read the information about the exhibit.

"Where's your meal ticket?" Bradford said, behind her.

"Excuse me?" Ravyn turned sharply.

"Where's Linder?"

"Inside, networking. Why aren't you in there doing the same?"

"Oh, I pretty much have my capital locked up. I don't have to go around begging for it."

Ravyn could feel herself getting flush. Bradford was making her very angry, and uncomfortable.

"May I refresh your drink, Miss Shaw?"

Ravyn looked down and realized she had drained her glass a little too quickly. "Oh, I can get it, thank you."

"No problem, I'll walk in with you."

"Great," Ravyn thought inwardly. "I can't get rid of him!"

Ravyn ordered another red wine at the bar, determined to just hold this one. Bradford ordered another gin and tonic, drank it at the bar stand, and ordered another.

"They give you such small glasses," he said to Ravyn, as a way of an excuse.

Ravyn spotted some hors d'oeuvres being passed and made sure she took a few to get something in her stomach to go with that first glass of wine.

"Why are you here with Marc?"

"He invited me. And I've been doing some PR work for him. It's good for me to see the men and women who will be helping his company."

"Oh, these people aren't going to help him."

"Oh? Why not?"

"Marc's company isn't that fiscally sound. They aren't going to throw good money after bad. Is he paying you by check?" Bradford asked, leaning in. Ravyn could smell the gin on his breath. "If I were you, I'd ask for cash."

"That's not true. His company is sound. I've seen the company's third quarter numbers."

"Oh, you're his accountant now, too?" Bradford said, snidely.

Ravyn immediately regretted she'd said anything about seeing Marc's financial information. She'd seen those numbers for the brochure, and that was in confidence.

"No, I'm not."

"Then you've just seen numbers he wants you to see. It's a house of cards. He's nearly broke."

"I have every confidence in LindMark and Marc Linder."

"Suit yourself. But you'll regret it."

"Excuse me, Mr. Cunningham, I need to use the powder room."

Ravyn practically ran to the restroom to get away from Bradford. "What an arrogant asshole!" she thought.

She walked into the restroom, putting her wine glass down on a small table. As she was washing her hands, she looked to her right and saw Laura Lucas. "Oh great," she thought. "The night gets better and better."

"Hello, Laura," Ravyn said, realizing she'd have to acknowledge her.

"Ravyn, I'm surprised to see *you* here."

"I'm a guest of Marc Linder."

"I bet you are," Laura said, icily. "He tends to bring his latest conquests to events."

"Are you speaking from experience?"

"Why yes. How does it feel to be sloppy seconds?"

Ravyn wanted to slap the grin off Laura's face. She's never disliked Laura more than right now. Now it was personal.

"I'm second to no woman, Laura," Ravyn said through her teeth. "I'm here to support LindMark any way I can."

"I just bet you are," Laura said, looking Ravyn up and down.

Ravyn suddenly felt very overdressed for the event. Most of the men were in business suits, and the women were in business attire or career wear. Ravyn's little black dress was almost too dressy. Even Laura was in a skirt and blouse, even if the blouse was cut very low.

"If you'll excuse me, I've got to get back to the event," Ravyn said, brushing past Laura and grabbing her wine glass, nearly spilling its contents.

She took a large swig of wine as she exited the ladies' restroom. "Will this never end? Jesus! First Bradford, now Laura!"

She walked briskly back toward the reception area, looking for Marc. Ravyn was determined to plant herself next to him for the rest of the evening and not move. She didn't care if he liked it or not, she didn't want to be alone with either Bradford or Laura again tonight.

She found Marc, who was in deep conversation with a short, stocky woman with equally short spikey dyed red hair.

"Call me in two weeks and let's set something up," the woman was saying. "I'm out of town next week, but let's keep in touch."

Marc shook her hand and she strutted off.

"That sounded promising," Ravyn said.

"I'm not so sure. Gwen Burton has funded some companies, but word is she's stretched too thin and doesn't have much more money to back anyone else."

"Oh. Sorry to hear that."

Marc looked at Ravyn, puzzled. "What's up with you?"

"What do you mean?"

"You look…" he started. "You look flustered."

"You have *no* idea. Bradford Cunningham is an ass and Laura Lucas is a bitch."

"Laura?" Marc gave Ravyn a startled look. "Is she here?"

"She sure is. I had the displeasure of her company in the ladies' room."

"What happened?"

"Let's not talk about it now. You need to network. Can I get you another drink?"

"Sure, another Scotch and soda. We should be going into the ballroom soon for the program."

Ravyn queued up again to the bar. She was beginning to feel a little unsteady on her feet. She wished she hadn't downed those glasses of wine so fast. She needed some food. Where were all the hors d'oeuvres? She got Marc's drink just in time. The doors to the ballroom opened and everyone began moving into the spacious room for the program.

Ravyn saw the set tables and was relieved. This was a seated dinner! Thank God!

"You didn't tell me it was dinner," she said to Marc as they sat down.

"I'm sorry. I thought I had. Oh, there's Joe Collins. I want to speak to him. I'll be right back."

Ravyn remained at the table, watching Marc move toward a tall, thin man in a gray suit. She took a deep breath and took a long drink of the water at her place setting. Out of the corner of her eye she saw Bradford walking into the room. She prayed he did not sit at her table.

He continued to walk toward the center of the room and took a seat three tables over. Then she saw Laura and felt herself get angry again. Laura walked by her table without a glance. Ravyn's eyes followed her, watching her wave at, then sit down next to, Bradford. "That's interesting," she thought. "But I guess two snakes would find each other."

Marc finally sat down at the table, which was nearly filled. Ravyn had quickly put his napkin over his chair back to reserve his seat as more and more people entered the ballroom asking if his seat was taken.

Ravyn introduced herself to the man on her left, Sean Cullen, who spoke with a slight lilt. The man to Marc's right was Paul Givens. Ravyn knew of him, but had never met him in person.

They started in on their salads, as servers came around with bread and more wine. Ravyn asked for another glass of red wine, and Marc asked for a glass as well.

A dinner of roasted chicken breast, scalloped potatoes and asparagus spears eventually made its way to their table. Ravyn smiled. "Ah, 'chamber chicken,'" she mumbled to Marc.

"What?"

"Oh, sorry. When I worked in South Georgia I sometimes covered the Rotary or Chamber of Commerce meetings and it was always rubber chicken. We called it chamber chicken at the office, and I've called any banquet chicken that ever since."

"Oh," Marc said, with a half-smile, then turned to talk to Paul Givens.

Ravyn felt like she'd said something wrong. This evening was not turning out the way she had hoped. She was not having fun at all and she felt more and more out of place.

"What do you do?" Ravyn heard that lilting voice to her left ask. She turned to Sean, who had clear blue eyes and a shy smile.

"I'm a freelance writer," she said. "I've been doing some public relations work and writing for LindMark. What do you do, Sean?"

"I'm a lender with Georgia Community Trust. I'm here to pick up some business when folks realize they're not going to get venture capital."

"Do you specialize in small-business loans?"

"Yes, some, through the SBA – the Small Business Administration," he said.

"I know what the SBA is," she replied, slightly annoyed.

"Sorry. I didn't mean…"

"No, that's fine. I used to be a reporter for the Trib. I've covered a lot of different things, including some SBA events and stories about small businesses that got their start with SBA loans."

"You're not with the Trib anymore?"

"No. I was a victim of the layoffs a few years ago."

"Sorry to hear that."

"Tell me more about Georgia Community Trust, and how you came to work for it. You don't sound like you are a native Atlantan."

"No, I'm not," Sean said, smiling shyly again.

"Damn, he's a cutie. If I wasn't involved with Marc…", Ravyn thought impishly.

"Where are you from?"

"Ireland, originally, but my family moved to the States when I was a teenager," he said.

"To Atlanta?"

"No, Boston. I went to university there and met my wife there," he said.

It was then Ravyn noticed the wedding ring. "Damn, I'm getting lax. I usually spot the ring right off," she thought.

"And how did you two end up in Atlanta?" she asked.

"My wife is from Atlanta. She wanted to be closer to her family when our first son was born," Sean said.

"Of course, that's understandable."

Ravyn and Sean continued chatting through dinner until the program started. One last round of wine came around the table before the speaker began. Ravyn's glass was topped off, but she made no move to drink any more wine. She was thankful she'd eaten all of the chicken and wasn't feeling quite so flustered.

Two speakers and three award presentations later, the event was over. Marc excused himself from the table to meet a couple more people. Ravyn remained seated as attendees moved toward the doors to leave. She was in a good spot to people watch.

She spotted Bradford and Laura standing up from their table. Laura looked unsteady on her feet and Ravyn could hear her loud laugh, almost a bark, across the room. She appeared to be fawning over Bradford. "Or maybe she's using him for support," Ravyn thought.

Laura started to walk and stumbled. Bradford quickly caught her.

Marc was walking back to the table and saw the couple. Laura reached for Marc, catching his arm.

"Hello, Marc. Good to see you," she said too loudly and slightly slurring her words. "You're here with your new girlfriend?"

Marc looked over toward Ravyn and Ravyn recognized the "help me" look. She quickly stood up and made her way toward him.

"Laura, good to see you, too. You remember Ravyn Shaw, don't you?" Marc said as Ravyn approached.

"Yes, I certainly know Ravyn," Laura said, leaning forward and swaying, her eyes narrowing at Ravyn.

"Laura, I hope you aren't driving tonight," Marc said, concerned.

"What business is it of yours?" she shot back.

"You don't have to worry about her," Bradford interrupted. "I'll see to it the little lady gets home OK. Come on, Laura. Let's go. Let's leave the lovebirds alone."

Ravyn felt her face flush and Marc looked angry, but before either of them could speak, Bradford began guiding, and half carrying, Laura out the ballroom doors. They got to the front doors and Bradford handed his claim ticket to the car valet.

"Where did you park, Laura?"

"I valeted the car. I think it's in the parking deck," she said, fishing out her claim ticket.

"Will the lady's car be OK in the deck tonight?" Bradford asked the valet.

"Yes, sir, as long as it's removed by 9 a.m.," the valet replied.

Bradford handed him a $20 bill and Laura's claim ticket. "We'll come get it by then."

"Very good, sir," he replied, handing Bradford the keys to Laura's Toyota.

"I can drive home," Laura protested, trying to reach for her keys.

"No, you can't," Bradford said, steadying her again, and pocketing the keys. "Besides, I think we have some things to discuss."

"Such as?"

"Marc Linder and LindMark."

Bradford's late-model black Lexus pulled up, and he eased Laura into the black leather passenger's seat. "I promise I'll be the perfect gentleman tonight."

"God, I hope not!" Laura said, barking another laugh.

Bradford grinned widely as he shut the passenger's door and walked to the driver's side.

Marc and Ravyn arrived at the front door in time to watch Bradford and Laura drive off.

"I hope she's alright with that guy," Marc said softly.

Ravyn thought the same thing, but was unsettled that Marc seemed to care so much what happened to Laura.

"Let me go get the car and come get you here," he said.

"No, I'm alright. I can walk with you."

"Are you sure? It's a long walk."

"I'll be OK."

The night had turned cooler, and Ravyn was glad she had her shawl, which she pulled tighter around her shoulders as they walked down Paces Ferry Road.

"Are you cold? Here," Marc said, taking off his jacket and putting it around her shoulders.

"Won't you be cold?"

"I've felt like I was sweating all night. My shirt feels wet. It feels good to be out of that jacket and feel the cool air."

"Did you make some good contacts?"

"I'm not sure. It's so hard to read these people. They all say they want to hear more about my company, but when I try to call some of them next week they won't even return my voicemail."

"Why? Don't they like your company?"

"It's not just my company. I think they say it to nearly every company CEO. I've learned it's not personal. But it *feels* personal."

Ravyn wondered if what Bradford said was true – that LindMark would never get funded because the VC community didn't believe in Marc's company.

Ravyn and Marc finally arrived at his BMW. Marc had been right, it was a long walk, and Ravyn could feel a blister forming on her right foot. Marc opened her door, helping her into her seat.

When they pulled away, Ravyn slipped off her shoe, rubbed her aching toes and asked herself, "What if Bradford is right? What happens to LindMark? What happens to Marc? What happens to us?"

She looked over, and Marc seemed to be as troubled as she was. This had not turned out to be the evening she had expected.

When they arrived at his house, Ravyn asked, "Do you want me to stay tonight?"

"I think I'm going to have to do some work tonight. Maybe tonight's not a good night to stay."

"I understand," Ravyn said, trying not to look disappointed. She slid Marc's jacket off her shoulders and handed it to him. "I'll talk to you tomorrow then. Good night."

"Hey," Marc said, pulling her close as they stood on his front porch. "Thanks for coming tonight. Having you there kept me focused, and probably kept me from punching out Bradford and getting arrested."

"I don't know. I might have decked him first."

"What did he say to you tonight?"

Ravyn's face clouded. "He just bad-mouthed LindMark, and me for working for you."

Now it was Marc's turn to scowl. "That goddamned bastard!"

"What is it with him? Why does he dislike you and your company so much?"

"He wanted to be my partner once, when the company was really young. He wanted to buy into LindMark. But I didn't want to give up control, so I said no. I don't think he likes to hear the word 'No.'"

"I think you're right. Listen, that just means he's jealous, because you are making something of yourself and the company, and he can't be a part of it. Try not to let him get to you."

"I can say the same thing to you. Don't let him get to you."

Ravyn smiled, her arms wrapped around Marc. "Yeah, easier said than done." She kissed him once more. "I'm proud of you. Now go work and I'll talk to you tomorrow."

Marc looked down at her. "Ravyn, I love …that dress." He cleared his throat. "I love that dress. It looks great on you."

Ravyn's heart skipped a beat and Marc suddenly looked uncomfortable.

"Thanks," she said, trying to sound calm, when in fact she could feel her heart pounding in her chest.

Ravyn drove home in a daze. Did Marc really mean to tell her he loved her?

Just as Marc had explained to Ravyn, none of the venture capitalists from the event a week ago took any of his calls the following week. He knew as it got closer to Thanksgiving, his chances of locking up any funding before the end of the year would be harder.

It was the holiday effect. People who had worked hard at their jobs all year seemed to want to kick back during the holiday season, especially if they had already made good fourth quarter numbers.

Marc wished his company was making good fourth quarter numbers. Third quarter they had broken even. He wasn't sure he would in the fourth quarter, which meant he'd take a loss for the year. Another year of negative numbers. That was not going to impress any investor.

He could not keep bleeding this way. He didn't like to think he might have to ask his father for another loan. He already owed his father $150,000 and wasn't sure how he would repay the first loan. And he knew the loan discussion would come with another lecture from his father that Marc should close the business and go back to practicing law, where he would make money.

Marc did not want to go back to practicing law.

Marc knew he could not get another mortgage on his house. When the recession hit, Atlanta's home prices fell dramatically, eating up any equity he had left in the house. He was very nearly underwater on his mortgage. He knew he could try to sell his house, but there was a chance he wouldn't make any money on it, which would defeat the purpose of selling it.

Marc rubbed his forehead. He felt a headache coming on.

Thanksgiving was in a week and a half. He'd see his father then and could ask about a loan. It made Marc dread the holiday. He wondered what Ravyn was going to do for Thanksgiving. Maybe she could come with him to dinner with his parents.

They'd be thrilled to meet her, even though he hadn't told them he was dating anyone. They'd be surprised, but pleased.

"That will soften the request for money," Marc thought to himself.

He dialed Ravyn's number.

"Hi there," she answered brightly. "What's up?"

"What are you doing for Thanksgiving? Are you going to South Carolina to see your parents? Because if you aren't, I'd love for you to join me at my parent's house for dinner."

"Oh, I'm sorry, Marc. I am going to South Carolina. I'm probably going to leave Tuesday to try to beat some of the traffic. But I'll probably be back on Saturday. I'd love to meet your parents, though. Can I join you the Sunday after Thanksgiving?"

Ravyn was surprised Marc had invited her to meet his parents. He so rarely talked about his family. She barely knew anything about them, and certainly had never met them, even though they lived in the Atlanta suburb of Dunwoody.

"Oh," he said, sounding disappointed. "Well, I don't know if Sunday will work. I'll see and let you know. I'll call you later tonight, OK?"

"OK. Bye."

Marc hung up, now really dreading the holiday. With his sister Brooke busy with her new job in Phoenix, it would just be an awkward dinner with him and his parents. He wondered if his brother Bruce would be out of rehab by then.

If so, Marc could expect a shouting match between his father and Bruce at some point during the day. If they were lucky, it would come after the meal. Maybe this year, no furniture would get broken.

Ravyn met Julie for lunch at Twist. It seemed to be their default lunch spot these days. Ravyn watched Julie come toward the table. She looked happy and Ravyn was relieved.

"Hey stranger! I haven't seen or heard from you in days. The sex with Marc must be good."

Ravyn blushed. It was, but she didn't want her friend to think she hadn't called because she'd been so busy with Marc.

"I've been busy with work. I got a couple of last minute freelance jobs last week that had quick deadlines. They paid extra for the rush job, so that was a bonus."

"Sure, sure, busy with work. Busy with Marc is more like it," Julie smiled broadly.

"Can't fool you, Julie," Ravyn laughed. "How are you? Things OK with you and Rob?"

"They actually are. I took your advice and asked him why he'd cheated. He said he really didn't know why. Some of it was the excitement of an illicit affair, but it scared him afterward. The secrecy, the uncertainty of another woman. What if she got pregnant? What if she blackmailed him? What if I found out? He said affairs are not all they are cracked up to be. I wouldn't know about that, but we had a good talk. We really did. We talked about how we'd gotten into a rut in our marriage and talked about ways to fix that. We talked about how little we'd been having sex, and how to fix that, too. And we talked about all of this in our house, not the therapist's office, so we didn't come to this revelation at $150 an hour! You saved me at least $300, so lunch is on me today."

"Well, you don't know what my hourly rate is, but I barter, so lunch it is." Both women laughed.

"What have you heard about the *Cleopatra* job?"

"Nothing yet. I haven't heard from James in a while and I haven't seen anything posted on the company's website or any journalism job sites yet. I'll call him later today and ask if he's heard anything. I updated my resume and I've added a few more story clips, including some magazine work. I really want this job, Jules. I want to work full-time again. I'm tired of just scraping by."

"I know you do, but are you willing to give up your freedom?"

"Let see, giving up being my own boss and getting jobs haphazardly against being able to pay my bills and eat? Yep. I'm willing to give that up."

"Just as long as it's what you want."

"It is, Julie. It really is."

"Gosh, a new man and a new job! It will be a whole new Ravyn Shaw! How has it been going in the new man department?"

"We went out about a week and a half ago to this networking event."

"As a couple?"

"Sort of. Umm, not quite. The evening wasn't all that great. I ran into that bitch Laura Lucas."

"What? What happened?"

"She was being her usual bitchy self. She called me sloppy seconds."

"What?! What in the hell did she mean by that?"

"Well, you know she and Marc were an item before me and Marc were an item. She told me I was second best. She seriously called me 'sloppy seconds' to my face."

"That bitch! With you, Marc has *improved* the quality of woman he's dating, not the other way around."

"Thank you. I wanted to punch her in the face, or at least throw my glass of wine in her face, but that would be wasting good alcohol. Plus, I was there at this event that was so important to Marc. I couldn't get into a cat fight with Laura and embarrass him, but God knows I wanted to! Get into the cat fight, that is, not embarrass him."

"Did you tell Marc about her?"

"No. I mean, he knows she and I had words, but I didn't tell him what she said. And here's the part that kind of pissed me off. She got pretty drunk at the event, and then Marc showed all this concern for her, about her not driving home and if she'd be OK with Bradford Cunningham driving her home."

"Why did Bradford Cunningham drive her home?"

"She sat at his table."

"Why would Marc even care?"

"My point exactly! Why should he care?"

"Did you ask him why he made a big deal about it?"

"No. Like I said, the evening was so stressful and odd. I didn't even stay over at Marc's house that night. I just went home. But here's the thing, Julie. I think he nearly told me he loves me."

"What!" Julie nearly shouted, causing several restaurant patrons to turn and look. "Once again, Ravyn, you are completely burying the lead! Tell me everything!" she said, lowering her voice.

"Well, we get back to his house and I ask if I was staying over and he says, no, he's got to work. Whatever. And we're on his front porch kissing goodnight and he starts to say 'I love,' and then he says 'your dress.' What the hell?"

"Oh my God! He was totally going to say 'I love you.' You know you have to let him say it first. Don't you go and say it to him first."

"Oh, I know."

"Do you love him?"

"I don't know that I'm there yet. I really, really like him, but I won't be blurting out 'I love you' just yet."

"That's good, but what if he says it to you first? What are you going to say back? You can't not say anything."

"I know," Ravyn said. She thought for a few seconds. "I'll tell him I love him. Maybe by the time he says it for real I'll be ready to tell him I love him back. In the meantime, that little black dress is my new favorite dress!"

"How were the shoes?"

"Oh, I had a blister by the end of the night, but that's only because we had to walk about a half mile to get back to his car."

"Why the hell were you walking in those shoes for a half mile? That's a good way to ruin good shoes. And your feet."

"The parking deck was full when we got there, so he had to park kind of far from the Atlanta History Center."

"So what? Does the man not know to get the car and pick you up?"

"He offered. I was just ready to get in the car and go. After my evening with Laura and Bradford, I just wanted to get out of there."

"What do you mean? What the hell happened with Bradford?"

"Well, he's just a snake. We were in the bar line together and he started bad-mouthing Marc and Marc's company to me, even though I told him I was doing freelance work and public relations for LindMark."

"Jesus! You did have a really shitty evening."

"Don't I know it."

"Hell, I wasn't there and I'm upset about it."

"Well don't be. It's over, thank God. I just pray I don't run into either one of them any time soon. My blood pressure can't take it. And if I do run into them, get ready with the bail money, because I'm liable to end up in Fulton County jail. I *will* strike first."

"That's my girl. And if I catch the bitch my husband slept with, we might be cellmates."

"Deal."

The women laughed again.

"What are you doing for Thanksgiving? Driving up to see your parents in South Carolina? If not, you know you have a standing invitation at our house," Julie said.

"I'm heading to South Carolina. I think Ward and June Cleaver would flip if I didn't go home for the holiday. But I was already invited to Thanksgiving – at Marc's parents' house."

"Really? He invited you to his parents' house? Where do they live?"

"Right here in Atlanta. In Dunwoody."

"Have you met them?"

"Nope. He rarely talks about his family and even though his parents live here, I've never met them. He's got a couple of siblings, but I don't know where they live."

"Hmm… That means family trouble. Maybe one of them is in the witness protection program."

"Oh, Julie, stop. No one is in the witness protection program. It is odd that he's never introduced me, but he did ask me to join him for Thanksgiving, so I would have met them then. I asked if I could meet them the Sunday after Thanksgiving. I'll be back on Saturday. He said he'd see, but he's never brought it up again, so I don't know if that's going to happen."

"Marc Linder, international man of mystery."

"What about you? Is your sister going to come to Atlanta for Thanksgiving, too? What about your mom?"

"My mom is coming. Dad and my stepmother are staying in Ohio. I'm not sure if Janice is coming or not. She's got a new boyfriend, so maybe she won't come. If she comes and brings her boyfriend, I'll have a very full house. I'm going to have the full meal: turkey, stuffing, cranberry sauce, mashed potatoes, the works. I'll start baking some things this week and freezing them, so I don't have to do it all Thanksgiving morning."

"I know you are going to have a spread."

"There will be lots of leftovers, so if you get back in town Saturday and are hungry, stop by. We'll have lots to share."

"You know my mother is going to make too much, too. She'll send me home with enough food for the next two weeks. But thanks, I appreciate the offer."

"Is Jane going to be at your parents' house?"

"I think so. It's been so long since I've seen her. I hope she's going to be there. We can get caught up. I need to call her to find out."

"Oh, God!" Julie said, jumping up. "Is that the time?"

Ravyn looked at her phone and saw it was nearly 2 p.m. They'd been at the restaurant for nearly two hours.

"I've got to pick up the girls," Julie said, laying money down to cover the bill. "I'm sorry to rush off. One more week and they are out of school. What am I going to do with them over the holidays? They are so full of energy!"

"Go! Go! Give the girls a hug from Auntie Ravyn."

"I will," Julie said, hugging her friend. "I love you. Thank you for being there for me."

"I'd do anything for you, Julie. You know that."

"I know. You'd help me bury the body." They laughed again and Julie dashed toward the exit.


Ravyn called James later that afternoon but got his voicemail.

"Hey James, it's Ravyn. I was just calling to see about the job at *Cleopatra*. Just wanted to see if you'd talked to your friend over there and if he knew anything. Call me. Thanks."

James called back 10 minutes later.

"Sorry I missed your call, Ravyn," he said. "I think there is a dead zone in my apartment. Your call went straight to voicemail."

"Oh, that happens at my place, too. I wonder why that is. What have you heard about the job? Anything?"

"Yes. Craig said the publisher was going to post the position after the holidays, so you should send him your resume and cover letter and he'll give it to Samantha. Do you know her?"

"I've met her just once, but I've done a couple of freelance articles for *Cleopatra*, which I'm going to include in my clips. I want them to remember they've worked with me."

"Good, good. I'll send you Craig's email. He's a good guy, so he'll put in a good word for you."

"Thanks, James, I really appreciate it."

"No worries. Hey, if you're free tomorrow night, I have another restaurant gig. I can invite a guest. It's a new menu tasting at Tin Can Taqueria in Sandy Springs. Do you like Tex-Mex? I think we get one drink free."

"You know me, James, I'll never turn down a free meal or a free drink. And I love Tex-Mex. Just let me check with Marc to make sure we aren't doing anything tomorrow night. I don't think we are."

"Oh, so you and Marc Linder are an item now?"

"Well, yes," Ravyn said, realizing she'd never told James she and Marc were dating.

"We've got a lot to talk about tomorrow then."

"What do you mean?"

"I've met someone, too."

"Oh, James! I'm so happy for you! Who is he? Do I know him?"

"No, you don't know him. His name is Carl. He's an architect. We met in a gay chat room. He's really great. I'll tell you all about it tomorrow."

"Can't wait. I'll text you for sure that I'm coming. I don't think it's a problem."

"Great. I'll text you the address of where we're going. See you then."

Ravyn hung up, disappointed.

"Crap! They are going to wait until after the holidays to post that job. That's almost two months!" she thought. She was hoping to try for the *Cleopatra* job sooner rather than later.

She texted Marc next to make sure it was OK to have dinner with James. It was. Marc said he would have to work late. Then she texted James she would meet him at Tin Can Taqueria.

Ravyn called Marc on her drive back from her parents' house following Thanksgiving. Ravyn's holiday had been full of food and family.

Ravyn drove up the Tuesday before the holiday, and her sister Jane got to the house Wednesday night. Ravyn's two elderly aunts and a younger cousin drove over from North Carolina Thanksgiving Day.

The Shaw family squeezed around the dining room table, which was loaded down with food. Ravyn wasn't surprised to peek into the living room later that evening to see her aunts both dozing in recliners while a football game blared on TV.

Ravyn stayed up late each night catching up with her sister, and was a little sorry she'd decided to leave Saturday. She felt the long weekend go by so quickly.

"Where are you?" Marc asked by way of a greeting.

"Well, hello to you, too. I'm still on I-85 coming south. I'm almost to the Georgia line."

"Sorry, I've just had a crazy holiday. I'm looking forward to having you back in Atlanta. What time do you think you'll get in? Want to have dinner with me? Stay over?"

"I should be home in another two hours if the roads aren't bad. Let me just unpack. My mom sent me home with so much food. I've got to get it into the fridge. Did you have a nice Thanksgiving?"

"It was OK."

"That doesn't sound very positive."

"Well, my brother showed up, drunk. We ended up having to call the cops."

"Oh, Marc. I'm sorry."

"Don't be," Marc said, angrily. "Bruce isn't worth being sorry about."

Ravyn didn't know how to respond. Marc never talked about his family. Until now, she didn't even know his brother's name.

"Are your folks OK?" she asked.

"My mother's pretty upset. My father is just angry, like me." Marc sighed audibly. "Bruce just got out of rehab. My mother always hopes he's cured and she is always disappointed."

"What about you?"

"I'm never disappointed in Bruce. He never fails to fail."

"That's pretty harsh."

"Well, you don't know him like I do."

An awkward silence fell between them.

"Well, call me when you get to your place. I'll get some salmon steaks, is that OK?"

"Anything that isn't turkey and stuffing is fine with me."

"Right. Talk to you soon," and Marc hung up.

Ravyn was baffled, but at least she understood why Marc never talked about his family. "Julie was right," Ravyn suddenly thought. "Family trouble."

The Shaw family wasn't exactly immune from family trouble, but hers always seemed to involve an unintended pregnancy, and recently a cousin shot a man in the ass during a domestic dispute. Ravyn made a mental note to call her cousin Bobbi to see when her court date was.

Ravyn turned up the radio and tried to watch her speed the rest of the ride home. The last thing she needed was a speeding ticket right before Christmas. She'd gotten a ticket about three years ago on the drive back to Atlanta, so she was always careful as she got close to the outlet malls.

She got back around 5:30 p.m. She had a lot to haul back up to her condo, so she didn't call Marc until almost 6:30 p.m.

"I was beginning to wonder if you were OK," he said.

"I had about three loads to bring up to my condo and I think one of the elevators is out of service. It seemed to take forever."

"Are you coming over soon?"

"Yes. Can I take a shower at your place? It will save me time and I just want to freshen up."

"Sure. Maybe I'll join you."

"Well, it would be nice to have someone wash my back."

"I'll make sure I wash that, too."

"I'm walking out the door now," Ravyn said, sprinting for her condo's elevator. "Have the soap ready."

Marc and Ravyn didn't finally eat supper until nearly 10 p.m. Shower sex turned into languid sex in the bedroom. They both fell asleep and might have slept all night had it not been for a car alarm somewhere in the neighborhood.

"Mmmm, are you hungry?" Marc asked sleepily.

"I am," Ravyn replied, rolling over. "I'm ravenous. What about you?"

"We worked up an appetite."

"I'll say. Do you still want to cook those salmon steaks, or should we scramble up some eggs?"

"Let's have those steaks. It won't take long. I'll go light the grill."

Marc reached for his gym shorts and padded out of the bedroom. Ravyn heard noises in the kitchen, then the sliding glass door open and close.

Ravyn got up and wrapped a towel around herself. She wished she'd thought to bring a robe. She found her yoga pants in her overnight bag and a sweat shirt. Ravyn wondered if it was too soon to ask Marc if she could leave some items in a drawer at his house.

As they ate, Marc asked if Ravyn was going to go back to South Carolina for Christmas.

"Yes. My mother really goes all out for Christmas. She likes to have family around for the holidays. What about you?"

Marc's face told Ravyn he wasn't looking forward to the holiday.

"Ah, I'm not sure what I'll do."

"Do you want to come with me?"

Marc looked surprised.

"To your family's house? To meet your family?"

"Oh, well, not like that. Not to *meet* the family, but yes, they will be there and you would meet them. I've talked about you, and my mom asked about you over Thanksgiving. My sister Jane asked about you, too."

"I don't know," Marc said with hesitation.

Ravyn sensed Marc pulling back, drawing inward.

"It's OK," Ravyn said, trying to sound casual about the offer. She would like her family to meet her boyfriend. Marc was her boyfriend, wasn't he? "Think about it," she continued. "My family would love to meet you, but it's OK if it would be weird for you."

"I'll think about it."

Ravyn knew he might think about it, but Marc would not be meeting her family any time soon.

# Chapter 9

The holiday season seemed to fly by, but Ravyn basked in the glow of having a steady boyfriend to share it with.

She didn't seem to mind the crushing traffic around Buckhead's two shopping malls, Phipps Plaza and Lenox Square, where all of Atlanta seemed to be headed to buy holiday gifts.

Normally, she tried to avoid the malls at all costs during the holidays, where it could take 30 minutes or better to find a parking space, but this year it was different. Even the valet lots in front of the malls were full.

Ravyn found herself humming to some of the Christmas tunes she heard in the crowded stores as she shopped for a necklace for Julie, and a new coffee pot for her mother, as well as other gifts for friends and family. She even found a trendy, very metro-sexual scarf for her friend James.

She smiled inwardly and outwardly. Ravyn was happy.

She spent Christmas with her family in South Carolina but made sure she was home a few days before New Year's Eve. She wasn't sure what Marc had in mind, but she didn't care. She was just happy she would spend the end of the year, and the start of the new one, with him.

Ravyn had called Marc on Christmas Day to wish him a merry Christmas. He didn't sound all that merry. In fact, he'd sounded tired. His voice sounded strained.

"Is everything OK?"

"Just trying to put some preliminary fourth quarter and year-end numbers together. I need to get those to the VC guys by mid-January. I'll need you to work up a new brochure the first week of January. Do you think you can do that?"

"Of course, Marc."

"Thanks. I just wish the numbers were going to be better."

"Are they bad?"

"Well, they aren't horrible. I was hoping I'd be able to show a little more revenue growth. It's going to be flat. Investors want to give money to companies that are growing, not flat. My company is flat."

Marc gave an audible sigh. Ravyn could almost see him rubbing his hand across his forehead, trying to undo the tension knots above his hazel eyes. It was a habit of his she had noticed.

"I just know my company would grow if I had more capital."

"You'll get it," Ravyn said, trying to be supportive, but her voice sounded too soft, as if she weren't sure he would. "You'll get it," she said again, this time more forcefully.

"I hope you are right." Marc sighed again.

"I am."

"How is your Christmas going? And when will you be back in Atlanta?"

"Miss me?"

"Yes."

Ravyn's heart leapt. "I miss you, too."

"So when will you be back?"

"I'll be home in a couple of days. Tomorrow my mom, my sister and I will do our post-Christmas bargain shopping. We do it every year. We hit the stores for the mark downs and then have lunch and catch a chick flick. My dad can't stand that stuff, so he stays home. I think he likes to have the house to himself after all the hustle and bustle of the holidays, though, so everyone wins."

"Sounds nice."

"What about you? How's your day going?"

"Oh, pretty boring. I spent Christmas dinner with my parents, but I'm home now. Just crunching the numbers."

Ravyn, already tucked into the guest bed at her parents' house, looked at her phone and saw it was 10 p.m. "Well, don't stay up too late. Get some rest, Marc."

"I will. You, too. Good night, Ravyn."

"Good night, Marc."

Marc poured another Scotch and water and tried to focus on the spreadsheet on his laptop, but no matter how he looked at it, the numbers showed lower revenue in the fourth quarter, not flat. He'd lied to Ravyn about his company's numbers. He'd lied to himself.

He knew lower fourth quarter numbers weren't unusual for many companies, but for one that counts on retail clients, it was bad news.

Retailers often make their entire year's goals in November and December, the final two months of the fourth quarter.

Since LindMark's software was so dependent on retail clients, his company ought to have had better revenue this quarter, or at least promising numbers for the quarter. Final numbers would come in early January.

Marc closed his laptop and closed his eyes, leaning back into his brown leather chair. He took another sip of his drink, then a bigger swallow.

Christmas Day hadn't gone too badly, he recalled, but it was only because his brother, Bruce, hadn't shown up. Marc knew his mother was worried about where his younger brother might be.

Bruce was doing it again – being evasive about where he was and what he was doing. It probably meant he was drinking or on drugs again.

Marc opened his eyes and sighed, remembering his family waited until almost 3 p.m., a full two hours after the time they planned to eat Christmas dinner, for Bruce to show up. His sister Brooke had had the good sense to stay in Phoenix.

Marc's mother had disappeared for nearly 20 minutes and they knew she was crying. When she returned to the kitchen, her eyes red and her face strained, she quietly served Christmas dinner. Hardly anyone talked during the meal.

And yet all Marc could think about during the Christmas dinner was LindMark Enterprises and its financial straits.

Marc had intended to speak to his father at Thanksgiving about a loan for the company but couldn't stomach it with the drama provided by Bruce. He then thought he'd ask at Christmas, but the mood was so dour, he decided against it.

He'd helped his mother clean up after the meal and left for home, where he spent most of the evening pouring Scotches and water and pouring over his financials. The numbers never changed. The amount of Scotch he drank did.

Late that night, he called Ravyn, wishing she was in town and not a state away. He just wanted to hold her in his arms.

Ravyn got home in the early afternoon of Dec. 27, quickly unpacked and drove over to Marc's Buckhead home. She'd talked to him the day after Christmas and he still sounded so tired. She suspected he had not gotten any rest Christmas night or last night, but had stayed up worrying about LindMark Enterprises.

Marc met her at the door and wrapped her in a big bear hug before giving her a long kiss, his whisker stubble scratching her face.

"I missed you," he said.

"I missed you, too. Have you been working all Christmas and today?" she asked, brushing his wavy brown hair with her hand.

"I didn't work all day on Christmas. Just most of the night."

"You look tired."

"I am tired," he said, taking her overnight bag and leading her into the house. "But let's not talk about work now. How was your bargain shopping?"

"Not that I think you really care, but we found some great buys. I got a couple of new sweaters and some really cute boots," she said, sticking out her right foot to show off her new footwear.

"Nice. I bet they would look great with this," Marc said, reaching for the wrapped gift on his living room end table.

"Oh, Marc, you shouldn't have. The company, the numbers…" Ravyn started to say.

"I can buy you a Christmas gift," he said. "Open it. I hope you like it."

"I'm sure I will love it," she said, knowing if he'd given her a rock she would have loved it.

Ravyn unwrapped a beautiful teal blue cashmere sweater.

"Oh, Marc! It's beautiful!"

"I hope I got the size right. I took a peak at the size of one of your shirts when you were here last month."

Ravyn ran back to Marc's bedroom and changed into the sweater. It fit perfectly.

"You got it exactly right," she exclaimed, giving a little twirl in the living room as she showed it off before giving Marc a kiss. "Look at it! It's beautiful."

"It's beautiful on you," he said, smiling.

"I got something for you, too," Ravyn said, reaching into her overnight bag. She pulled out a heavy, gift-wrapped box.

Marc unwrapped a set of lowball glasses with his initials, MEL, engraved on them.

"How did you know my middle name?" Marc asked, looking at the E on the glasses.

"Your middle initial is on some of the paperwork you gave me, although I don't know what E stands for."

"Edward. Marc Edward. Edward is my father's name."

"I know how you like your Scotch and I thought it would taste better in these," Ravyn teased.

"I should try it out now, since you are already trying out your present."

Marc went to the kitchen to wash out one of his new glasses and fixed a drink. "You want one?"

"I've never had Scotch. Don't fix one for me, but can I try yours?"

"Sure. Here."

Ravyn took a sip and felt the liquor burn down her throat. She made a face. She gasped, then coughed. "Must be an acquired taste," she sputtered.

Marc laughed. "I guess it is. What can I fix you instead? A glass of wine?"

"Let me have some water first to put out the fire going down my throat."

Ravyn went into the kitchen and took a long drink of cold water and felt recovered. Marc pulled a bottle from his wine rack, opened it, then handed her a glass of red wine, and she took a sip. "That's more my speed," she said.

"Let's eat in tonight," Marc suggested. "Is pasta and meat sauce OK?"

"Sure, sounds good. I can make up a salad if you have some lettuce and stuff."

"I don't think I do."

Ravyn opened Marc's refrigerator, which was mostly empty. "Why don't I run out and get some salad stuff and a loaf of Italian bread. I can drive over to the grocery store."

"You just got here," Marc said, rubbing his hand on Ravyn's back.

"I won't be long," she said. "And once I'm back, we won't have to go out again tonight."

"I like that idea."

"I thought you would. I'd like to stay put tonight, too."

Marc gave Ravyn a long, deep kiss. "Don't be long."

Ravyn felt her body respond to Marc's kiss. "I won't."

The couple ate on a small table off the kitchen. Ravyn was glad she had gone to the grocery store. She had ended up getting a few things for breakfast in the morning, as well. Marc's bare refrigerator made that a necessity.

Marc refilled Ravyn's wine glass as she dipped another slice of bread into the marinara sauce on her plate.

"Do you have plans for New Year's?" he asked.

"You mean the day? I usually run the Atlanta Track Club's Resolution Run 5K that morning. I always want to feel like I'm starting the year off healthy. Even if the rest of the year isn't, I start it out healthy," she said, smiling with the thick slice of bread in her mouth.

"Does it start very early?"

"No, it starts at 11 a.m., which is good. It was cold last year and the later start time let the temperature get up another two degrees. Ugh, it was cold last year!"

"But no plans for New Year's Eve?"

"No, do you?" she asked warily.

"I was hoping we'd go out to dinner," Marc said.

"I'd love that. Have you made reservations anywhere?"

Marc's face looked blank. "No. Am I supposed to?"

Ravyn nearly rolled her eyes at him. Who doesn't make reservations for dinner for major holidays? "Men who haven't been out much on major holidays in a while," she thought to herself.

"Yeah, we'd better make reservations or we won't get into one of the nicer restaurants. Unless you were planning on taking me to IHOP."

Ravyn was teasing, but without reservations, a pancake house might very well be where they ended up.

Marc smiled sheepishly at her. "No, let's not go to IHOP."

"Well, what did you have in mind? I might be able to call in a favor to get us a table somewhere."

"I don't know any of the popular places. You pick."

"OK. What kind of food are you thinking of? Indian? Italian? French? Asian?"

"What about a place where I can get a good steak."

"Sure, a steak place."

"No, not necessarily. Some of the seafood places do good steaks, too."

"That's a great idea. I could get some fish, something a little lighter before the race in the morning, and you can get your steak. I'll check tomorrow to see if there are any open reservations. I know of a couple places to try. What time do you want to eat? Early? Late?"

"Let's go a little later. I don't know if there are any places where we can go after dinner to enjoy some live music or something to ring in the New Year. But I don't want to keep you up too late if you've got that race."

"If I'm home by 1 a.m. or so I'll be OK. I'll call James tomorrow. He'll know where to go. He writes about all of that stuff for his blogs, so he'll know."

"Sounds great."

Ravyn was thrilled. She couldn't remember the last time she'd actually had a date for New Year's Eve. When she was still working at the daily newspaper, she usually had dinner with other single co-workers, and sometimes ended up at a party at someone's house or apartment. But she was always wary of staying out too late that night and made sure she didn't drink too much.

There was always the chance back then that she'd have to work New Year's Day, or get called in even if she had the day off. It was always quiet at the newspaper that day.

Half of the staff came in hung over, and a few times she had been among them. She'd hear some wild stories of parties and naughty behavior. Work that day normally amounted to checking the police reports for bad wrecks or accidental shootings from people celebrating the New Year.

One year, a young boy was killed while sitting in church at a midnight service when a stray bullet from celebratory gunfire hit him. She was glad she didn't have to cover that story. She knew she would have cried while trying to write it.

After Ravyn was laid off, she stayed out longer on New Year's Eve, but always with friends. She never seemed to have a steady beau during the holidays.

When she started making the Resolution Run a tradition, she made sure she was home shortly after the clock struck midnight so she was rested for the race later that morning.

Ravyn smiled. She was going to spend New Year's Eve with her boyfriend.

"What are you smiling about?" Marc asked, startling Ravyn out of her reverie.

"I was just thinking it has been a while since I've had a date on New Year's Eve. I'm looking forward to it."

Now it was Marc's turn to smile. "Well, I bet it's even longer since I've had a date for New Year's Eve. I think I was still married the last time I went out on New Year's."

"How long ago was that?"

"Hmmm…Five years."

Ravyn waited for Marc to say something else about his married life, but he didn't. She'd never heard him talk about his divorce or ex-wife. Of course, she never talked to him about any of her ex-boyfriends, either.

"Well, I'll call James and see about the reservations. We'll get in somewhere that doesn't serve pancakes."

New Year's Eve arrived cold and damp in Atlanta. After such a mild fall, it seemed winter had finally taken hold in the city.

Ravyn awoke in her condo, pale gray light just managing to peek into her bedroom window and pulled the duvet tighter around her. Felix stirred next to her, stretched, then leapt off the bed in search of his food. Ravyn knew if his cat food bowl was empty she would hear a yowl of displeasure in the next few seconds. She strained to listen, but all she heard was some crunching of the cat kibble in the kitchen.

Ravyn rolled over and considered going back to sleep, but looked at the clock and decided she should get up. She could take a nap later today to be ready for her big date with Marc tonight.

She was excited. She'd gone shopping with Julie yesterday and found a dressy jacket on clearance to wear with her new sweater from Marc. She'd decided to wear her black denim skirt with black tights and new black ankle boots to finish out the outfit.

Her friend James had been able to help with a dinner reservation for the night, and even then it was tough to get squeezed in at Atlanta Fish Market in Buckhead. She and Marc would be eating a little earlier than they had planned. But she was pleased. Marc would get a nice steak and she could get some seafood.

She'd even managed to score a couple of seats at a local hotel's event, which included live jazz and a midnight toast and light buffet. All she would need to do in exchange for those tickets was post a couple of reviews and mention the hotel in an upcoming hospitality brochure she needed to write for the local convention center.

Ravyn had never felt so happy.

The evening turned out cold and crisp, with the earlier dampness gone.

Ravyn got to Marc's house around 7 p.m. and they got to the restaurant in time for their 7:30 p.m. reservation. The place was packed.

Not a large restaurant to begin with, Ravyn noticed extra tables were squeezed in. They got to their two-seat table, which thankfully was at the end of the row. Other couples, she noticed, were just as cramped as she and Marc were.

"Sorry. Looks like it's a full restaurant tonight," Ravyn said as she hung her coat over the back of her chair.

"Not your fault. I'm glad you were able to get us something at all. Since I don't go out much on holidays, I didn't remember this sort of thing. I'll do better at Valentine's Day."

Ravyn smiled. Valentine's Day! He was already thinking of Valentine's Day!

They each ordered a cocktail and began to look over the menu, which also listed a special prix-fixe menu for New Year's Eve. Each ended up ordering what they had initially wanted. Marc ordered his filet mignon steak and Ravyn ordered the stuffed flounder. They split a spicy tuna sushi roll as an appetizer.

The restaurant was noisy, making it hard to have much of a conversation. When the meal was over they headed over to the Marriott in Buckhead and enjoyed the music and more drinks.

The hotel was noisy, too, but they managed to find a quieter area where they could still hear the music, but not have to shout to one another.

"This is turning out to be a lovely date night," Ravyn said.

"I agree. That steak was really good. We'll have to go back to celebrate when I get some good news about the funding."

"That would be wonderful."

Ravyn watched couples moving toward and then off the dance floor. She was tapping her foot to the music and wondered if Marc was much of a dancer.

Marc's voice broke her reverie. "Do you mind terribly if we go home early?"

"What? Is something wrong?"

"No, I'm just tired. I think that big steak and the potato is putting me to sleep."

"Oh, sure."

Ravyn tried not to hide her disappointment, but she looked around at the party and realized they didn't have any friends here and weren't interacting with other couples. Clearly, Marc wasn't a dancer, since he never even offered to hit the floor with her. Ravyn sighed. They could easily just celebrate the new year at home.

"Let's go then," she said, standing up and heading toward the coat check. "We can celebrate by ourselves."

"Thank you. I'm sorry," he said, as they walked down the hall. They retrieved their coats and Marc helped Ravyn put her coat on. "I hope I'm not ruining the night."

Ravyn turned to face Marc. "As long as I get to kiss you at midnight, my night is not ruined."

"You can do more than kiss me at midnight if you want," Marc teased.

Ravyn blushed. "Well then, let's go!"

Ravyn and Marc waited outside the hotel for the valet to bring their car around and they saw they were not the only ones with the same idea. It took about 15 minutes to get Marc's BMW.

When they got into the car, Marc noticed the time. "Maybe we should have stayed. I didn't think it would take so long to get the car. We'll get home just in time to celebrate the new year."

"Don't rush. We'll make it."

They got home with just a few minutes to spare before midnight. Marc turned on the television and found one of the New Year's programs live from New York City.

"Have you ever been to Times Square for New Year's?" she asked.

"No, have you?"

"Never. It always looks like a fun thing to do, but I imagine it is very cold. I'd probably find it fun for about 10 minutes and then want a warm hotel room."

Marc poured them a couple of glasses of wine and sat on the couch next to Ravyn. "I don't have any champagne. This will have to do. Do you want a fire?"

"No, I'm fine. I'll be warm enough next to you." She smiled at him. He smiled back.

"Thank you for being so understanding about tonight."

"It's fine. This is better."

A few moments later the New Year's countdown began. The noisy crowds on television erupted as the ball began to drop in Times Square.

"Happy New Year, Ravyn," Marc said, moving his wine glass toward hers.

"Happy New Year, Marc."

Marc kissed Ravyn passionately, nearly spilling his wine glass. Marc moved both glasses to the end table and then laid on top of Ravyn on the leather couch. Ravyn could hear Auld Lang Syne being sung as Marc began deftly removing the Christmas sweater he had given her. Ravyn responded, wiggling out of her skirt and tights. They made love on the couch before moving to the bedroom, where the passion started again.

"Ravyn, Ravyn," Marc moaned. "Oh Ravyn, I love you."

Ravyn felt tears well in her eyes. "I love you, too," she whispered.

They held each other close, not saying another word. Ravyn could hear Marc's heavy breathing begin to even and slow. Soon she heard his soft snoring. As Ravyn fell asleep in Marc's arms, she could not remember a better holiday.

Ravyn awoke with a start to the faint sound of her phone's alarm. The race! Thankfully, she had set her phone to wake her up, but she'd left her purse, and phone, in the living room.

"What time is it?" Marc said groggily.

"I'm not sure, but I may be late for my race. Where's your clock?"

Marc rolled over, peering at his phone. "It's 8:30." He rolled back and pulled her close. "Don't go."

"Marc, my friends will be there. I've got to leave by 9:30."

"Good, that gives me an hour."

Ravyn started to protest, but decided she'd rather make love to Marc than get up. Forty-five minutes later she was rushing to pull her running shoes and clothes out of her overnight bag and grabbed a piece of buttered bread and some water as she sprinted for her car. She made the race with not too much time to spare.

Marc pulled himself out of bed after Ravyn left.

"Well, if she's going to start the new year healthy, I might as well do the same," he thought. He dressed and headed over to the gym.

He was surprised to see so many people there for New Year's Day, then remembered it would be crowded for the next few weeks.

New Year's Resolutioners, the regulars called them. Those folks who make a New Year's resolution to begin working out at the gym and crowd the facility for the first four to six weeks, before their resolve is gone.

Not that all of the resolutioners quit. Some of them did keep their promises to themselves and become regulars, only to gripe about the new batch the next year.

Marc hit the weights first, for the first time in a long time having to wait twice for a couple of the machines.

Then he grabbed some water and towel and headed for the treadmills. He could see a crowd there, too. One lone treadmill was empty over in the corner and he started it up.

He'd forgotten his headphones, so all he could do was watch the small television in front of him with the close captioning. CNN seemed to be doing a rehash of the New Year's celebration around the world. Images of fireworks in Sydney, Australia, then Paris, then London, then New York, and finally Seattle sped across the screen, before the reporting turned to global conflict.

Soon Marc lost interest in the television set and began to think about last night, and how he'd told Ravyn he'd loved her. He hadn't really meant to say it. He did love her, he just wasn't sure how she felt about him. He was glad she had told him she loved him, too. She was the only thing going right in his life right now, he thought.

"God, with my company going to hell and Bruce screwing up again, I'm glad I have Ravyn," Marc said to himself, as he pushed the treadmill speed a little higher. He kicked it up and ran hard for the next 25 minutes.

With the holidays over, Marc returned to worrying about LindMark in earnest.

"Can you work up a new one-sheet with these fourth-quarter numbers and my first-quarter projections?" he asked Ravyn over the phone.

"You know I will."

"Great. Try to put as positive a spin in the projections as you can. Can you get this back to me by next week? I'd like to get it out to a couple more VC guys in California. My deadline to them is January 20."

"Sure thing. You want me to pick up dinner tonight?"

"Better not. I'm not sure how long I'll be," he said, reaching for another set of papers and a manila folder on his desk.

"OK, but don't work too late. You need your rest."

"I won't. I promise." Marc and Ravyn both knew that was a lie.

Ravyn was disappointed she wouldn't see Marc that night. They'd only been together once this week. He was putting in very late hours. She worried about him.

Ravyn was also a bit worried because since New Year's Eve, he hadn't told her he'd loved her again. She was beginning to think he'd only said it because they were in the throes of lovemaking. He won't be the first man who'd shouted out he'd loved her during sex. But this was the one time she wanted it to be genuine.

Ravyn looked through her emails. She was hoping she would hear something back from *Cleopatra* magazine, but there had been nothing. The holidays were always rough when it came to freelancing. Hardly anything came her way the last three weeks of December. Her bank account was running on fumes.

"What bill am I going to pay late this month?" Ravyn wondered.

Ravyn knew she should invoice some of her work to Marc, but he was so stressed out about his company, she felt like she couldn't ask him for money, even though she really needed it. And she was doing the one-sheeter for him and saw the revenue numbers weren't all that great. He was only slightly in the red for the fourth quarter, but it was still negative income. He probably didn't have funds to pay her anyway.

Ravyn sighed again. She could ask her folks for a loan, but she'd done that two years ago, and finally paid it off six months ago. She didn't want to ask them for money again.

Ravyn started trolling some of the freelance websites, looking for some quick work, even if the pay was a bit low. She knew through experience what to avoid. She'd been burned by fly-by-night companies that wanted some contract work, but then never paid. She knew they preyed on freelancers like her that wouldn't take them to court over a $200 invoice that was never paid.

She didn't see anything promising on the freelancing websites she knew, so she composed a couple of emails to her more regular publications, including Atlanta Trend and two in-flight magazines.

"Please, please, please have something for me," she whispered as she hit the send button on her laptop.

Next, she called her friend James, to see if he knew anything about the *Cleopatra* job or when it might be posted.

"Hey, Ravyn, what's up?"

"Hi, James. I was just wondering if you'd heard anything from your friend at *Cleopatra*. I haven't heard anything and I'm dying over here. I'm hoping they haven't filled it yet."

"I haven't heard from Craig, but I'll ask him again. How were your holidays?"

"They were good. I spent Christmas with my family and New Year's with Marc."

"With Marc, huh?"

"Yes," Ravyn couldn't help from smiling. "Me and Marc. We're officially a couple."

"Congrats!"

"Thanks. It feels good. And thanks for your help with the New Year's reservations. How were your holidays?"

"Kind of quiet. I spent Christmas with my mother in Birmingham. But I was back here for New Year's Eve. I went out to the Eagle and got home way too late."

"Way too late in a good way, or a bad way?" Ravyn teased, thinking of her friend dancing the night away at the Eagle, one of Atlanta's popular gay bars.

"Let's just say way too late."

"OK, have it your way."

"Let's do lunch soon. I'm sure I'll have to try a new menu in the next couple of weeks. Be my lunch date and let's catch up."

"Sounds wonderful. You know I'd love that."

"And I'll check with Craig. I'll let you know what I hear."

"Thanks, James. I really appreciate it. I want that job."

Marc kept pouring over the spreadsheet. Realistically, he would need at least a half-million dollars to get his new retail software developed and launched. He'd been developing it for the past six months, but only able to pay his programmers minimally, and he certainly didn't have cash to market the product once the bugs were out.

He'd met with a couple of local angel investors, but he realized he'd need more than they could offer. He'd have to go to venture capitalists, who would be willing to offer more money, often for a piece of the company. Marc was willing to have investors buy into LindMark Enterprises, as long as he could retain control.

If he couldn't get the financing, there wouldn't be a LindMark to buy into. Marc's ugly realization was he had about a year, maybe less, before he'd likely have to declare bankruptcy. He knew from being an attorney, once a company declared bankruptcy, it rarely came out of it with success. And if it did, he likely wouldn't have control of LindMark. It made him more discouraged.

Marc had lined up a conference call meeting with two more venture capitalists in California. He couldn't even afford to meet them in person. But they were busy men and women, too. Conference calls were quicker, but they were also more impersonal. "Easier for the VC to decline a request," Marc said to himself.

Marc saved the spreadsheet file, then closed the brief description he'd written up about the software and what he expected it would do for the retail world. He'd have to give that to Ravyn soon to be part of the package he'd give to the prospective investors. He looked at the clock on his computer – 10:30 p.m.

He shut down his computer and turned out the lights, walking toward the office elevator and then to his car. He'd call Ravyn when he got home, if only just to tell her good night.

Marc arrived at the gym before 7 a.m. the next morning. He was tired, but restless. He wanted nothing more than to hit the treadmill and then the weight room.

Even at this early hour, the gym was crowded. The "resolutioners" were out in full force.

He wrote his name on the whiteboard for the next available treadmill and went to the weight room to see if anything was available. Maybe the leg press or the Smith machine, he thought.

Marc turned the corner toward the weight room and was unpleasantly surprised to see Bradford Cunningham. Marc scowled.

"Hey, Linder," Bradford called out, wiping his forehead with a white hand towel. "Working out?"

"Of course," Marc said flatly. "Why else would I be here?"

Bradford cackled, putting the towel around his thick neck. "Oh, I don't know. Maybe you are here sniffing around for pocket change."

"What do you mean by that?" Marc asked, angrily.

"Oh, no offense, Marc," Bradford said, putting his hands up defensively. "It's just everyone knows your fourth-quarter numbers suck. Maybe some lost change in the parking lot will help."

Marc grabbed Bradford by the arm, hard. "What do you MEAN by that?"

"Take your hands off me!" Bradford shouted.

Patrons turned to look at the pair. Marc tightened his grip on Bradford's arm. "Why do you think my numbers are bad?"

Bradford jerked his arm away from Marc. "Listen, you asshole! Everyone in this town knows your company is nearly bankrupt! Everyone knows you are down this quarter and your projections show negative! No one is going to give you money! Why do you even have those meetings next week with the VCs? You're finished, you fucking shit!"

Bradford stormed off toward the locker room. Marc stood near the weight room, people staring at him, or trying to avoid him, and he physically shook.

"How could he know about my numbers?" Marc wondered. "How could he know about my meetings? Only Ravyn knows all of that. She wouldn't tell him. She wouldn't." But suddenly Marc felt cold. "Or would she?"

Marc went into the men's locker room, careful to make sure he didn't run into Bradford. He collected his things and left the gym as quickly as he could. When he got to his BMW, he started the engine, but just sat in his car. He felt like he couldn't breathe.

How did Bradford know his numbers were bad? Marc wondered. How could he know? Marc wracked his brain to think if he'd told anyone about those numbers other than Ravyn. He didn't think he had. But why would she tell a snake like Cunningham? He had no idea. But he was determined to ask her.

# Chapter 10

Marc got the first call from the venture capitalist about noon. He glanced at the Caller ID on his office phone and recognized the California number.

"Linder here," Marc answered.

"Marc, Ryan Dodd here. Wanted to talk to you about the conference call we're supposed to have next week. I think we're going to pass."

"Pass? Why?" Marc asked, stunned.

"We're not sure your company is right for us," Dodd said flatly.

"Well, let me send you my projections. I can have them to you by the end of the day. I think you'll see my company is a good investment."

"I don't think so, Marc. We're going to pass."

And just like that, Dodd hung up. Marc sat at his desk, unsure of what had just happened. Why had Dodd decided to back out of the meeting?

Marc put in a call to Ravyn, but got her voicemail. "Ravyn, it's Marc. Call me when you get this. It's urgent. I need to talk to you about that fourth-quarter report today."

Marc had an uneasy feeling. With the confrontation with Bradford Cunningham at the gym that morning and now the lost meeting, Marc felt something had happened, and he didn't know what it was.

Marc's phone rang again in about an hour. He expected it would be Ravyn, but it was a second California number.

"Linder here," he said.

"Linder, Tom Fosse. Wanted to talk to you about your company's numbers. They don't look so hot."

"My numbers? You mean my third-quarter numbers?"

"Yeah, I've got those, and they don't look good. When are we going to get your fourth-quarter numbers? I hope they are better."

"Close of business today. You'll have them today."

Marc felt unnerved. Why where the venture capital firms calling asking about his fourth-quarter numbers? He hadn't given them out yet and they knew they were coming.

Ravyn called him later that afternoon. "What's up, Marc?"

"Ravyn, have you given anyone the fourth-quarter numbers?"

"No, of course not," she answered, surprised he would even ask.

"OK. I need them today. I need to get the materials to a venture capital firm by close of business today."

"I'll send it over in an hour. I have it in a PDF."

"OK. Thanks. It's just…" He went silent.

"Marc, what's wrong?"

"Nothing, nothing," he said, trying not to sound so tense. "I've just had a bad morning. I lost one of the meetings with the VCs. I've got some calls to make to see if I can set some other meetings up. Ravyn, I've got to go. Send over the numbers soon. Thanks."

Marc hung up without saying goodbye. He started making cold calls to some smaller VC firms in Raleigh, North Carolina, one out in Denver, Colorado, and two more in Portland, Oregon. He was about to call one in Seattle, Washington, when he received the email from Ravyn with the PDF file of his company's fourth-quarter financials and the new brochure. He glanced quickly at it, but everything looked in order.

He emailed the files Ravyn had just sent to Tom Fosse's firm, along with a message reconfirming their conference call the next week. Marc looked up at the clock. It was nearly 7 p.m., which meant he still had time to call a few more West Coast companies.

Two hours later, he still hadn't heard back from Fosse, but Marc's rumbling stomach and pounding head were telling him it was time to eat. Marc shut down his office computer and turned out the lights. Everyone else in the office had left long ago.

Ravyn tried not to panic. She hadn't heard from Marc in two days. It wasn't like him. They had been talking every day, at least a couple of times a day.

She wanted to call him, but he was so short with her the last time they spoke. She knew he was worried about his company and his meetings. She also knew his financials weren't that great. It would make convincing others to invest in his company more difficult.

Ravyn paced her condo. She hadn't been out for a while. Atlanta's weather had been cold and dreary. She didn't feel much like running to Piedmont Park for exercise. She didn't feel much like doing anything. She was feeling very blah.

Ravyn sat at her breakfast bar, her laptop in front of her. She checked her email again, hoping for responses to come with recent freelance queries. Nothing.

"I've got to get out of here," she thought. Ravyn called Julie. It had been ages since they'd gotten together.

"Hey, stranger," Julie said, answering her cell phone. "What's up?"

"Hi Julie. Just feeling stir crazy and haven't talked to you for a while. Want to meet for coffee?"

"Can't. The girls are both out of school today with colds. But why don't you come over? I can make coffee here. And I'll keep the girls quarantined in their rooms. You won't get sick, I promise."

"Sounds good. What time should I be there?"

"Come whenever you are ready. I'm house-bound, and, quite frankly, I'll enjoy some adult conversation. There's only so many Disney movies I can see at a time. See you soon."

Ravyn eased her Honda into Julie's driveway. Julie's beautiful Buckhead home was well-manicured on the outside, colorful pansies a stark contrast to the brown Bermuda grass waiting to spring back to color at the first hint of warmer temperatures.

Her home was even more beautiful on the inside, even with two young daughters to leave toys, clothes and fingerprints throughout the house.

Ravyn always envied Julie's sense of décor. Everything was in its place. Everything matched. Ravyn inwardly smiled at her lack of such skill. Ravyn's condo was almost a mish-mash of things she had found that were affordable, some at thrift shops, some at discount stores, some on clearance. Many things she'd had since she was a college graduate, but that was almost 10 years ago. Which meant things rarely matched. Ravyn joked her décor was shabby chic, but it was really just shabby.

Ravyn knocked on the door, then tried the door knob, finding it unlocked.

"Hello!" she called, poking her head in. "Anybody home?!"

She heard high-pitched giggly shrieks from upstairs. "Coming!" Julie called down. "You girls need to settle down!"

Ravyn heard the pounding of several feet coming down the stairs and Ashley and Lexi rushed to hug her in the foyer.

"Hey, I thought you both were sick. Are you feeling better?"

Both girls looked up at Ravyn, grinning. She could see they had runny noses, but their eyes were bright.

"We've got colds," Ashley said, sounding stuffy.

"But we're getting better," Lexie chimed in. "We can have ice cream for lunch."

"Ice cream for lunch? Really?" Ravyn asked, arching a skeptical eyebrow.

"Not for lunch, girls, after lunch. If you eat all of your soup," Julie said, coming down the stairs with a full laundry basket in her hands. "Clean up for lunch."

The girls pounded back up the stairs. "Have you eaten?" Julie asked.

"No."

"Well, have some lunch with us. It's just soup and sandwiches."

"Sounds perfect for this kind of day," Ravyn said, taking off her coat and scarf and hanging them in the nearby coat closet. "Can I help with anything?"

"Why don't you set the table. That's usually Ashley and Lexie's job, but I don't want the girls to touch plates and silverware while they are sick."

"On it," Ravyn said, pulling perfectly matched plates and bowls out of the kitchen cabinets.

"How are things with you?" Julie called out from the laundry room just off the kitchen.

"Eh, not so good. No freelance coming in. I haven't heard from Marc in two days."

"You haven't heard from Marc? Has he been out of town?"

"No, he's here in Atlanta. He's so worried about his business," Ravyn started to say, now helping her friend fold some towels just out of the clothes dryer. "Julie, I really shouldn't say anything about his business."

"Who am I going to tell? Lexie and Ashley? The gerbil? Spill."

Ravyn stopped folding and looked at Julie. "His company is in trouble. Financial trouble. Not bankruptcy trouble, I don't think, but real cash flow trouble. He is trying to raise money from some investors, but because his financials don't look so good, it is hard. He's stressed out and it's spilling over into our relationship, I think."

"I'm sorry. Is there anything I can do?"

"No. Just thanks for listening."

"What's with the freelance problem? I thought you were going after that job at that magazine, *Cleopatra*."

"Well, I've got my resume and cover letter in, but I haven't heard back at all. It's so frustrating!"

"I still think you would be great for that job. Let me see if I know anyone over there. I'll put in a word, if I can."

"Would you? That would be great. What about you?" Ravyn lowered her voice to be sure Lexie and Ashley couldn't hear her. "Everything OK with you and Rob?"

"Yes," Julie smiled. "It is OK with us. Thank you for asking. And thank you for supporting me. We're still seeing a counselor, but I really think we are doing OK. I wouldn't have thought that a couple of months ago. And we still have a way to go. There are trust issues on my part, for sure. But we're working on it and it's OK."

Ravyn hugged her friend, right over the laundry. "I'm so glad. I was really worried about you."

"I was, too."

Just then both women heard the pounding of feet down the stairs again. "Is lunch ready?" Lexie asked. "We're hungry!"

"In five minutes," Julie said, heading into the kitchen to finish up the sandwiches. Minutes later, lunch was served.

"Oh, this all tastes so good," Ravyn said, with her mouth nearly full. "And it's nice not to have just plain tuna for a change."

"What do you mean? Aren't you eating steaks over at Marc's house every night?"

Ravyn picked up her napkin and wiped the little bit of mayonnaise she could feel on her lip. "Well, no," she admitted. "Things between me and Marc have been a little weird lately. I haven't actually seen him in nearly a week."

"A week?!" Julie exclaimed. "You get your ass…"

Julie glanced over at the stunned look on her daughters' faces and blushed. She so rarely said a bad word in front of them. "I mean, you get yourself over to Marc's house this evening! Seduce him if you have to."

"What does seduce mean, Mommy?" Lexie asked innocently.

"I'll tell you when you are 30, honey."

Ravyn and Julie both laughed then.

"I'm not so sure that will help. He's been working really late. I just hate that he's so stressed about his business. I wish it was going better for him. Then I think it would be going better between us."

"Trust me. One has nothing to do with the other," Julie said. "If he's really into you, he needs you more than ever if his professional life isn't so hot. That's kind of how Rob and I got together."

"Really? Tell me."

"Well, you know I went to interview him for a story."

"Yes, that part I know. I always envied that that's how you met him. I interviewed tons of guys and never fell in love with any of them."

"What about Marc?"

"Oh, right! I guess I did!"

"You're in love with him?"

"I think so. But how did we get to talking about me? We were talking about you and Rob. How did it happen?"

"OK, I interviewed him for a story, and I thought he was really hot."

Ravyn looked over at Lexie and Ashley, who were as rapt as Ravyn was at the story.

"He called me up after the story to complement me on it and we got to talking and agreed to meet for coffee."

"Coffee? Really? No big first date?"

"No, we met for coffee. I was still dating Todd, remember? I wasn't looking for a romance with Rob."

"Who's Todd?" Ashley asked. "Was he your first husband?"

"No! Your father is my first and only husband. Todd was just a boy I was dating before your father."

Ashley rolled her eyes. "But you probably kissed him before you kissed daddy."

"Well, of course, I … I really need to finish this story later," Julie said, getting up from the table and collecting empty plates. "Do you want more soup, Ravyn?"

"If you have more, I'll eat more. I told you I'm on the tuna diet."

"What's the tuna diet? Is it some new fad?"

"No, it's all I can afford at the moment. Peanut butter and tuna. It's getting kind of boring."

"What do you mean? You are working for Marc, right? Is he not paying you?"

"Well, no. But I haven't turned in an invoice in a while. I'm afraid to. He's so broke! I've seen the company numbers. It's bad."

Ravyn stopped. "I shouldn't have told you that. I'm sorry. I'm breaking a confidence."

"Oh, who am I going to tell? You need to invoice him. You need to get paid, Ravyn. You are doing the work. Don't sell yourself short. You are worth every penny he *should* be paying you."

"I know you're right," Ravyn said, collecting more plates and bringing them into the expansive kitchen. She laid the water glasses and her plate in the sink, keeping her soup bowl. She ladled out another portion and sat at the kitchen's island, finishing up the soup.

"Go wash your hands and then I want you girls to read quietly in your rooms for a half hour," Julie called out to her daughters.

The sound of small feet pounding up the stairwell was followed by the sound of running water, and then the sound of a slamming door.

"Those two! I don't think they know how to close a door softly," Julie said, looking up at the ceiling.

"OK, finish your story about Rob. I want the gory details."

"There's not much to tell, really. We went out for coffee and it was really nice. I still thought he was hot, but I was still seeing Todd. After the coffee, I couldn't stop thinking about Rob. But his personal life was a wreck. He was divorcing his first wife, or maybe they had just separated. No, I think they were divorced. He talked about that at our first coffee. I think I told him I was dating Todd, and maybe I told him it wasn't great between me and Todd. I can't remember."

"Things weren't great between you and Todd? You know, I thought you two would get married. You were inseparable! You were living together, weren't you?"

"Yeah, and maybe that's what ruined the whole thing. I tell you, it's all love until you see how a man lives. Todd was a complete slob. I couldn't stand that!"

Ravyn looked around Julie's kitchen, the beige granite counters with the neat countertop appliances in a row. Everything was in place here, too. *Southern Living* magazine could walk in the door right then and take professional photos.

"OK. I can see how that would drive you mad."

"Mad? It drove me insane! The man would drop his disgusting dirty underwear on the floor. Never even put them in the hamper."

"C'mon, Julie, lots of people do that," Ravyn said, thinking of how there was probably a pile of dirty clothes in her bedroom.

"No, I mean this was disgustingly dirty underwear. I don't think that man knew how to wipe his ass. There were tire tracks in his tighty whiteys."

"Ew! I don't want to know that! I just ate!"

"Hey, I didn't want to know that either. Once we started living together, he just expected me to cook and clean everything and he was a damn slob!"

"I never knew you felt that way. You never let on."

"I know. At first, I was just too in love with him. That curly blond hair, blue eyes and dimple in his cheek when he smiled." Julie's face softened. "I really was in love with him at first. But once I saw his habits, I fell out of love with him. And there I was talking to Rob about it, and he was telling me about his ex-wife and all he went through. We sort of bonded. His personal life was a wreck and he wasn't all that happy with his job at the time, and he told me that I was the light in his life. I was what kept him going. You need to be that for Marc. Don't let him withdraw. Don't let him pull away. He needs you."

"I hope you are right. It's just our relationship is so new. It feels fragile. I'm afraid of breaking it. I'm crazy about him and I won't want it to be over."

"Don't be afraid of the relationship, Ravyn. And don't think of it as fragile. You've got to fight for it to make it strong. Fight for yourself, for what you want. You deserve it."

"Are we really talking about my relationship?" Ravyn said, her voice low. "Or are you talking about your relationship with Rob?"

Julie's brown eyes got misty and her voice caught. "I am talking about me and Rob, but it should be how you feel about your relationship with Marc, too. You deserve to be just as happy as me and Rob. And we are getting there. We are getting our relationship back. We really are. I'm so grateful that we are working on it. I don't want to live without him. He's my best friend."

Ravyn hugged her friend, who began to cry softly. "This is so silly," Julie said. "I really am happy. Why am I so weepy all of a sudden?"

"You've been under a lot of stress. It's natural to feel a bit emotional."

"I haven't been this weepy in therapy. The past few days I have been, though."

"Is it that time of the month?" Ravyn asked. "I'm always weepy then."

"Oh, maybe," Julie said, looking puzzled. "Maybe that's it. Just leave the dishes. I'm going to rinse them and put them in the dishwasher."

"I can do that. Let me. It's the least I can do for lunch. And that soup was wonderful."

"Publix's finest!"

"I'll have to get some," Ravyn said, stacking the last of the bowls in the dishwasher. "You know, when I have money again."

"Invoice him," Julie said, wiping her eyes with her dish cloth. "You can't work for free. None of us can."

Julie stood on the front porch waving as Ravyn pulled out of the driveway. Ravyn was so glad she had met her friend for lunch and caught up. She felt refreshed. She felt re-energized.

She got home and drew up invoices for her work at LindMark Enterprises and hit send via email before she could think twice about it. Then she got on some freelance sites and put in proposals for three jobs that offered a decent hourly rate. All in all, it turned out to be a good day.

Ravyn emailed James to ask if he'd heard about the *Cleopatra* job. That was one she didn't want to slip through her fingers.

Then she opened the file on the last of LindMark's financials. She just had to get the rest of the fourth-quarter numbers out of a spreadsheet and into some sort of marketing wizardry, where the revenue didn't look quite so bad. Or rather, so flat. Fourth-quarter numbers in retail really should be positive, if the company is healthy.

After all, so many retailers make their year from fourth-quarter sales. There is a reason retailers keep pushing holiday sales into October.

It didn't help that LindMark's revenues were flat for November and December. As a software company that sold to retailers, it should have been better. If those companies made money, LindMark should have made money. Why hadn't they? What was off with the numbers? Ravyn thought.

Well, it wasn't necessarily her problem, other than she needed to spin the marketing materials so it didn't look so bad to the money men. And what could she say?

"Our customers made money, but we didn't, so give us some of yours," Ravyn giggled at that idea. That wouldn't work. It might be honest, but it wouldn't get LindMark financial backing.

Instead, Ravyn decided to write up how the software helped retailers gain revenue, leaving out entirely the fact LindMark didn't for the fourth quarter. All she wanted potential investors to see was that customers were making money, and hope they realized eventually Marc's company would make money too.

Ravyn suddenly realized how stiff she felt working on her laptop. She stretched and got off the breakfast bar chair in her kitchen. She looked down at her iPhone to check the time: 9:12 p.m. How did it get so late? And why hadn't she heard from Marc again today? Should she be worried? Ravyn considered calling him but decided against it.

"I don't need to chase him," she thought. "He needs to chase me."

Ravyn woke up late Thursday morning, and stretched. She could see pale daylight through the blinds of her bedroom windows. Maybe today was a day to run down to Piedmont Park.

She got her warmest running clothes and shoes on and headed out the door. The weather men were starting to chatter about snow coming into Atlanta.

Ravyn knew what that meant: Atlantans would head to the grocery stores in droves to buy up all the milk and bread. She smiled. There was no need to panic.

It was a brisk morning, and traffic was a little heavy along Peachtree Street, and then again on Piedmont Road as she headed north to the park. But the air was crisp, and the sun felt warm as she made the first loop around the oval. By the time she got home around 10:30 a.m. and showered, she was ready to start searching for more freelance jobs.

Ravyn booted up her laptop and was pleasantly surprised to see five emails from publications that had accepted her proposals. She had five freelance jobs that would pay from $300 to $500 per gig. With a sigh of relief, she realized she'd be able to pay her February rent.

Ravyn's phone rang and she was pleasantly surprised to see it was from Marc.

"Hey, stranger," she said, hoping she sounded playful, not annoyed.

"Hey, yourself. I got your invoice. I'll get the check out soon."

"Thanks. No rush," she said, trying to sound casual, but knowing that it really was a rush for her.

"Any plans this weekend?" Marc asked.

"None unless they include you," she answered.

"Why don't you come over for dinner Saturday? Stay the weekend?"

"I'd love that. I'll pack a bag. Have you been listening to the weather report? Says we might get snow."

"When? I haven't been watching the news."

"Early next week, I think. Not this weekend, though. I don't have to pack my snow boots."

"Do you have snow boots?" Marc asked.

"No. I barely own a heavy coat."

"Well, we can get a fire going this weekend and keep cozy."

"That sounds lovely," Ravyn said, and she meant it. Sitting snuggled up with Marc on his leather couch by a fire sounded just about perfect. "Do you need me to bring anything? Wine? Some groceries? I can pick them up on my way."

"Maybe get some breakfast stuff like you got before. That would be great."

"Sounds good. I'll see you Saturday."

Ravyn hung up and could not stop smiling. Marc had called. He wanted to see her. Even though it was Friday morning she began packing her overnight bag. "Felix, buddy, you are on your own this weekend," she said as she scratched her cat behind the ears.

Saturday and Sunday were nearly perfect, Ravyn thought. She and Marc stayed in, warm with the fire in the living room and the fireworks in the bedroom. Ravyn didn't want to leave Monday morning back to her condo, but Marc was getting more anxious about getting back to making more calls to VCs in other areas, trying to drum up meetings. "If they will just take a meeting with me," he had said Sunday evening. "I know I can show them what we are doing and it's worth investing in."

"I know. Have you looked at the fourth-quarter stuff I sent over?" Ravyn asked.

"I glanced at them, but I haven't proofed them yet. I will, I promise."

"OK. Let me know if you need anything else from me," she said, standing at Marc's front door.

"I just need you to keep me grounded," Marc said, wrapping Ravyn up in his arms, bending down and kissing her deeply.

"You make me happy," she replied. It was as close as she was going to get to telling Marc she loved him before he said it again. She looked up into his hazel eyes. "You make me so happy."

By Monday evening, Atlanta's weathermen had gone into full-blown snow mode, talking about the snow that was supposed to start Tuesday. Ravyn had made a quick run to the grocery store, which was a mob scene. She had plenty of milk for her coffee and breakfast cereal but picked up another bottle of wine and a few other items that could be eaten cold, if necessary.

Living in a condo, which had an electric stove, Ravyn knew if she lost power she wouldn't be able to cook anything, unless she wanted to trudge down to the courtyard and use the communal gas grills. All fine and good if it was a warm spring day, but the thought wasn't as appealing in colder temperatures. The worst part would be not being able to have a hot cup of coffee in the morning. She was glad she'd grabbed some bottled Starbucks frappuccinos. It would have to do in a pinch, if necessary.

She called Marc on her way home from the store. "Are you ready for the snow storm?" she laughed.

"Rachael, my assistant, is all in a panic. She said she wouldn't be coming in tomorrow. Is it really going to be that bad?" Marc asked.

"I don't know, but if the grocery stores are any indication you'd think the apocalypse was happening."

"Grocery store?"

"Yeah, I just went to Publix and the place is a mad house. There isn't a single loaf of bread left on the shelves, other than some sad squished thing I saw, and someone grabbed it anyway!"

"Should I go to the grocery store on the way home?" Marc asked.

"Well, if you haven't gone by now, I'd say you are out of luck," Ravyn said. "Bread and milk are gone by now. Listen, I went and got a few things. Why don't I come over to your place tomorrow and we can ride out the storm together?"

"Will it really be that bad?" Marc asked, sounding worried.

"I don't think it will amount to anything. It might mean the roads will be a little slick until the snow melts. I think they are just calling for up to two inches. You'd think we were going to get two feet the way people were acting at the store."

"Yeah, come over. We'll get a fire going again."

"We certainly will," Ravyn thought, smiling.

In the end, the weathermen were right. There wasn't that much snow that fell in Atlanta. Unfortunately, that few inches of snow melted and immediately froze on the roads, coating everything in a couple of inches of solid ice.

Ravyn and Marc remained warm and cozy at his Buckhead home, but the rest of Atlanta was paralyzed. Children had been trapped on school buses that became stuck on icy roads. Some children ended up spending the night at their schools when officials realized it was too dangerous to send them home and frantic parents were unable to pick them up.

Motorists were trapped in their cars overnight, unable to navigate the icy highways or side streets. News crews showed overhead helicopter shots of tractor-trailers jackknifed or overturned on highway ramps. Numerous vehicles were abandoned on highways and roads, many dented and smashed following icy encounters with either other vehicles or guardrails. The news coverage made the city look eerily like a ghost town. Essentially, it was. There was even the surreal news shots of people ice skating down abandoned Peachtree Street.

While the rest of Atlanta struggled, Ravyn felt bliss, spending each night in Marc's arms. Marc, however, became more and more anxious. He'd managed to reach other VCs and set up two meetings for mid-February, but he didn't like having his office shut down for two days. Some of his employees, he knew, had taken their laptops home and were working, but it was sporadic. Not everyone was able to work outside of the office. He needed to get back to work and he needed his employees to get back to work, too.

By Friday afternoon, Ravyn knew she'd better try to get back to her condo, as well. She'd called her down-the-hall neighbor Jack Parker to check on Felix, but with Marc getting more antsy, she was feeling antsy too. "So, this is what they mean by cabin fever," she thought.

"Listen, I'm going to head home in a bit," she told Marc as they cleared breakfast plates.

"Are you sure? Will you be safe?"

It was nice he was thinking of her safety, but she was out of clean clothes and needed to let him get back to work.

"I'll keep the car in low gears. I'm sure Peachtree Street is probably cleared by now. It's been two days. As long as I can get there OK, I should be fine."

"OK, but call me when you get home."

"I will."

Marc held her in a tight hug, then kissed her. "I love it when you stay over."

Ravyn could feel her heart beat more rapidly. Love. He'd said that word again, just not quite in the way she wanted to hear it.

"Me too," she replied.

A week stretched by and once again Ravyn heard nothing from Marc. No calls, no texts, no emails. What kind of relationship was this, she wondered. She ached for him. She ached to hear his passionate whispers as they made love. She ached to feel his hands caress her skin. She ached to feel his body next to hers, inside hers.

Ravyn saw that Valentine's Day was just a bit more than a week away and she didn't even know if she and Marc would be going out, celebrating as a couple.

# Chapter 11

Marc couldn't believe what he was reading. Another email from a West Coast VC firm had just canceled a meeting with him set for Feb. 17, more than two weeks away. The email simply said after reviewing LindMark's fourth-quarter numbers, they were no longer interested in investing in him.

Marc finally pulled up the PDF file Ravyn had sent over and began going through the marketing materials more carefully. Something about the numbers looked off.

Next Marc pulled up his Excel spreadsheet and started to compare the numbers. There! One of the figures in November had been changed. And there were incorrect numbers for December, too. The erroneous data made his fourth quarter look worse that it was. Why had Ravyn changed the numbers? Hadn't she proofread the materials before she sent them? How could she be so careless?

Marc was furious. This had cost him a chance at investment money.

He dialed Ravyn's cell number.

"Hi, Marc!" Ravyn said, brightly, thinking of the time they had recently spent together.

"Ravyn!" he shouted, not even trying to hide his anger. "You completely fucked up the marketing materials. You put in incorrect numbers and now I've lost a meeting with the VC company!"

"Marc, Marc," Ravyn tried to break in.

"How could you do this? How could you be so careless?" he continued shouting. "Are you there?! Ravyn!"

Suddenly, there was silence on the cell phone. Ravyn spoke in a quiet voice: "Marc, I didn't put in wrong numbers. I looked them over very carefully and I checked the document more than once. I used the numbers you sent over."

"You couldn't have!" he shouted. "I'm looking at my Excel spreadsheet and the numbers for November and December are different than what is in that PDF you sent me! You cost me that meeting! I can't believe I ever trusted you with those figures! How could you? How could you betray me?!"

"Marc, I didn't betray you," Ravyn said, her voice cracking. "I'm pulling up the Excel file you sent me on my laptop. Those numbers are what you gave me. I can send you back the Excel file you sent me."

"Don't bother," he said, icily, his voice narrow and tight. "I know what I sent you. I have it right here in front of me. I thought I could trust you."

"Marc," Ravyn cried. "You can trust me. I'm looking at the Excel file right now. What you sent me is what I put in the PDF. I don't understand why you are so angry. I put in exactly what you sent! I'm sending you the original Excel file right now."

Marc's computer pinged with a new email and he saw Ravyn had attached a file, but he didn't open it.

"You couldn't have. And I can't believe you are lying to me about it! I thought we had something, Ravyn. I really did. But I can't be with someone who lies about something this big. Goodbye."

Marc wished he'd had an old-fashioned phone he could slam down. Instead, he picked up his empty coffee mug and threw it across the room. It hit the wall, leaving a dent in the drywall, then hit the carpeted floor and bounced. He didn't even get the satisfaction of it being smashed into pieces.

Ravyn felt physically sick. Marc had just accused her of sabotaging his company. It wasn't true. It simply wasn't true. She was looking at the Excel spreadsheet and the numbers matched what was in the marketing brochure she'd created. What was he talking about? The November and December numbers were different? Which numbers? She hadn't transposed any figures. She had double checked everything before she'd sent it to him. How could they be wrong? Had he really just broken up with her? Over the phone? After the time they had just spent together?

Ravyn felt numb as she walked around her condo. She wanted to cry or scream, but she felt like she was in slow motion. She gulped for air. She blinked, then blinked again. She felt the first tear roll down her face. She put her face in her hands and sobbed.

The next two days were something of a blur. Ravyn had two other freelance assignments, and somehow managed to get the interviews and writing done, but she felt like she was in a fog.

The cutting blow came later that week, when a check from LindMark came for "services rendered. No further assistance needed" the invoice read. He really had broken up with her, she realized. She'd wanted to call him, text him even, but thought she'd better let him cool off. Now she realized she was too late. It was over. She felt hollow.

Julie was furious when Ravyn finally confessed what had happened.

"That *asshole!*" Julie yelled. "What an *asshole!* You are so better off without him."

"I don't feel better off without him," Ravyn said, her voice weak.

"Well, you are. Believe me. He didn't even give you a chance to show him he was wrong, or find a way to correct the mistake! His mistake! What an asshole! It's a good thing I never got to meet him, or I'd go right over to his house and punch him in the nuts for you. I can still do that. What's his address?"

Ravyn gave a small laugh. Then she started to cry again.

"Oh, God, I'm sorry, Ravyn! I'm just so angry for you. And he hurt you, and that hurts me. Come over. Come over and I'll get a bottle of wine and we'll just drink and bash him."

"No, I can't. I've got one more freelance gig I picked up for the police foundation. A couple of quick stories for their monthly newsletter. Shouldn't take me long, but I've got to get on it. It will pay the cell bill, so I've got to get them done."

"OK, but the door is always open," Julie said. "I'm so sorry, honey. You deserve so much better."

Ravyn hung up the phone but wasn't so sure she did deserve better. She loved Marc. She deserved him, and he deserved her. She'd probably never admit that to Julie. She had hardly admitted it to herself, she realized. Ravyn began to cry again. "This wasn't the way it was supposed to turn out," she whispered to herself.

Ravyn realized, dully, that this Valentine's Day would be just like so many others: She'd spend it alone.

Marc wasn't feeling much better. He'd fired off the invoice payment, with the note saying he wouldn't need her services again. It made him feel better at first, then angry again. If he'd never used her services he wouldn't be in this mess, he thought. He also wouldn't have met her; gotten to know her; made love to her; loved her. The thought was painful.

His anger was slow to subside as the week went on. He was still angry with Ravyn, but he also missed her. Several times during that awful week he wanted to call her to tell her something. He'd even pulled her phone number up on his cell. But he never connected the call. He hadn't been ready to delete her contact information, though. Not yet.

Instead, he got into the office early and worked late, went to the gym to blow off steam, then went home and drank Scotch. Work, gym, Scotch. Work, gym, Scotch. He didn't see that pattern changing any time soon.

Late one evening, after a few glasses of Scotch, he thought he might still need some help with getting the venture capitalists to take a chance on him. He needed a spin doctor. He needed Laura Lucas.

Laura. She might be able to help him get out of this mess, in more than one way, Marc thought.

Marc picked up his cell phone and scrolled through his contacts, then hit dial.

"Well, hello, stranger," Laura's silky voice answered. "You are calling rather late."

"I need your help, Laura," Marc said. "I'm having trouble getting the VCs to consider funding LindMark."

"Your girlfriend not helping?"

"She's not my girlfriend. We're not together anymore."

"Oh really," Laura purred. "Do tell."

"I'd rather not, Laura, but I do need your help. Are you available tomorrow? I need some updated materials for my fourth-quarter numbers. I need them to look good. I need them to convince the VCs to fund me."

"I'm glad you called me," Laura said. "You know I can help you. You need me to come over right now?"

Marc looked at the time on his phone and hesitated. Laura coming over late in the evening would get the process started right away. But Laura coming over late in the evening might lead to other things. Did he want those other things?

"Sure," Marc said with a sigh. "Come over."

March in Atlanta started cold and windy.

Ravyn was digging into the closet for her lined windbreaker for a quick run in Piedmont Park when her cell phone rang. She didn't recognize the number, but as a freelancer, she almost always had to take the call.

"Hello, this is Ravyn Shaw."

"Ms. Shaw, this is Marcy Butler from *Cleopatra* magazine. We've reviewed your resume and we'd like to schedule a phone interview. Are you available next Monday?"

Ravyn nearly dropped her phone with excitement. "Yes, Ms. Butler. I'm free Monday."

"Wonderful. We'll call you around 10 a.m. if that is convenient."

"That's perfect. Who will be on the call?"

"Myself and Samantha Hunt. We'll talk to you Monday. Thanks."

Ravyn hung up and did a little dance around her condo. She looked at her phone. She wanted to call Marc to tell him the good news. She hesitated, then dialed.

"Hello, Ravyn. What do you want?" asked Laura. Ravyn looked down at her phone. Had she called Laura by mistake? No, this was Marc's number.

"Laura? I thought I called Marc."

"Oh, you did," Laura said, "He's in the shower right now, so I answered his phone. Is there something I can help you with?"

"Ah, no. No, just tell him I called."

"I don't think I will, Ravyn. You've done enough damage. Don't call again." And with that, Laura hung up Marc's cell. Ravyn stared at her phone in shock. Marc is back with Laura? She was hurt. "Didn't take him long to fall back in her clutches," Ravyn thought. Suddenly her good mood was gone.

"Was that my phone?" Marc asked Laura, as he carried a small stack of boxes from his garage into his house.

"Yes," Laura said, quickly deleting Ravyn's call history from Marc's phone. "I didn't think you'd mind if I answered it. It was a wrong number anyway."

"No, that's fine. Just don't make a habit of it," Marc said. "Here are the printed materials I got from the printer. I need to get them in a couple of packages to go out in the mail tomorrow morning."

"Don't worry, darling," Laura said, practically purring. "I'll take care of you. I'll always take good care of you."

Laura took the boxes out of Marc's hands, placing them on the kitchen table. Then she took him by the hand and led him back to the bedroom.

Monday morning Ravyn was a jangle of nerves. She could feel the sweat under her arms and in her palms as she paced her condo waiting for the call from *Cleopatra* magazine.

"Please let this go well. Please let this go well," she intoned. She jumped when the phone did ring at 10:02 a.m.

"Miss Shaw, this is Ms. Butler and I have Mrs. Hunt on the line as well."

"Good morning to you both," Ravyn said brightly. Maybe too brightly. Inwardly she winced. "Tone it down a notch," she said to herself.

"As you know, we are looking for a managing editor for our Atlanta magazine. Are you familiar with it?" Marcy asked.

"Yes, Ms. Butler…"

"Call me, Marcy, please."

"Yes, Ms., ah, Marcy. I am familiar with *Cleopatra* magazine. I've written a few freelance articles for you. It's been several years ago, though."

"Well, then, you are familiar with our style and tone," Marcy said. "We are a chain of lifestyle magazines. Atlanta's *Cleopatra* is just one of our many publications. Our headquarters is in New York, where we also have a magazine, two in fact, but we also have magazines in Los Angeles, Boston, Chicago, Dallas, Phoenix, Miami and elsewhere. They are similar in that they are lifestyle magazines focusing on home, fashion and dining, but they certainly have their own flare for their respective markets."

"I can certainly see that," Ravyn said.

"We're looking for someone who can handle the work in Atlanta, which will be extensive. It's probably not a 40-hour a week job, Ms. Shaw. It will require hard work, some long hours, and a great deal of organization to keep the production schedule humming."

"Please call me Ravyn."

"Very well, Ravyn," Marcy said. "Is that something you are still interested in?"

"Yes, Marcy. Very much. My background is newspapers and early in my career I was the editor of a small daily newspaper, so I know about hard work and long hours."

"Yes, that's one reason we wanted to talk to you. May I ask why you are a freelancer now?"

"Ah, well, I was part of the downsizing of the daily newspaper here in Atlanta a few years ago. I started freelancing to pay the bills as I looked for other work, but there wasn't much other work at the time for a writer and editor. I do enjoy the freedom that freelancing gives me, but there are good months and bad months. I'd like something a little steadier. And I'm ready for a new challenge. Working for *Cleopatra* would certainly provide that challenge."

"Are there references from your clients that we can talk to?"

Ravyn hesitated for a split second. "Why yes, I am sure any one of my clients would be happy to talk to you." "Well, all but one," Ravyn said inwardly.

"Wonderful. If you will email those contact names and numbers over."

"Certainly, I'll do it this morning."

"Ravyn, this is Samantha Hunt. We're looking for someone who can start relatively soon. Our current managing editor is leaving us at the end of next month and we'll want to hire someone soon, very soon, in hopes that he can do some in-house training before he leaves. I take it since you are freelancing, you can start relatively quickly?"

"Yes, of course. I have a few projects I'd need to finish up, but that would only take me a week, two at the most, to finish," Ravyn said. She was lying through her teeth. The freelance jobs she had wouldn't take more than a couple of days to finish up, but she didn't want to sound desperate.

"That sounds good. Do you have time later this week to come in and see the operation?" Samantha asked.

"Yes. I can make myself available. Just let me know what is good for you."

"How about Thursday, say around 11? You can tour the office and then we can head out to lunch," Samantha said.

"Sounds perfect. I'll see you at 11 on Thursday," Ravyn said, hopping from one foot to the other with excitement.

"Wonderful. See you then and thank you."

Ravyn hung up and could feel tears behind her eyes. She was so happy she was getting a second interview. She ran to her closet to start thinking about what she would wear to make a good impression.

The week was a blur as Ravyn finished up her freelance work and got ready for her face-to-face interview with Samantha Hunt and Marcy Butler. She realized as she got ready Thursday morning that she hadn't thought as much about Marc in the past few days.

"I guess it means I'm getting over him," she sighed to herself.

She checked some local news sites and blogs on her laptop and saw a brief item on a technology blog that Bradford Cunningham's BC Enterprises got $2 million in funding from an

Atlanta venture capital firm. She didn't see any mention of LindMark getting any money. But that didn't mean he didn't get any, just perhaps not from any local firms.

"I can't think about that now," she thought. "I've got to move forward."

Samantha Hunt was dressed in a cream silk pantsuit, with a chunky gold statement necklace that had tiger's eye stones. She was slightly taller than Ravyn, but it might have been because of her open-toed high-heeled sandals. Samantha extended a hand in greeting. "It's just you and I today, if you don't mind," she said.

"Not at all," Ravyn said.

"Marcy had to head back up to New York for some meetings," Samantha said.

"Oh, she's not based here in Atlanta?"

"She's based out of New York, but she's been here quite a bit lately as we get ready to transition our managing editor."

Samantha gave a quick tour of the office, which was small. There was a small reception area and behind a frosted glass wall there were several small offices surrounding a more open area with several cubicles. A large table and chairs sat behind the cubicles. Ravyn was introduced to the advertising and marketing staff, who took up most of the cubicles. The director of advertising had his own office. She also met the production staff, where she saw Craig Taylor, the one who had told her friend James about this job opening. She'd have to remember to take him out to lunch as a thank you.

Samantha then introduced Ravyn to the outgoing managing editor, Jeff Black. The three sat in his office talking about the duties, hours, highs and lows of the job.

Ravyn tried to come prepared with several questions that she hoped didn't sound too simple. She so wanted this job and she could feel the perspiration down her back, the result of her nervousness.

"You certainly come highly recommended from your clients," Samantha said at last.

Ravyn smiled. "That's great to hear. I certainly am happy when they are happy."

"We'd like to have you join our team, Ravyn," Samantha said.

Ravyn almost didn't understand what she was hearing. "I'd love to join *Cleopatra*," she said, blinking in disbelief. "I think I'll be very happy here and I think I can bring my expertise to the magazine."

"We think so, too," Samantha smiled, extending her hand. "Welcome aboard. Let's go to lunch to celebrate."

# Chapter 12

March and April flew by as Ravyn learned the ins and outs of her new job. Jeff Black trained her as best he could in his last few weeks as managing editor, but Ravyn knew she'd be learning more by the seat of her pants, and to her, that was almost the best way to learn: in the heat of the moment.

She got her first magazine to production on her own in May. It was a thrill to hold the magazine in her hands. But it was no rest for the weary. She had July deadlines to meet. She was getting used to the magazine deadlines of 60 days ahead. It wouldn't be long before she'd be working on fall and holiday issues. Ravyn realized she'd be the one thinking of Christmas in July as she thought of stories and photos that might appear in the November and December issues.

Ravyn met Julie for lunch in Midtown, since *Cleopatra*'s offices were more downtown, and Julie was more in Buckhead. It was a nice way to meet in the middle.

Ravyn was recounting how she was now drumming up story ideas and photo possibilities for the fall fashion issue, which would come out in August.

"Who wants to think of fall fashion in May in Atlanta?" Ravyn said, as they sat out on the patio of Tin Lizzy's, a couple of baskets of fish tacos demolished on their table. It was a beautiful afternoon in Atlanta: warm, but not yet too warm and humid. A perfect day for lunch on the patio of any restaurant in town.

"Well, I guess you'd better," Julie laughed. "Ravyn, you are absolutely glowing. I haven't seen you this happy in a long time."

Ravyn smiled. "I haven't been this happy in a long time. I am loving this new job. It's a lot of work. I'm putting in long hours, but I think once I get the hang of the production cycle and get the freelancers into a groove, it won't be as bad. But, working long hours right now is OK. Keeps me from thinking of other things."

"I wanted to ask but wasn't sure how. Since you brought it up, have you heard from Marc?" Julie asked, taking a sip of her margarita.

"Not a peep," Ravyn said, looking down and running her finger around the salted rim of her glass. "But I hear through the grapevine he's back with Laura Lucas."

"No! Really?"

"Yes, really. I'd like to say they deserve each other, but I'm not sure even Marc deserves Laura."

"Speak of the devil," Julie said, her eyes going wide.

Laura Lucas walked onto the patio with Bradford Cunningham, the two of them following a hostess to a table in the far corner. Ravyn turned her head to look.

"Hmm. Wonder what that is about. Funny that she should be having lunch with Marc's competition," Ravyn said, turning back around to face Julie. "Well, not my business anymore."

"You still love him?" Julie asked softly.

"No. I don't think so," Ravyn said. She could feel herself starting to blink back tears. "I have to move on. I have to move on without him. He made his choice and it wasn't me."

Julie took her friend's hand. "It's his loss. I'll still go punch him in the nuts if you'd like."

Ravyn burst out laughing, putting her credit card down for the bill. "Thanks. I knew I could count on you."

"Hey, let me get this," Julie said, reaching for the check.

"Oh no you don't," Ravyn insisted. "I've got a steady paycheck again and it feels good to start repaying a few lunches you bought when I had no income."

"Well, I could get used to this!" Julie laughed. "Next time we'll have lunch over at the Ritz!"

"You've got it," Ravyn said.

She threw one last glance over at Laura and Bradford as she and Julie were leaving. Laura and Bradford were sitting very close. Ravyn then saw Laura reach up and stroke Bradford's cheek, then heard her loud, barking laugh. "Very odd, indeed," Ravyn thought.

Marc sat in his office turning his laptop on and off. It was running so slowly. He hoped he wasn't going to have to buy a new one. It really wasn't that old.

He called one of his guys over, one he knew was good with computers.

"John, I am having a lot of trouble with my laptop. It's running really slow. Slow to boot up, slow to connect to the WiFi. Just slow. Can you figure out what's wrong with it?"

"Yeah, I can take a look. Why don't you let me have it when you get ready to leave this afternoon."

"That would be great. Thanks."

Marc looked at his calendar. Not much on it today. He leaned back and thought about Laura. He didn't expect that they would be an item again. He wasn't complaining, really. She was great in bed. But sex with Laura was like a sporting event. It was all high adrenalin and then a big crash. There were no soft edges. There was no cuddling afterward or whispering in the dark after making love. He realized what he missed was being with Ravyn.

"Well, can't go back now," Marc thought, though wishing he could. He rubbed his hands down his face, feeling the start of his afternoon stubble. "Maybe I'll just knock off early today."

Marc shut down his laptop and walked it over to John's desk. "Here you go. I think I'll head over to the gym since I can't do much work on this thing. I hope I don't have to buy a new one. Not really in the budget."

"I'll take a look at it. Maybe it's a virus or something slowing it down. Or it could be a corrupted file or program in the background that has a glitch."

"Thanks again. Hey, don't stick around too long yourself. Looks nice out there," Marc said, looking out the window at blue skies. "Good day to be out of the office."

As Marc got to the parking deck, he decided against driving and opted for a short walk. He headed down Peachtree and then turned onto 10th Street. As he passed Tin Lizzy's, he thought he heard Laura Lucas's distinctive laugh. He looked up to see Laura and Bradford Cunningham seated at a table on the outside patio.

Marc was taken aback. What was Laura doing with Bradford?

He slowed his walk. He didn't think they saw him, so he stopped just beyond the patio. He could only hear a few words, since traffic noise and other sounds overwhelmed their conversation. The words capital, bogus, and year-end were all he heard. Then Laura's laugh again, along with Bradford's laugh, which sounded like a horse whinnying.

Marc felt uneasy. He'd have to ask Laura about this lunch and why she chose to have it with Bradford Cunningham. His good mood was gone. He walked back to his office.

John Deevers, the IT guy, caught Marc as he came through the office door.

"Hey, Marc, I thought you were out of here for today," he said.

"I was. But then I wasn't. You know how it goes," Marc said, giving what he hoped was a smile, but might have been a grimace.

"Well, I think your laptop might have a virus," John said.

"Great. More good news."

"I should be able to clean it up fairly quickly, but you might want to shut down other access to your laptop," John said. "Looks like it might have come in from someone else's remote access."

Marc was startled. No one was supposed to have access to his laptop but him.

"What do you mean? No one is authorized on this laptop but me."

"Oh, man. That's bad. Then you might have been hacked. Let me see," John said, opening up that laptop and pulling up files. "Yeah, I can see someone remotely accessed your computer back on Jan. 15. It looks like the hacker got into some spreadsheets. Ah, looks like your year-end data. Can't tell for sure what was done or changed. I would need to check the version history of those spreadsheets. Let me see if I can identify that."

Marc could feel himself getting cold. "Someone hacked into my year-end spreadsheet?" he asked himself. "And changed data? The data I yelled about to Ravyn? The data I accused Ravyn of changing?"

Marc was starting to feel sick. "But who would hack into my laptop?" he wondered. Then it struck him. "Bradford! That slimy bastard Bradford would do it. Or pay someone else to do it."

Now Marc was getting angry. "Is this something I should turn over to the police?" Marc asked John.

"Umm, not sure yet. Maybe. Let me take a look at this a little while longer, now that I know you might have been hacked or accessed remotely. You are sure no one else is authorized to access this computer?"

"Well, no. Just me. Not since I fired…" Marc went still. "Not since I fired Laura Lucas about a year ago."

"That was your PR gal? The one with the blue eyes?" John asked.

Marc blinked. "No, no, not Ravyn. Ravyn never had remote access to my laptop. The one before her. The dark-haired one."

"Ah. Did you change her remote access after you fired her? Or change your password?" John asked.

"No. I didn't think I'd need to," Marc said, groaning inwardly, wondering why he hadn't done any of those simple things to block remote access.

"Well, if she still had remote access, she could have gotten in if you didn't change your password or unauthorize her account," John replied, his brown eyes blinking behind his thick glasses.

Marc let out a deep, defeated sigh. "OK. Keep checking. I need to know if she's the one who hacked in."

"Do you have an email from her that you know she sent you from her laptop?" John asked. "I can check to see if the IP addresses match."

"I think so. You should be able to find that in my laptop."

"Great. I'll look into that. Don't worry, man. We'll figure it out."

"You bet we will," Marc said, suddenly angry again.

Marc walked back into his office and nearly slammed the door.

Capital. Bogus. Year-end. Were Laura and Bradford talking about what they had done to his spreadsheets? Had the two of them worked together to ruin his company? Bradford doing that he could believe, but Laura? Marc shook his head, trying not to think of Laura deliberately trying to ruin him and his company. Did she do it out of spite for their break-up? He wondered.

And what did that mean about Ravyn? She had been telling the truth. The numbers he'd given her were wrong, especially if someone – Laura – had gone in and changed them. He needed to check the Excel spreadsheet Ravyn had sent him when she was trying to tell him the numbers weren't wrong. Did he still have it? He thought he'd deleted it in anger. Maybe not. He'd need to check his laptop again, when John was finished with it.

Marc blew out hard, puffing out his cheeks. "What a mess," he thought. Ravyn had been right. Ravyn. Marc sighed deeply again and sank back in his office chair. "I really screwed up this time," he said out loud, staring up at the white office ceiling tiles, "in more ways than one."

Marc's week did not get any better. A late-night call on Thursday from his parents that his brother Bruce had been arrested in Johns Creek, a suburb of Atlanta, for drunk driving led to more stress. He sat on his leather sofa drinking this second scotch Friday evening, rubbing his forehead, trying to relieve the tension.

He wished he could call Ravyn, but he felt he couldn't. Not now. Not after the way he'd treated her.

Marc had to get ready for the venture capital meeting in Atlanta next week, where some decent investment in startups would be announced. He'd hoped his revised numbers that he'd sent over would improve his chances of getting some funding for the second half of the year. If it didn't make him look like a complete rank amateur.

Marc gulped down the last of the scotch and contemplated fixing another. That would probably only lead to a bad headache in the morning.

"Fuck it," Marc said, as he got up for a third glass.

Marc was nervous as he stepped into the ballroom of the Peachtree Westin. He affixed the name tag to his sports jacket lapel and began scoping the room for familiar faces. Unfortunately, the first familiar face he saw was that of Bradford Cunningham.

Bradford was laughing loudly, almost braying, to the man next to him. Marc didn't recognize the companion, but he felt sorry for him.

Marc walked over to get a cup of coffee from the urns set up along the side of the ballroom.

"Hey, stranger," he heard a soft woman's voice say. He turned to see Laura Lucas. "I've missed you," she said, placing a hand on his arm and rubbing it. "I've missed you a lot."

Marc's eyes darkened. "Well, I've been busy. Getting ready for this meeting and checking through some files on my laptop. I found some unauthorized activity on it."

Marc saw the brief look of panic in her dark brown eyes. "Gotcha," he thought.

"Ladies and gentlemen," the meeting organizer said through a microphone at the podium at the front of the ballroom. "If you will please be seated, we can get started. We know you are all anxious for the announcements."

Marc had no intention of sitting anywhere near Laura or Bradford, but Laura was determined to stick close to Marc.

As he took a seat, Laura slid in next to him. She reached for his hand and gave it a squeeze. "Good luck," she said as she smiled at him.

"And in the category of startups, three to seven years, our award goes to Bradford Cunningham of BC Enterprises," the announcer said.

A whoop went up from the middle of the room as Bradford stood up, did a fist pump, and walked to the front to accept his accolades and check.

Marc winced. Laura looked over at him in surprise. "Oh no!" she said. "I was sure you would get it. I'm sorry, Marc. We can work on some other marketing materials and get them out to the West Coast VCs next week."

"No, you will not," he said, through gritted teeth.

Laura looked puzzled. "But we need to…"

"We will discuss this later," he cut her off.

The room was buzzing as attendees were making their way out of the ballroom, the meeting over. Marc saw several people glad-handing Bradford, but Marc had no intention of being one of them.

He tried to quickly walk past Bradford, but the crush of people prevented that.

"Linder!" Bradford barked. "I guess the best startup got the spoils!"

"Not necessarily, Bradford," Marc said, not wanting to discuss anything with him.

"Well, I have to thank that little lady for helping me today," Bradford said, pointing at Laura.

"What do you mean?" Marc asked, getting angry.

"Oh, she just helped me with some numbers," Bradford smirked. "Really helped with my pitch today."

"Don't you mean she helped me with *my* numbers, Bradford?" Marc said. "I know what she did, Bradford, and I know you had a hand in it."

"I don't know what you are talking about," Bradford sneered. "If you don't know what your own fourth-quarter numbers are, I can't help that."

Bradford suddenly realized what he'd said, but Marc was already wheeling around to face Laura, a look of horror on her face.

"You, bitch!" Marc shouted, as people began to move away from the fracas.

"I didn't know," Laura said, tears filling her eyes. "I didn't realize…"

"What, Laura? You didn't realize what? That changing the numbers would cost my company? That you would ruin my career? That's sabotage. That's a criminal matter now."

Laura looked stricken. "Criminal?"

"Yes, Laura," said Marc, his face dark with anger. "I have the evidence that it was your computer that hacked into my laptop. I have the evidence that it came from your IP address. You're done, Laura! You're done! I'm turning everything over to my attorney and the Atlanta Police."

Laura grabbed Marc by the arm, tears now streaming down her cheeks. "No, Marc. It was a mistake. I just wanted you to be mad at Ravyn. I didn't mean for it to go this far."

Marc wrenched his arm from Laura's grip. "Well it did. It did. You're done."

"Just admit it, Linder," Bradford stepped in. "You're a chump and always will be. Come on, Laura. You don't need to listen to this crap."

Laura spun around and slapped Bradford hard in the face. "You, bastard! You put me up to this! I'm not going down alone!"

September in New York City had to be close to the most perfect time to be there.

Ravyn flew up for meetings with *Cleopatra*'s parent company. She was meeting with other managing editors from the other publications and firming up the editorial calendar for the coming year. Although the meetings could be tedious, she could hardly complain since the weather was superb, the company was treating everyone to great restaurants, and she loved the little boutique hotel she was staying at in Midtown Manhattan, not far from Bryant Park.

She was sitting in Bryant Park with a morning cup of coffee, catching up on emails, when a news alert popped up.

The venture capital firm of Axel Capital was suing Bradford Cunningham's BC Enterprises for the return of its investment given out just this past May. The news alert went on to say that Axel Capital believed BC Enterprises, and Bradford in particular, had provided overinflated figures, which led to the award. Toward the end of the article, it said Axel Capital was instead funding LindMark.

Ravyn closed her cell phone and smiled wanly. "Good for Marc. I'm glad he finally got his funding."

A slight pang went through her heart. Marc. She still thought about him, about what they had had. She put both hands around the warm cup of coffee, wondering whether she should contact him.

"Well, I could congratulate him," she thought. "There would be nothing wrong with that."

Ravyn put her coffee down on the bench and picked up her phone again, typing in a text to send to Marc. "Congrats on the funding. I know LindMark will be a great success."

Ravyn hit send and then put her phone down on the park bench, picking up her coffee again. She then heard a muffled "Hello? Hello? Ravyn?"

Ravyn looked around, wondering who was calling her name. Then she looked down on the bench and saw Marc's number on her phone.

Alarmed, Ravyn picked up her phone. "Marc?"

"Ravyn, is everything OK?"

"Yes, why? Is everything OK with you?"

"Yes. You called me, and I thought it might be an emergency," Marc said, rather groggily.

"Called you? I didn't call you. I just sent you a text."

"No, you called me. My phone just rang."

"Oh no! I must have accidentally called you when I put my phone down. Sorry."

"That's OK."

"You sound funny. Is everything OK?" Ravyn asked.

"Well, it's 5:30 a.m. here in California."

"Oh no! I'm so sorry. I woke you up. I'll hang up."

"No, don't, Ravyn. Don't hang up."

They both were suddenly silent on the phone, but a NYC fire engine roared by with sirens blaring.

"What was that? Where are you?" Marc asked.

"New York City. I'm up here for meetings this week," Ravyn replied.

"Meetings? For a freelance job?"

"No. I'm the new managing editor of *Cleopatra* magazine. I'm up here for meetings with other editors and meeting the corporate big wigs at the parent company."

"Congratulations! I didn't know you'd gotten a new job."

"Well, yeah. Congrats yourself on the funding. I saw Bradford Cunningham had his funding rescinded. He faked his numbers?"

Marc sighed. "Ravyn, I owe you a huge apology. Bradford and Laura, well Laura mostly, with Bradford's encouragement, hacked into my laptop and changed those quarterly numbers. I blamed you for it, but it was Laura. Laura did it."

Ravyn was shocked. "She did? I can't believe she'd do that."

"Well, she did. Essentially she wanted me to fire you so she could get back in my good graces."

"Mission accomplished," Ravyn said bitterly.

"Well, sort of. I figured it out and turned the information over to the police, but they wouldn't prosecute. Said it was more a civil matter."

There was silence between them again.

"Ravyn, I'm so sorry. I should have believed you. ...I miss you."

Ravyn didn't know what to say. So much had happened since then, and Marc had been so angry with her.

"Are you there?" Marc asked.

"Yes. I'm here. Just stunned is all. I've missed you, too."

Marc sighed, clearly relieved. "Will you let me make it up to you?"

"Marc, I don't think…"

"Dinner, at least. When you get back to Atlanta. When will you be back?"

"I get back late Friday."

"OK, how about dinner Saturday then. Anywhere you want to go."

"Marc, I don't know…"

"Hey, it's dinner. Besides, you owe me."

"I owe you?" Ravyn said, incredulously.

"Yeah, you are the one who is always calling me at odd hours, waking me up from my much-needed beauty sleep."

Ravyn laughed out loud.

"Well, I do have a smartphone. I'm just a dumb user. See you Saturday."

Made in the USA
Monee, IL
19 January 2022